And Then That Happ

Liam Livings

First edition, copyrigh

Second edition, copyri   .y Liam Livings

Third edition, copyright 2018 by Liam Livings

Paperback edition 2018

Cover design by Meredith Russell

Edited by Val Hughes

Dedication

This is my first gay romance book to be published and I really hope you enjoy it. But before I let you meet Dominic and Gabe, first there are a few people I'd like to thank.

Thanks to my lovely beta readers: Charlie Cochrane, Jane Wilkinson, Elin Gregory, Ian Phillips and Tim Westcott. You all brought your own particular type of feedback to the story, which helped me when I could no longer see the wood for the trees. I know how time consuming beta reading is, and I thank you all for your time and sensitive, constructive feedback.

Thanks to my wonderful, complicated, enthusiastic, friend N, who through meeting you, gave me the inspiration about writing the story in the first place.

Thanks to Callie who came up with the concept of an *and then that happened*, way back in 2005 in Canada.

Thanks to Hannah, who, when I explained this concept, completely and utterly got it, and has kept the concept alive since then, and helped me think it was a concept worth putting in a story.

Thanks Val Hughes, the wonderful editor who's worked polished and corrected the mistakes I made, and pointed out things that had never occurred to me, to make the final version a better stronger story than it was originally. It has always felt like a great team effort working with you on these edits.

Thanks to Meredith Russell for making a beautiful cover to illustrate one of my favourite scenes from the story.

And lastly, thanks to you, the reader, who's bought this book, I hope you enjoy reading it, as much as I enjoyed writing it.

Lots of love,

Liam Livings xx

Chapter One

Now

It was all so clear and simple. I knew where I was in my life: I was exactly where I wanted to be. Everything in its place, and in its place, everything. Until it wasn't. Until it threw everything up in the air just to see where it all landed. Yes, me, Mister Organised, Mister Stable. I knew what I thought, what made me happy, what love was — until I met *him*. And then I didn't know anything; I didn't know anything at all.

31 December 1999

I stepped out of the shower, walked to our bedroom and closed the door. Music and laughter filtered upstairs as I walked across the hallway. The sound of the party starting to get up and live. Our New Year's Eve party.

Every newspaper ran panic stories shouting about the Millennium Bug. At work the nurses worried about our holiday records and shift rotas being lost when the clock hit midnight as the ancient IBM computer in *matron's office* freaked out and lost everything.

I'm a matron, it's *my* office. Well, I'm a charge nurse really, as I'm male. Charge nurse for two medical wards in a district general hospital in west London. Okay so it's not a big teaching hospital with a double barrelled name or one of those you hear about on the TV all the time—'A patient was air lifted to St Anthony's after suffering a gunshot wound...' We're more, 'An elderly man who'd spent his whole life living on clarified butter was wheeled to the cardiac department *slowly* for a long-term care plan.'

We'd drawn straws for who would work over the New Year. I drew a long straw, so worked an early shift and finished at three pm. I stayed afterwards looking after the patients and caught up with paperwork in my office, periodically interrupted by colleagues poking their heads around the door, asking me about my plans for the night.

'Sitting in a bath of my own tears' didn't have much of a ring to it, so instead I told them we were having a house party, then became embarrassed with my lack of knowledge about it when they asked.

Luke had organised the party: invited most of our friends, decorated the house, bought the food, chosen the music; he'd even picked a film to run in the background for the whole evening, said it reminded him of Heaven, the London nightclub, not that we'd been there in years.

Although, *I* had been recently. I had been and I'd loved it. But not with Luke.

The party was all to keep up appearances. All to continue the show of being normal, nothing to see here, move on.

'Dominic, are you nearly ready? I need a hand with the cheesy pineapple sticks,' Luke shouted upstairs.

How long could I get away with ignoring him until he eagerly ran upstairs to meet me, bounding around the room like an enthusiastic puppy, despite what we'd been through at Christmas? I closed my eyes and counted slowly in my head: one, two, three, four, five, six, seven…

'Did you hear me?' he repeated.

I wiped the salty tears from my face with the towel and forced a reply to avoid him seeing me like this. 'Nearly done, be down in a bit.'

Silence. I'd bought myself another half an hour's delay before facing the party. Our party really. Although he'd done all the prep, it was still my house, our house — for the time being. Why was I dreading facing the party so much? It wasn't the normal New Year's Eve dread, the indescribable pressure to *have a good time* which suddenly thrust itself upon everyone, young or old, gay or straight, male or female, vegetable or mineral. People who'd never dream of going to a nightclub found themselves queuing up outside in the frozen December air, grabbing onto their friends and boyfriend for dear life, desperately hoping to *have a good time*. People who'd spent the whole year avoiding hosting dinner parties, suddenly thought it a good idea to invite their whole mobile phone address book to one. The pressure to put on a shiny happy face and *enjoy* yourself became larger than anything else in the room. It was bigger than the party itself.

And this wasn't just any old New Year's Eve, it was The Millennium. The New Year's Eve to end all New Year's Eves: computers would crash, traffic lights would stop working, and entire countries would cease to function all because of the millennium bug. A friend of a friend who 'worked in computers' — I didn't know any more than that, despite having known him for more than ten years — had made an absolute killing by charging other companies huge amounts of money, each working out of grey offices, making nothing, but selling information, to ensure they were millennium bug-proof for the big clock switch over. 'So much money I won't have to work for most of the year two-thousand,' he'd proclaimed a few nights ago over jovial drinks.

Luke had laughed and told him how envious he was and mentioned our party to him again, recounting the preparation he'd done, the special millennium hats, glasses, tinsel, little bits of sparkly glitter he was preparing to scatter in corners of the house I didn't know had any business having them. I'd just smiled and internally rolled my eyes, dreading the party even then. *If I do nothing for it, it'll just not happen, it'll pass without note and the year 2000 will come and we can both get on with our lives.*

Only now, I'd met *him*, I didn't want to just get on with my life. Now, it wasn't okay to just plaster on a fake smile, repeat 'teeth, tummy and tits' to myself and walk out into the party. Now I'd had a glimpse of what was possible and how that contrasted with what was reality. Now it was so much harder to just *teeth, tummy and tits* my way through my life. Now it all felt so fake, because the life I would be pretending to get on with didn't really exist any longer.

I imagined pasting on a false smile and telling all our friends how 1999 had been such an amazing year again. 'You're so lucky,' they'd say, gesturing around the house. 'Ten years, it's like a proper married couple. You're so lucky.' I would nod, and Luke would hug me from behind and smile over my shoulder. We would both continue the charade for all our guests.

Our double bed, perfectly made, with an indentation from Princess, our dog, stared back and mocked me. I couldn't remember the last time we'd done anything other than sleep in it. I thought about the house; every room was a scene of perfect domestic bliss, like a show home at the Ideal Homes Exhibition.

Why *this* room? Why *this* house? Why *those* clothes?

I dried myself and threw the towel on our double bed, caught myself, stood naked in front of the mirror. Not bad for twenty-eight; I mean, I wasn't eighteen anymore, but no love handles, a bit of muscle in the right places. *I'd fancy this, not bad!*

He had fancied this.

And Luke too. At one point we couldn't keep our hands off each other. I turned around and glanced at my bum. 'Perfect and peachy' Luke used to say. I blushed briefly at a memory from the first few months together, then tried to remember when anything similar had happened recently.

Blank.

He'd laid clothes out for me on our bed, for me in the shape of a man. White long-sleeved T-shirt with dragon motifs down the arms, smart dark flared jeans. Even after Christmas Eve, he was still being so *nice* to me, so sickeningly *nice*. But now I knew that wasn't enough. Not enough, if there was no clothes ripping, blood rushing grrrr about it.

I closed my eyes and pictured *his* face. The face that hadn't quite launched a thousand ships but had, in a few short months, made me question everything I had, everything I thought was constant and perfect. I opened my eyes and pushed away *his* face into a dark corner of my mind. Looking around the room, all my previous choices taunted me, laughing, mocking, taking the piss.

'Are you nearly ready? I need a hand with the nibbles.' Luke's voice drifted up the stairs.

'I'm having a shave. Be down in a bit,' I shouted. Was I going to have a shave? I'd not bothered for a while and now had quite an impressive bit of facial foliage. Not quite a proper beard saying, 'I'm not shaving and this is a beard,' more like, 'I've not bothered shaving, so this is what's happened.' Less a committed beard, more of a laissez-faire facial hair.

I walked to the en-suite and ran the hot water, gathered up my shaving things. *It's another ten minutes alone before having to face the reality of the party, so I'll shave. It'll help with the pretence of everything being normal.*

Every time I looked at my reflection in the mirror, another thought popped into my head. *On the one hand, this is good… but on the other, this isn't so good…*

Reflection, shave. But at least tonight I'd see my friends. That would make the party worthwhile, wouldn't it? We'd recount memories of times during the past year, laugh at shared jokes, promise to keep in touch better next year than this. Adding at the end of each conversation that we'd see each other next year, and look at the clock as it approached midnight, the joke never became tired with some and we'd all laugh together. That would be something to look forward to; I could do that, couldn't I?

Rinse the razor, reflection, shave. But there was so much I couldn't tell them. So much I wanted to ask, but hadn't dare tell any of them. Have you ever had a secret, or a thought so unthinkable, that you daren't even say it out loud, never mind to someone else? Luke and I had agreed it was best to keep it all quiet until after the party.

Rinse, reflection. There was nothing more I could say to Luke; we'd already had that conversation and done it to death. I couldn't say it to any of our other friends, friends we'd grown up with as couples during our life together. Friends who only knew Dominic and Luke, the perfect couple, the couple who never argued, never fought, had been together through thick and thin, through others splitting up and worse, we'd been a constant.

Shave, rinse, reflection. There was no way I could spoil that impression for them. It would be like telling a four-year-old there was no Father Christmas or that the Tooth Fairy was all bollocks. I could just imagine our friends' faces, surprised at the revelation. 'Completely out of the blue,' they'd say. 'I had no idea,' they'd add. It was much better to get the party out of the way and tell them all in January. No sense spoiling the party, not after all the work Luke had put into it. It was a good plan: Luke and I had made a good plan together.

Reflection, shave. Of course Luke had had no idea, cos I'm all teeth, tummy and tits about everything. I've had a life of putting up with it, not causing a stink, just getting on with it, for the sake of everyone, even if it's my happiness which suffers. Is it dangerous to regret your whole life? Could it cause cancer? What would I tell my GP if I wanted to speak to her about it? Where do you go with something like that?

Reflection. My normal face stared back at me, my non-caveman face.

He entered the bedroom. 'That's better,' Luke said. 'I wondered if you were ever gonna get rid of that. It didn't suit you.'

Thanks! I smiled weakly and made eye contact with him in the mirror. *Take off the towel and throw me onto the bed. Now. Go on, throw me about a bit, like you used to. Bend me over and remind me what it feels like. Go on.*

'Did you like the clothes I chose?' He walked to the bed.

I nodded. 'Very nice, thanks.'

'You okay?'

I'm stood here in just a towel, freshly shaved, and it would have only taken a few skilful manoeuvres before I was primed and ready for sex. Men are always only ever a few moves or thoughts away from a full shag: any man who's ever sat on a bus with an erection will testify to that.

'Tired.' I shrugged. *Kiss me, kiss me, kiss me. Show me it's not all dead.*

'I'll make you a coffee. I know you don't want to do this, but we did agree we'll tell them all in January, not now.'

I nodded. *Yes, that was what we'd agreed Christmas Eve after exhausting all the other options and talking until we couldn't speak any longer.* After that night, my previous position of disinterest about the party had seemed like nirvana, a state of perfection.

'See you downstairs.' He walked out of the bathroom, my towel still round my waist.

Chapter Two

November 1999

Luke had been going on about the New Year's Eve party for months, and I *mean* months. Literally since September all he spoke about was the bloody party. I think the combination of hosting a party and it being The Millennium, with all that entailed, had combined to become an irresistible opportunity for a party. And Luke had grabbed it with both hands.

'Shall we get some year 2000 hats and glasses?' Luke asked as I pushed a trolley around a party shop.

I nodded and he threw some in the trolley.

'What about a trifle? Or a special cake? Which is more Millennium, do you think?'

'What sort of special cake were you thinking?' I said, trying to understand the concept myself. Could a cake *be* Millennium?

'Some sort of celebration cake, something with sparklers on top, layers of different coloured sponge. Maybe some bright-coloured icing.'

'Sounds perfect.'

Every night he would approach me with some more extraordinary ideas, asking for my opinion. Each time I just nodded then, he continued with more plans. It all seemed so pointless next to the thoughts swirling around my head.

'Have you invited your list of friends?' he asked over dinner.

The concept of 'my friends' and 'your friends' becomes quite blurred after ten years with someone, hence he referred to the list.

'When was I supposed to?' I asked, confused, searching my mind for the conversation when he'd asked me to make this particular thing happen.

'Oh, Dominic, I asked you two weeks ago. I need to send out the invites tonight. You remember them, don't you?'

I nodded.

'So where are they?'

'Where?'

'Yes, as in, what have you done with them, we need to put them in envelopes, write people's addresses on, and post them.'

'Why would I have them?'

Luke stood up and put his hands on his hips. I knew I was in trouble now. 'You are shitting me, aren't you? We agreed the wording and clip art, and I asked you to print them at work during your lunch.'

Lunch, now I remember that concept, but not intimately. 'I said I'd do that?'

He nodded.

I reached in my bag and found a three and a half inch floppy disk, covered in biscuit crumbs and dust. 'Is it on this?'

He snatched it from me and walked out. 'I don't know what's wrong with you.'

No, you don't, and you really can't see it, can you?

After that, Luke hadn't given me any mission-critical things to do, he'd just asked my opinions on various things: colours, shades, numbers, locations, cakes, that sort of thing. And I'd nodded and made all the right noises, and he'd run off excited and made things happen. After all, it was his party, I was just along for the ride. But he didn't seem to think that. 'It'll be great to see all our friends together. We're the perfect hosts, aren't we?' he'd asked, not wanting an answer. Which was fortunate, as I didn't give him one.

I hadn't really been involved in any of it; Luke had simply dragged me through it with my eyes shut. I'd given my opinions, but not fully understanding or listening to each one. I never fully believed it would really happen. I spent my days at work at the hospital completely absorbed, making sure I didn't inject someone with the wrong drugs and kill them. So when I got home, I just floated through until bedtime. It won't really happen. It can't happen. Christmas felt like it was ages away. A different century even.

I just went along with it, for an easier life. That was what I did. That was what I'd always done.

Like I had gone along with Mother staying the previous Christmas.

Big mistake.

Huge.

This time last year, I was sitting on the sofa, alternating between the TV and one of Luke's work problems, something to do with sales targets, when the house phone rang. On speakerphone, her voice filled the room: 'Darling, I thought I'd call and ask what your plans were for Christmas. I wondered if you had space for little old me to squeeze around your table. Just a few days, I promise I'll help cook. I'm sure that boy Luke won't mind...'

Luke smiled at me before tackling his mother-in-law. 'Hello, Carol Anne, this is Luke. Do you want me to pass you on to Dominic?'

I frantically made waving movements with my hands and patted my head.

'I'm sorry, he's not feeling well, he's got a headache, can he call you back later?' Luke smiled at me.

'Darling, it won't take long, just a little yes is all I require.'

He shrugged, mouthing 'sorry,' and left the room.

'Mum, I'm not well so can we make this quick?'

'*Mother*. I've no idea why you insist on calling me *Mum*. It's *so* common.' She said the last word as if it pained her even to utter its syllables. 'Repugnant. I've spoken to you before about this, if you can't bear to use my name, then it must be Mother.'

Since my grandmother had died in 1995, leaving Mother a sizeable inheritance, content that by then Mother had severed all ties from the ex-husband she'd married disastrously beneath herself, Mother had suddenly — overnight actually, the day after the funeral — climbed from proudly working class to upper middle class. Overnight, corned beef hash was no longer an acceptable meal in her house. Gone was her little Ford Fiesta, replaced by the first of a series of silver Mercedes cabriolets. Light kisses on both cheeks replaced warm lingering hugs. She threw out all her C&A and M&S clothes, replacing them with bright shoulder-padded suits and dresses from Hobbs, as well as acquired her own tailor 'for special occasions, darling.' Even the mere mention of the fact she'd at one point been joined to Dad made her shudder with disbelief.

And then that happened.

I was first introduced to this concept by a friend at work: we were at the nurses' desk and she was telling us about a holiday she'd had with her boyfriend. 'We were walking along the beach, holding hands, and he stops and says he wants to split up with me, he's moving out next week. I asked him where this had come from, and he just shrugged. So he packed his stuff and moved out last Wednesday.' My colleague had paused as we all took in what she'd just said. Before anyone could jump in with the usual 'Oh, poor you,' back rubbing and tilted head action, she added, 'So yeah, and then that happened! Who's doing tea?' before returning to the kitchen for a round of tea and coffee.

Some people think there's some cosmic plan for our lives, someone orchestrating what happens, like an ethereal puppet master. I don't. I think it's all random. I think you can plan until you're exhausted, and something will still come from the side and knock you over. Because life's random like that. You know when something happens that comes out of nowhere or is so big and shocking there's nothing more to say, no 'oh it'll be fine,' back rubbing. It is what it is. And that's all there is to it. Because sometimes life's like that. Well, that's *And Then That Happened.*

Now, Mother knew I couldn't bear to call her Carol Anne, since I was neither a new age hippy nor someone living in a 1970s sitcom. We had been through this, so I refused to repeat myself. 'Anyway, what did you want?' I had asked, rolling my eyes at myself.

'Just a few days, I'll be no trouble. I'll bring food, presents for you both, cook, everything. You'll hardly know I'm there at all.'

'You didn't want to know us last Christmas.'

'Rosemary's on holiday this year, so… And you know how I get in winter. The doctor said it's important I get out and see people, socialise, talk, laugh.'

There was a pause while I considered her offer.

'Dominic, darling, are you still there?'

'Of course, you can't be on your own at Christmas. We can make a cake together.' I imagined us in the kitchen, stirring the cake mixture, little bits of flour on our faces, Christmas songs playing in the background. Both wearing bright red festive jumpers, Luke walking in with reindeer antlers on his head. *Where did that come from? We're hardly the Brady Bunch.* 'And are you…?'

'All under control. No need to worry darling.'

'Don't forget your light box and tablets.'

'Of course darling, I simply can't drag myself through winter without them.'

'Come Christmas Eve, we'll bake a cake.'

'See you on the twenty-first, can you make sure there's space for my car. I don't want to leave it too far from the house, did I tell you how much Mercedes charged me for that scratch last time I stayed at yours?'

'You can come on the twenty-fourth, we're both working before that.'

'You won't notice I'm there at all. I will just disappear, a little apparition in the corner.' The phone clicked and that was it.

So for an easier life I'd just gone along with Mother's suggestions. I didn't have the energy to argue with her, which at the best of times had always taken all my strength.

She had turned up on the twenty-first of December, empty handed, complained about having to walk from her car to the house. 'It's a very expensive car, I need it in sight from your drawing room. Can't you ask someone to move their car? Some of them are more than four years old, and not a Mercedes in sight. I'm sure the owners wouldn't mind.'

I'd requested the day off to prepare for her arrival, expecting to settle her in, then watch some TV, or read companionably in silence together. Instead, she took up the entire day. We drove around most of west London and the Home Counties looking for ingredients for the cake. 'The recipe says ninety percent cocoa and so that's what I'm getting. I'm not compromising. It's not my fault your silly little Morrisons doesn't sell it. And I want *natural* glacé cherries, not the common red ones, they're full of E numbers. Terrible for your body.'

I didn't mind that really. I was actually quite looking forward to some Mother and son bonding over cake batter, with or without natural glacé cherries. Just as long as she didn't ask to buy some wine.

We returned to our house, this time parking just outside as someone had vacated a spot. She put the roof up on her Mercedes coupe, carefully folding up her bright red scarf before it caught in the window. I shivered from the cold, which she'd insisted was character building and good for the circulation. 'Why buy a convertible if you're not going to use it,' she exclaimed as I pointed to the vapour our breath made in the cold air.

'Be a darling and carry the bags for me would you.' A statement, not a question. 'I'm not as young as I used to be… Just off to pick up a little something for the table.'

'I thought you said it was all under control, after what your doctor said.'

'I am, but it's Christmas darling, and how much harm can a little sip of wine do? I don't ask much, just a few little crutches to prop Mother up.'

I knew as soon as she started referring to herself in the third person, it would be downhill all the way.

I wasn't wrong: she started with a little sip the next day. 'Just to get me in the mood while we bake.' And by lunchtime had finished the first bottle and two more for good measure. I made the cake alone while she slumped in the armchair, a party hat askew on her head, sleeping all afternoon. I put her to bed in the recovery position.

On Christmas Day she opened the gifts we'd given her — from a list sent to us in October, nothing costing less than forty-five pounds or available from anywhere which could be described as 'high street'. She smiled and piled them up next to her gin and tonic on the table, before returning her gaze to Luke as he handed out presents from under the tree.

We reached the final gift and had yet to find any labels proclaiming 'Best wishes Carol Anne' or 'Merry Christmas, love Mother,' so Luke asked the unaskable question.

'Carol Anne, do you have any gifts for us?'

'Me?' she asked, incredulous, sipping her drink and swaying slightly.

I bit my tongue and noted the fairy lights twinkling in the tree.

'I'm sure I've got something, I'll check in my room. Can you help me up, I seem to feel a bit dizzy, is the central heating on too high?'

I helped her up and she wobbled to her room, returning with two immaculately wrapped gifts. She sat and asked for a top up, gesturing to the presents, then told us to help ourselves.

Mine was a silk handkerchief, bright pink and blue, with my initials D W: Dominic Wilson, and silver cufflinks, again monogrammed with my initials. Perfect for all the black tie dinners I went to every evening. I smiled weakly at Luke.

And Luke's was a checked, padded lumberjack shirt. Luke held it up and said he'd hang it up with all the tailored jackets in the wardrobe. 'For when I'm cutting up wood…' He rolled his eyes at me, as Mother took another generous glug of wine.

We both smiled at each other, then Mother, before Luke looked at me and asked for another drink. 'It's going to be a long day.' He smiled through gritted teeth. I went to the kitchen to make two strong gin and tonics, excluding Mother as she was already suitably soused.

We finally waved goodbye to her on the twenty-seventh at nine pm.

So this year, when Luke had suggested the New Year's Eve party, I hadn't the strength to refuse, my mind was too full of other thoughts. The first time he mentioned it, I was in the middle of a long soul searching bath with the lights off and eyes closed, quietly sobbing, away from Luke. He had shouted the suggestion and I'd just said, 'okay' from the bath. I didn't have the words to talk to him about how I really felt; it was too large to grapple, and he always struggled a bit with my black moods. And this was an extended supersize version, with added complications—well, one complication, in the form of *him*—on the side. As the only place in the house where I could cry and be sure of not being disturbed, I was taking to the bath quite a lot at the time.

During these baths I flashed back through my memories with *him* of the previous six months and contrasted them to the ten years with Luke, then quietly sobbed. Why had I chosen Luke? Why *this* house? Why *this* dog? Why *these* friends? Why *this* life? Everything in my life felt like it didn't quite fit, like a jumper bought in the sale, one size too big as it was an unbelievable bargain, which taunted you every time you wore it with baggy sleeves and shapeless body. My whole life felt shapeless and baggy, all aspects of it. Except *him*. Except he wasn't in my life anymore, we had decided that would be best. So instead, I lay in the bath, tears streaming down my face as I remembered every little decision that had led me to this moment now, in this bathroom, with this man outside, asking me if we should have a New Year's Eve party.

I climbed out of the bath and walked to our bedroom. Luke came in, I covered my body with the towel, self-consciously.

He frowned. 'What's wrong? Nothing I haven't seen before.'

I smiled weakly and leant awkwardly against the wall.

'You okay? Your eyes look red. You were in there for ages.'

'This party?' I replied, ignoring most of his questions.

'I thought we could have a party here? Fun, eh?' And he told me all his ideas for the party, where he'd got the idea from, and how much fun he knew it would be.

I caught the odd word, through my black fog. I shrugged. 'Could be.' I forced a smile.

'You sure you're okay? You look…' He looked me up and down.

'Winter, you know what it's like.'

Somehow we'd continued to move further away from the Dominic and Luke we first were, further away from the Dominic and Luke we settled into as we both started our careers, to where we were now. If I was honest with myself, I didn't really know how we'd got here. It hadn't been one big thing, no big arguments, no door slamming, just a gentle slide into this place we found ourselves in now. I say a place, but it felt more like a non-place: not lovey dovey 'Do you still love me,' at the end of every phone call; not 'I hate your guts, you can fuck off,' doors slamming; and not even night in with a DVD and takeaway, cuddling on the sofa, love.

I felt alone, marooned while being in a relationship. Alone yet attached. Not connected to Luke, but not separated from him.

We were just there, with each other, like air is just there, all around you.

And up until I had met *him*, I hadn't really noticed that, I just thought, this is how it is when you've been with someone so long. But now I wasn't quite so sure.

Chapter Three

One of the other reasons I was dreading the party so much, apart from an ongoing ache, missing *him*, was Matt. He had faithfully promised me he'd come to the party. That was at least one familiar face, among the legions of others, mainly Luke's friends, who I'd have to *teeth, tummy and tits* my way through the evening for. Matt *had* confirmed, *was* on the spreadsheet, then during my shift on New Year's Eve, he called and announced he wasn't coming.

'I can't come. I can't face anyone. Me and Marcus have split up, I'm going to Morocco, to meet some nice Arab boys. I'm gonna shag them all over the sand dunes, up *their* sand dune. You wanna come with?'

'I didn't know anything was wrong.'

'It wasn't, but then it was, so I told him I'd had enough and I booked a flight. Coming?'

'I've not heard from you for ages and now you want me to come away with you.'

'Why not, perfect opportunity to catch up. Get away from the boyfriends, kick back, just like old times. We could get some costumes and dress up like we used to back in the day. Put Michael Alig to shame. Come on, you know you want to,' he purred.

I stared at my office wall, covered in staff notices about parking and the canteen's prices. 'I can't let all the guests down. They're expecting me and Luke to host. It's our party, what would it look like if only Luke was there? And I can't afford it.'

'Fuck the guests, fuck the money, come with me. You know you want to.'

I looked around my office, piles of paperwork on every available surface and thought about the party. Root canal work felt like a better option at that moment. But if you needed root canal work, you should plough on and have it done. And plough on I would. 'A bit of notice would have been nice.'

'I didn't know we were going to have that row. You can't timetable splitting up. It just sort of happened.'

'Would have been nice to hear from you with good news.'

'Well I'm sorry my news is upsetting you, I'll remember not to split up with someone again on your watch.'

'That's not what I mean. I haven't heard from you in a month, no replies to my texts, you haven't called me, nothing since we were at your parents' place, and now this has happened and you want to see me.'

'I'm a good friend, you hear from me all the time, when me and Marcus met we came round yours for dinner. I remember it well, you did pasta. It was nice.'

'What about me?'

'What about you?' he threw back.

'Exactly, you don't have a clue do you? No idea what's going on in my life, and you still don't even ask me. I could have been dead for the past few weeks and the first you'd know is now, when you called.'

'It's called being busy. You're not my only friend, you know. Newsflash, Dominic, people have other friends too.'

'I know that.' I let the silence hang between us.

'Look, you're not coming, so that's that. I'll call you when I'm back. Everything else okay?'

'That's what I wanted to talk to you about, face to face, not now, while I'm at work.'

'Sure you don't want to talk now? I'm all ears, I can fit you in.' I could hear the smile in his voice.

I started to gather my thoughts, all the things I wanted to tell him, realised I didn't know where to start, that it was too big for *I can fit you in*. 'Don't wanna tell you on the phone, here.'

'What is it, Dominic? I'm here before the taxi arrives, come on. Chat.'

'I can't just launch straight into it. I've got to explain how it happened. The back story.'

'Back story, what's this, some ITV drama with an actress from a soap?'

'I'm in love.'

'I know we're friends, but I never knew you felt that way!'

'Not you…'

'Tell me it's Luke. Although lord knows why.'

'I do love him, you know.'

'I should bloody well hope so, you've been with him long enough. How long is it, eh?'

'Ten years. I'm not talking about Luke. This is different. It's something I've never experienced before, not even when I first met Luke. It's been four weeks and I can't stop thinking about *him*.'

He was silent after I finished speaking. 'Big. Heavy. So it's about *him*. I told you you're spending too much time with *him*. It's not normal. I'd love to talk, but I've got a flight to catch and I've not packed yet. My taxi's coming in… ten minutes. Call you as soon as I'm back?' And he was gone.

It'll wait till I come back. It'll have to.

My friendship with Matt was complex, and long standing. After our club kid phase I met Luke, and Matt watched me settle down while he continued to search for what to do with his life. Through tens of jobs, moving home, and various boyfriends, he still hadn't found what he was looking for. Probably because he didn't know what he was looking for. We'd spent days deconstructing relationships, flings, men he'd seen in clubs who'd not called him back, over vats of tea and mountains of cigarettes in his parents' house, every holiday I came home from university.

Now, he was back living with his parents in Hampshire, working in a call centre, after losing his job in another call centre and having to leave his flat. Despite me spotting that he didn't earn enough to live on his own, Matt had ignored me: 'It'll all be fine, bit of overtime and I'll be away.' That was until he realised on top of rent you also had to pay: council tax, water, electricity, gas, phone, and buy food too.

I was twenty-eight and realised, and welcomed the concept, that I wasn't eighteen anymore. Matt still chased after being an eighteen-year-old again. I was perfectly content with approaching thirty; in fact some parts of me really couldn't wait. I'd noticed a gentle satisfaction in the things that once would have caused me horror (a night in with a film and takeaway instead of clubbing, taking pride in my home rather than it just being somewhere to rest my head each night) and I gradually allowed myself to lean towards these as I approached the big three-oh. While Matt was in complete denial the concept of being thirty would ever actually happen to him.

Marcus, his latest boyfriend, was everything Luke wasn't. Which was why Matt continued to ask me out to clubs and pubs in Southampton and Portsmouth, keen for us to relive our club kid days. He was content with frantically dancing to the latest songs, flirting with men, snogging them, and disappearing for a while as I fiddled with my straw. I was happy to look and not touch, knowing Luke trusted me completely and how powerful a deterrent that was to cheating. But every time we went out, 'club kids again' as he described us, I found myself looking around, feeling old among the barely shaving teenagers who surrounded us, longing for a curry and a good film on the sofa back at his parents' place.

Matt was part of my past, and I was part of his past. Unfortunately we hadn't yet worked out how to become part of each other's present very well: he ignored the fact I was with Luke, insisted on going out like two singletons; I didn't know how to be my twenty-eight-year-old pipe and slippers self around the eighteen-year-old version of Matt. The more we tried (in the clubs and bars,

I'd not yet managed to convince him of the benefits of a night in together) the more I realised we were two completely incompatible people, who'd never be friends now. We were only friends because of who we were all those years ago. We'd met as two teenagers on our own and he wanted to continue our friendship like that, only now I wasn't just one person, I was part of a couple. I no longer wanted to do those things.

What happens to clubbing friends, when you stop going clubbing?

Chapter Four

1976

During one summer holiday when I was five, I complained how I never saw much of Daddy, so Mummy took me to the building site where he was working at the time. We found him, sat on a bench, with a woman on his lap, giggling and stroking his hair, while he alternately fed himself and her sandwiches. Sandwiches Mummy had packed him that morning.

'What's this then, Dave?' Mummy asked, surveying the scene.

'Nothing, just having a laugh. Shirley forgot her lunch, so I said she could have some of mine.' He smiled at Mummy.

'You must think I'm fucking stupid. I knew you hadn't stopped. You dirty —' She hit him. '— lousy —' She hit him again. '— fucking bastard.' Shirley was off his lap by now.

'Leave it out, Carol, it's doing no harm.'

'And as for you, you trollop, you should know better. He's a married man, with a kid.' She looked at me. 'He shouldn't have to see this.' She grabbed my hand and led me away, shouting backwards. 'I want you home at four sharp, or I'll be round again, Dave.'

And we were off the building site and gone.

It all happened so quickly, at the time, I barely understood what was happening. I knew the young lady wasn't Mummy, and that it was usually Mummy he laughed with, but other than that, it felt like a scene from one of the soaps she used to watch every night.

When we arrived home, Mummy put the kettle on (her answer to everything then) and sat at the kitchen table, her head in her hands, crying quietly.

I stroked her arm and offered to make the tea, just like she'd shown me, carefully and slowly, only putting two cups of water in the kettle.

She nodded.

Sipping her drink, she told me how he had done it before, how he'd promised never to do it again, but she'd had suspicions, and now she knew. 'I've followed him to work before, checked his pockets for receipts, smelt his jacket for perfume. And every time he says it's the last time, he promises me he won't do it again. And I take him back, and he does it all over again.' She looked into my eyes, wiping tears from her own, her mascara smudged and mocking her for getting dressed up earlier to see Daddy. 'I'm so stupid, Dominic, such a stupid cow.'

'It'll be alright, Mummy.' I repeated what she told me when I was upset, not knowing what else to say. We sat there until the tea was cold, and Mummy had cried all her mascara off. I cleared up the kitchen, made more tea, and together we made dinner for when Daddy came home when I was asked to go to my room, as 'Mummy and Daddy have to talk without you, darling.'

Chapter Five

Summer 1999

Usually, I enjoyed my job. It gave me a sense of purpose. I enjoyed helping people; why else would you become a nurse? I didn't exactly relish the paperwork that came with management, but understood it was part of the job. All part of joining the 'skimmed milk level,' as my ex-matron, Helen, had described it: during a panic before the chief executive and trust board had arrived at the ward, Helen had realised we'd run out of milk for the tea and cakes reception she'd organised. I'd offered to buy some from the shop in the hospital reception, shouting 'full fat' as I left her office. She'd replied, like I'd just suggested I book a lap dancer for every trust board member, 'I don't think people at *that level* drink full fat. No, it must be semi skimmed at the very least, preferably skimmed. Quick sticks, Dominic, before they arrive. Quick sticks.'

Now *I* was at that skimmed milk level, but I still took full fat milk. Helen would be appalled at how common I was, sat in her old office, feet on the table, glugging full fat milked tea by the gallon, and poring over the off duty rota.

Even now, I found myself looking behind me when a member of staff asked me for some clinical advice, then I remembered, it was me they were speaking to. I constantly expected someone to uncover me for being a sham, as I was too young to be a male matron—and still drank full fat milk!

During the summer, I had signed up for a lot of extra shifts. 'It'll help pay for Christmas, the money'll come in handy, and they're really short staffed, so I'd be helping them out,' I breezed at Luke when he'd asked me why.

He didn't seem to pick up the fact that it was me who I'd be helping out, as the Keeper of the Off Duty. One of my least favourite jobs I'd acquired since becoming male matron a while before. Despite many efforts to delegate it to senior nurses and even the ward clerk, everyone told me with complete certainty that it was my and only my responsibility to do it, and they couldn't possibly begin to do it. The fact that I'd never done one before didn't seem to bother them, so I had quickly learned the mysteries of doing the off duty. It was a bit like reading tea leaves or runes. You'd align it all according to a complex 'requests book' system, where nurses wrote which shifts they'd like to work, when they definitely had to have a day off, all cross referenced with a 'minimum staffing levels table' that my director of nursing had electronically thrust into my hands, my first week as a matron. The planets would all be perfectly aligned, and I proudly reviewed the spreadsheet on my computer, then someone would get gastroenteritis, or lose a grandma, or suddenly have to go to a wedding three Saturdays away. So I'd have to reread the runes, move everything about, swap myself again another three times, until it was balanced. Honestly, it was practically a job in itself.

So, alongside arranging for agency and bank nurses to fill the black hole-sized gaps in the off duty, I signed up for some extra hours too. Entire weeks of nights, to avoid sharing a bed with Luke, afternoon shifts after being on since seven am, so I was working thirteen hours, morning shifts before an afternoon shift which ended at nine pm, so another thirteen hours.

I couldn't put my finger on *exactly* why I was doing it; all I knew was it was easier to be at work, forgetting the niggling issues back at home. Much easier to work all day, concentrating on healing sick people, dealing with staff issues, and being the Keeper of the Off Duty, than talk to Luke about our non-existent love life.

I'd learned from the master: my dad declined doing anything at home, except taking off his muddy work boots, as long as he had work. Every evening Mother (or plain old Mum as she was then) would try to speak to Dad about doing something with me at the weekend, and he'd finish his dinner, push the plate away and walk to the living room (lounge as we had called it). If pursued he'd reply, 'I've been at work all day, and all you do is get on at me. I'm knackered. Leave me alone will you. If you want to take him out at the weekend just do it, but don't waste money.'

Bang went a family outing.

So now, I continued working hard. I knew I was good at my job. Second day as matron, a care assistant and a nurse came to my office in the middle of an argument. The nurse complained that the care assistant wasn't working fast enough, it was nearly lunchtime with two patients not washed and dressed. The care assistant said she'd work faster if she wasn't doing all the *proper work*, not just *fannying around with the drug trolley*, on her own. She added how hard it was especially as more than half their bay were doubles, requiring two staff members. The nurse insisted she'd not stopped all morning and didn't even know what this fannying around was. Fortunately, I'd been on both sides of this argument before, having worked as a care assistant before doing my nurse training. I took a deep breath, remembered who was in charge (me, but I couldn't quite believe it) and said, 'You want to give good care, don't you?' Nods all round. 'So work together then. It's all needed, the drugs, the washes, everything. Think of the patients and get back out there and get on with it.' They left my office, heads high, proud to do what they'd come into nursing to do. I looked around, wondering where that little speech had come from; it didn't feel like it had come from me, but it had.

I had another nurse whose time keeping was awful: every morning he'd be at least fifteen minutes late. Excuses ranged from buses, trains, broken alarm clocks. I bought him a new alarm clock, setting it twenty minutes early to take account of transport, and he still arrived late. When I spoke to him alone he told me he was looking after his son on his own, as his girlfriend had left for bread one Saturday and never come back. He didn't get much sleep, so always slept through his alarm. I arranged for his little boy to have a subsidised place in the workplace day nursery, and changed his shifts to fit around family members helping out.

I wasn't too bad with patients either: noticing things others easily missed. Years of looking after Mother meant I could spot an alcoholic in denial miles off. The yellow pallor, disinterest in food, and fascination with nipping out for a cigarette (and swig of gin) all jumped at me so I referred the patient to the substance misuse team, and contacted the family.

I even tackled Di Anne the ward clerk—I say tackled, in fairness, she was more a work in progress, but anyway, I felt she was going in the right direction. She had worked on the ward since the hospital had opened in the mid-seventies, always in the same role, on the same ward. First week in, I asked her to photocopy some notes for me, and you'd have thought I'd asked her to perform open heart surgery on all the patients. Arriving at midday, after taking back some TOIL (time off in lieu) in lieu for what I never did find out, she sat down and replied, putting her hand in my face, 'Wait a minute, I've only just got here. Hang on a minute, I need to work out what I've got on today, I just don't know when I'm going to fit it in. I mean, I've got all this to do.' She gestured to a pile of two unopened envelopes. 'I've got all this extra stuff to do. I really don't know when I can do that. I've been on the phone all morning to the solicitors and estate agents about this house sale. Actually, I'll just nip out to make a quick call.' And she walked out. I cleared her backlog (in three minutes), showed her the photocopier and gave her the papers, told her not to do any of the 'extra things' that weren't in her job description, and concentrate on the things I asked her to do. She huffed and puffed at me but did eventually present me with the photocopied papers.

I was good at that, so why was I so bad at my relationship with Luke?

*****

The fourth of June 1999 at eight thirty pm, it was raining, as expected in a British summer. I looked up from my handover note in the staff room; he pushed the door open slowly and sat opposite me, smiling at everyone else.

It was my fourth of a string of extra nights, and I felt the sort of tiredness that comes from a series of night shifts where you grab hours of poor quality sleep during the day, between batting about with housework and other chores. The sort of tiredness only people with young babies or night workers can fully understand. *His* arrival immediately woke me back to more than normal levels.

My gaydar gave me mixed signals as he wore Timberland shoes and a very plain jacket over his nurses tunic.

He smiled at me, shook his curly dark brown hair so water sprayed around the room, then removed his jacket. 'Look at me, Ernest! Just look at me! I'm soaking wet!'

The day sister looked him up and down. 'Ernest, who's he?'

'A joke.'

'I'm assuming you're Gabriel, from the agency.'

He nodded. 'Gabe.'

But as soon as he quoted *Death Becomes Her*—I knew for definite, without a shadow of a doubt, he was as gay as bunting. No straight man quotes that film, not in this world or the next. 'Spanish, are you?' I asked, feigning disinterest.

'My dad is.' He stared at me, his long brown eyelashes framing his eyes perfectly.

I deliberately allocated myself at the far end of the ward from him. I didn't want to come across as too keen. Besides, I was *happily* partnered.

Once everyone was settled for the night, I met him in the kitchen, having noticed him walking in too, carrying an empty mug. Just on the off chance of meeting him obviously.

I stared at my tea bag intently. 'Dominic.' I held out my hand to him.

'Says on your name badge.' He smiled, shaking my hand.

'Sister wasn't impressed with your *Ernest, I'm soaking wet* line.'

'I wanted to see how she'd react. Looked like she was about to explode with no sense of humour. If she'd lost the plot it would have been perfect.'

'*These are the moments that make life worth living!*'

'I love that bit! Exactly.' He smiled and made eye contact.

Keen to continue with the Spanish conversation I persevered. 'So, Spanish father, what's your surname?'

'I'm just Gabe, or Gabriel.'

'What like, Cher, or Prince?'

'If you like.'

'You must have a surname.'

'I only tell it to people who deserve to know it.' His chestnut eyes flashed at me, one slightly obscured by a curl in his left eye.

I wanted, with all my body, to kiss him there and then. My groin was doing somersaults and I had to quickly regain interest in the tea bag to preserve my dignity. 'I'm going to the nurse station. I've got do to my notes.'

Between nursing I found out he lived with his boyfriend, A, (no more than that, what was with him and these odd names?) 'In a tiny flat in Acton, but the landlord told me it was Chiswick. It's about as much Chiswick as it is Kensington.'

As he left that morning, I asked him if he needed any more shifts.

'I've got plenty thanks, this week. I'm off to Lewisham tonight, then Guy's tomorrow night.'

'Nice to be in demand.' I forced a smile. 'If you need any more, I do the off duty, so…'

'I remember, you're the Keeper of the Off Duty.' He smiled and waved goodbye.

I didn't want to give him my number as we'd already established we both had boyfriends, and I wasn't ten, so couldn't say 'just to be friends,' like you did then. So that was it, he was there and then he was gone.

And then that happened.

Now, I stopped by my office on the way out, just to check if Di Anne was in yet.

She snapped shut her paperback and turned round to face me. 'I thought you were on nights.'

'I'm just about to go home. Try not to get crumbs on the keyboard please.' I looked at the family pack of croissants next to her mouse. 'I sent you an email with things for today.'

She opened the email, sighing like I'd asked her to climb a mountain. 'What, all this? I'll do it in a minute, but I'm in the middle of something.' She returned to her paperback.

'I'm back tonight and if it's not done, I want to know what you've done instead, which is in your job description.'

She mumbled, 'Git,' under her breath.

'And that doesn't include reading a book,' I added, closing the door and smiling.

I walked to the Tube, thinking whether I'd see Luke before he left, and felt flat. My mind put that thought into a quiet little corner, and instead, I brought out some conversations from the previous night, savouring their warmth in my mind, like a small kitten on my lap: favourite Goldie Hawn film quotes; Gabe telling me to fuck off loudly when I insisted Roxette were a good example of pop rock; me telling him to fuck off loudly when he still wouldn't tell me his surname.

I thought of Luke and a jabbing feeling came to my heart. Guilt? Anxiety? Something like that. But why should I feel guilty, I'd not done anything with Gabe. That had never been on the cards, we'd both mentioned the boyfriend word more than enough. But somehow, the laughs and quickly established pattern of in-jokes felt like cheating of a different type, *emotional* cheating.

Would I tell Luke about meeting him, almost definitely not? Another jab, yes, that's definitely emotional cheating. No point in telling Luke, it wasn't like I was going to ever see Gabe again was I?

Chapter Six

The night after meeting Gabe, I turned up for the night shift, vainly hoping he'd be there too, saving a seat for me at handover. Because my life wasn't an American teenaged drama, this didn't happen; instead I worked with a friendly woman called Charity, who came from Ghana. She didn't even know who Goldie Hawn was, so I gave up on that particular avenue of conversation.

That morning I travelled home, barely able to keep my eyes open as I sat on the Tube. I crawled into bed, set my alarm for a few hours and then nothing.

In my pyjamas, and after a strong coffee, I collected some laundry for a whites wash. I piled the towels into the machine, then checked the pockets of my nurses tunics, removing latex gloves, old handover sheets and a half eaten Kit Kat. When I was just about to bundle them into the machine I pulled out a small square of paper. Something I'd put chewing gum in after it was finished. But I hated chewing gum. I rubbed my eyes and longed for my bed, opened the piece of paper, on it was 'Gabe,' followed by a phone number.

I made another strong coffee and sat at the kitchen table, munching the Kit Kat, staring at the scrap of paper. I had no recollection of asking for his number, I certainly hadn't given him mine. Not after the guilt I felt afterwards, no way would I have let myself go this far.

And yet, here I was, holding his number in my hands. I could have thrown it away, but I hadn't. Not yet.

My mobile phone rang and I jumped to answer it.

'Hi babe, you okay? Thought I'd check you were up after last night,' Luke said.

I hid the piece of paper — *like he could see it?* — and burbled my response, 'Fine, bit tired. Just doing some washing.'

'It'll be nice to see you. Feels like it's been months.'

'Only three days.'

'Being away from home too, it doesn't help. I can't wait to see you and Princess.'

'Me too… not Princess, she's here… you know.'

'Anything funny happen at work?' He enjoyed me telling him about things I, by now, found everyday, but which never ceased to amuse and shock him.

'We lost an old lady's teeth,' I replied, not even amusing myself, feeling the piece of paper in my pocket.

'Tell me all about it when I'm back. See you soon, and don't do too much, you need rest. See you when I'm home. Bye.' He used to tell me he loved me, or how much he had missed me. It used to make me smile, how often he told me he loved me. He used to tell me what he wanted us to do together when he next saw me. Now it was nice to see me. How the lovesick mighty have fallen.

'Bye.' I put the phone down and took the piece of paper out my pocket.

After staring at the number for half an hour, sipping coffee, I realised I wasn't going to get a sign from above about whether I should call him or not. It also dawned on me that, as he didn't have my number I'd have to make *the next move*. Then of course, what followed after *the next move* would all be down to me. *The next move*, even in my head it sounded ominous. Anything that happened would all be my fault.

The night we met, Gabe had asked me how long I'd been with my boyfriend. I said, I hadn't told him I had a boyfriend at that point, and he explained he could tell. 'You're stable. You've been with him at least six to seven years. Some people change who they are as they move around the country, change jobs, change boyfriends and friends. But you, I can see you've been who you are for a long time, probably all your life.'

'And is that a good thing?' I asked, both perplexed and slightly insulted.

'It is what it is.'

I shrugged.

'It's not good, it's not bad. You are you, with your life and I'm me, with mine. So how long?'

'Ten years.'

Now, I folded and unfolded the piece of paper. Ten years of life together, ten years of problems and fun together. Ten years of my parents and his parents. All that held in my hands now. If he called me, I'd answer it, but me calling him, now that was a bit much. I thought back to my reasons for working the night shifts (not the money for Christmas presents, it was summer, the real reason). I tried to remember the last time Luke and I had had any kind of sex—not just sweat dripping down your back, mind blowing, should be illegal sex, but any kind, a bit of a fumble, a quickie in the shower — and I drew a blank.

I picked up my mobile phone and dialled the number. It rang, and at first, I felt relieved, *it's going to voicemail*, then he picked up. After establishing who I was, he asked me what I was doing.

'Laundry,' I replied, embarrassed.

'Exciting!'

'That's just the way I like to roll here. What about you?'

'Between shifts, nipping to Boots.'

'Yours is hardly *Terminator Two*, is it?'

'Fair comment.' I heard him lighting a cigarette. There was a pause as he inhaled. In a slightly higher pitched voice he said, 'What about that time I turned up to your ward, covered head to toe in red roses, with a red bow around my waist, as an apology for what happened with Brian, my ex. You were in the middle of the drugs round and you came to the ward entrance to tell me to go away, but as soon as you saw me, you couldn't be angry with me anymore. And last week when you came home from work, so tired, and late that I'd just ordered a Chinese, without you asking. And we sat together eating with chop sticks out of the containers, watching TV.'

'What?' I asked. I had no idea what he was talking about, at all.

'And the time you posted yourself to my flat on my birthday.'

'Seriously, what are you talking about?' Still completely lost.

'Don't make me say, or this could be a *very* short friendship. Think about it. I'm Gwen to carry on, pick up Gwen you can... But I'd forgotten you weren't at home that day, so instead I ended up being delivered to the Royal Mail depot, and you had to collect me the next day...'

'...and you were so hungry cos you hadn't eaten for a whole day, when I opened the box up, we went to my favourite Hungarian restaurant together!'

'I was worried there. It's my favourite of her films, you know?' he replied, smiling. I could tell he was smiling even down the phone. I could feel it *beaming* down the phone at me.

I noticed I was beaming, lighting up the room with my smile, for the first time in ages. 'I saw it three times at the cinema, and bought it on video as soon as it came out. First time we saw it, with Luke, he didn't get what was going on, and I kept explaining it to him, until a woman told us to be quiet very loudly. He came with me the second time, just to humour me, but still didn't get all of it.'

'Have you ever wanted to step into a painting or a picture, and see what it would be like to live there?'

'All the time,' I replied wistfully. 'Just like Gwen in *Housesitter*.' I stared at one of the straight off the shelf, instant art, Ikea photos on the wall, and wondered what it would be like to sit in one of the chairs in the front garden of the duck egg blue summer house, sipping a drink while my husband carefully ordered Chinese food, knowing we were both too tired to cook.

'So, you wanna meet? I mean, we could carry on like this, but I'm sure it would be better face to face, over something alcoholic.'

After an awkward bit where I explained I couldn't meet tonight as Luke was back and we hadn't seen each other in a while, Gabe added he was busy tomorrow night, so we settled on two days' time, a pub in central London.

I knew Luke would be away, which *may* have influenced my suggestion of that night, but I didn't allow myself to dwell on that thought. No need to tell him. Nothing to tell. We both have boyfriends, and we'd always been clear on that.

*****

I sat in a corner of a Victorian pub in central London, strategically placed to see the door, without having to crane my neck, or stand. I nursed a half pint of beer and checked my mobile. *Could I remember what he looked like?* Are you kidding, I'd not stopped thinking about those eyes since we met. *What would we talk about?* Did I need to remember some more good quotes from Goldie Hawn films for good measure? We'd done *Housesitter* to death, or would he want to continue with the made up stories? A sick feeling spread in my stomach: nerves, anxiety, guilt? Certainly a mix of all three.

My hands nervously fiddled with my mobile and I remembered two nights ago, when Luke had so looked forward to seeing me. All I could think about was meeting

Gabe. Luke had finished telling me about his trip away, something about a new winter collection, and the new black would be grey, and asked me what was wrong.

'Nothing. Work,' I replied, standard easy excuse.

'That Di Anne giving you problems again?'

'Yeah. It's boring, I don't want to talk about it.'

'No it's not, I'm your boyfriend, it's my job to be interested.'

I'd spun out the story about Di Anne, embellishing some details, and he gave me some good advice, which now I'd forgotten. We went to bed, and after I tried to show an interest, he brushed me off, saying he was too tired.

No need to feel guilty, it's only a drink.

With someone who I'd omitted to tell Luke about ever meeting. But that was a minor detail.

Now, I looked up and Gabe was stood opposite me, arms outstretched, ready to hug me. We hugged quickly, and he kissed my cheek lightly, so I reciprocated.

Are we doing both cheeks? I paused, then, relieved at not having to be all French about it, sat back down.

I decided to plunge straight in and tackle the metaphorical boyfriend in the corner: 'He's called Luke, we've been together since eighty-nine, so ten years, and we had a commitment ceremony a couple of years ago. He works for Dior doing marketing, brand, sales, that sort of stuff. What about yours?'

'We've been together since ninety-five, so just about four years. We live together, but none of that commitment ceremony stuff, not that I have a problem with it, it's just not for me.'

I told him about the house in the west London suburbs and Princess our dog.

'Does it have a white picket fence?' Gabe teased, smiling.

'It's nice. It's very nice. I like it. *We* like it.'

'Alright, alright, you don't have to defend it. I'm only joking.'

There was a pause between us, he smiled at me and I immediately forgave him. With those long eyelashes and that smile, I would forgive him an awful lot more than the picket fence remark.

I took a sip of my drink. 'Your boyfriend, he's called, A, was it? What's that stand for?'

'It's a long Spanish name, so it's easier to just say A.'

I nodded. 'What does A do?' I told him about Luke's job, travelling, the brand, everything (as much as I knew really). 'He's away tonight actually!' I said brightly, feeling the guilt stab me in the stomach.

'A doesn't work at the moment. He's doing an access course for the A levels he missed.'

'How's that going for him?' I leant forward.

'He's only just started. We'll see how it goes...' Gabe added, before explaining how he and A had an open relationship, with certain conditions.

Intrigued, I asked what the conditions were.

'No serial seeing someone, so it's only a onetime thing, or before you know it it's a relationship. No friends, or friends of friends. Oh, and the latest one, which I've only just found out, is *not at home.*'

'What does that mean?' It was like another world, part of which I'd never even glimpsed before.

'I met someone and took him back to our flat, while A was out, and when he came home we were just stepping out of the shower, *afterwards.*'

'*Afterwards*, afterwards?'

Gabe leant towards me across the table, looked to one side like a spy and said, 'Literally minutes afterwards. He looked at me, looked at the guy and went to the kitchen. I got dressed, said goodbye to the trade, and all he said was, he didn't expect it to be *this* in his face. I thought that was rich, since it was his suggestion in the first place, this open relationship thing. We agreed the rules, and that was it. Doesn't mean I don't love him, it's sex, not love. He kept saying it was in his face, and told me to change the sheets.'

'And did you?'

'Change the sheets?'

I nodded.

'Course, and we talked about the rules, and that's when he added the latest one. *Not at home.*'

'Interesting.' I looked at my hand then back to his eyes.

'Interesting, disgusting, or interesting, I'd like some of that?'

'No, just interesting. Not that I have a problem with open relationships, it's just not for me.'

He smiled at me, lifted the empty glasses and looked at the bar. I nodded and he left for another round.

He returned with our drinks, and asked what, apart from Goldie Hawn films, I liked; my favourite music.

'It's a bit of a cliché, but,' I paused, worried about telling him it. 'I like Erasure. Is that awful, to like such a *gay* group?'

He shrugged.

Getting used to this now, I continued, 'And I loved their ABBA covers—'Lay All Your Love On Me' and 'Take A Chance On Me'.' I pursed my lips, realising that was it, I'd fucked it right up.

'It was everywhere a few years ago, wasn't it? Erasure and ABBA this and that. Have you seen their videos, Erasure dressed up like ABBA?'

I nodded. *Had I seen the videos?* I only owned them all on tape, but I kept that to myself.

'I love them,' he said, 'all of them. Bought the EP of all four ABBA songs they did.'

We talked about other music for a while, gently teasing each other as we revealed the truly awful nature of some of our musical taste. You know, the groups and songs you listen to on your own, as a proper *guilty pleasure*.

Emboldened by my second drink, after a break from boyfriend talk, and after a long conversation about our political leanings—mine fairly nonchalant, his very left wing—I asked what A used to work as.

'He was a florist, for a hotel in London.'

'Why did he stop?'

'He had to.'

'But why?'

'I don't have to answer that. Do you want a cigarette, or have you got your own?' He offered me one.

'I'm fine thanks.' I reached into my jacket pocket and took out a cigarette. As a social smoker, I reserved my cigarettes for social or special occasions, and this definitely fell into the latter category.

Gabe lit his cigarette and passed me his lighter.

I lit my cigarette and looked at his eyes. 'I'm sorry, I didn't mean to…'

'It's fine. Let's not fall out over it. If we're going to fall out, let's make it something worth falling out over. Some big histrionic hissy fit, eh?'

I nodded.

'So where we going now?' He blew smoke out the side of his mouth, smiling.

'On a week night?'

'Yes, on a week night. Last time I checked it wasn't illegal. Have you got to be up in the morning? I'm on a late at Lewisham, so it's fine.'

'Off tomorrow, I was going to walk Princess in Richmond park…'

'Princess?'

'You remember. Our dog.'

He raised an eyebrow. 'I remember. I just can't quite believe it.'

'Long story.'

'We've got all night,' he replied. 'Heaven, it's usually pretty good in the week, full of students, usually glad of a bed for the night if you pull.' He stood up and grabbed my hand.

I suddenly had a vision of him sitting on a fairground ride, reaching out to help me aboard. 'Go on then, I can walk her in the afternoon.'

'If you're back then…' And we were gone.

We were in Heaven, on the podium, Gabe had taken his top off, so I was attempting to avoid looking at his pretty delicious chest, covered in lots of dark hair, and trying to copy his dance moves. Conscious of not having a school night hangover, I'd opted for water and soft drinks.

We took a break from nonstop dancing to smoke in one of the under the arches seating areas.

'Alright?' Gabe handed me one of his cigarettes.

I nodded.

'You've been here before, right?'

'Years ago. Me and Luke used to come here quite a bit. Until we didn't.'

'No boyfriend talk. Just us two, okay?'

I nodded.

He leant close and whispered in my ear. 'I'm going to kiss you in a minute and pass you something, just take it, and swallow it with some water. Trust me, okay?'

I nodded again. I'd done quite a bit of nodding, and just gone along with things, but it just felt right, I didn't feel worried; I just went along with Gabe's suggestion. He kissed me on the lips, not with tongues, and I felt something bitter in my mouth. I took a swig of water and leant back to look at him, now noticing his chest, dripping with sweat. 'What was it?'

'Half an E.'

My eyes widened and I started to shout, 'What!' until he put his hand on my mouth and held me tight.

'Just forget about it, keep drinking water, and stay with me. I'm not going to leave your side, not even for a minute. Okay?'

He sat on the car of the Ferris wheel, leaning forward, arms outstretched. I took his hands, got on board, as the wheel turned, lifting us to the sky.

He told me how he became really ill last winter; at first he thought it was another cold, but this time he couldn't shake it, no matter how much paracetamol he took. It went on for months, and months, getting worse, until he was admitted to hospital, collapsing at work one morning. He had a collapsed lung from pneumonia and he'd lost over a stone in weight—the cold suppressed his hunger so he'd just not bothered eating, between doses of medicine from Boots.

'A went to the hospital after I found out and when they told him, that's when he sort of went a bit off the rails. He stopped working, didn't pay the bills, didn't eat, slept all day, and didn't sleep at night. He's not worked since then. We used to fight for days, and we'd stop and forget why we started arguing in the first place.'

'Why don't you leave him?' I asked, trying to take it all in.

'It's not that simple.'

It took my breath away. I hadn't expected him to say anything more, after the last time. It felt like we'd fast-forwarded our friendship by two years in the two short weeks we'd known each other. Once someone shares like that, there's no point in holding anything back, no point sugar coating it when they turn up in an awful outfit, no point biting your lip when they spend their whole time with you checking their mobile phone.

I felt sick and stubbed out my cigarette.

Gabe rubbed my back. 'It's normal, nothing to worry about. It'll pass. Have a sip of water.' He handed me his bottle of water.

The sickness subsided and soon all I really wanted to do was dance: my legs tapping up and down gave Gabe the hint. He nodded to the dance floor, took my hand and led me there.

One of my favourite songs of the year, 'All or Nothing' by Cher, started to play and I felt waves running up and down my body. I closed my eyes and lifted my hands into the air, moving them in time with the music as my feet and hips swung in time too. It felt like I was teaching the whole club a *new way of being*, as they watched me dance to the music. I had invented a new way, and they would follow. I closed my eyes and imagined everyone copying my dancing, a huge smile spread across my face.

Gabe held my hands. 'Feeling okay?'

I nodded.

'Nicely pilled up?'

I nodded again, then stared at a muscly guy's chest an arm's length away. The guy smiled and continued to dance, looking at Gabe then back to me.

Gabe touched my arm. 'Not very subtle. Didn't your mum tell you it's rude to stare?'

'I'm sorry.' I walked to the muscly guy and touched his arm. He shook his head and smiled at me, then Gabe, who quickly led me away.

I danced so much my feet hurt, smoked a whole packet of cigarettes in three hours, explored all of Heaven's rooms and dance floors, the whole time Gabe never once left my side. Even when I went to the gents, he stood just outside, asking if I was okay as I swayed lightly at the urinal. We curled up in a seating booth, me resting my head on his lap and playing with his chest hair, while he held my other hand. It wasn't sexual, not one part of it was sexual, it was sensual, and comforting, but not sexual. Later, thinking about that moment, I knew Luke wouldn't be convinced, so was glad he wouldn't know, but I knew there was nothing sexual in that moment, as my groin could testify to.

We left the club, walking out into bright sunshine; so to celebrate my first all-night clubbing in years, we sat in the paws of the lions at Trafalgar Square, watching the buses pass.

'My night bus goes from there, what about yours?' Gabe asked, pointing to a corner of Trafalgar Square where groups of people gathered.

'There.' I pointed to my corner.

'You okay to go home on your own, or do you want me to come with you, or you could come back to mine? Sofa bed…'

My mind tried to make sense of all the options he'd presented me with. 'I'm fine, I feel fine. Not sick, not tired, just a bit floaty. I know which bus to get, I know where to get off, look, I've even got the right money for it.' I showed him some change, proud at how simultaneously together and floaty I felt.

'Sure?'

'Sure.' I hugged him hard, kissing his cheek, and skipped to my bus stop.

I thought about the night, how we'd started in a pub, just for a drink, and now, having not gone home, I was floating my way home on a night bus. It could have been an early day bus actually, I'd not noticed if it had a N in front it its magic number which I knew would take me all the way back to my corner of suburban Middlesex. One minute I was in a pub, next in a club, and now here. *And then that happened.* I couldn't remember the last time I'd just gone with the flow of a night out—never mind that, I couldn't remember the last time I'd actually had a proper night out.

Chapter Seven

I finished handover to the morning staff, having worked another night shift. Ostensibly to help pay for Christmas, but in actual fact, when I'd allowed myself to think about it that night, to avoid seeing Luke and telling him about Gabe. There was only so long I could legitimately keep Gabe a secret from him without it becoming suspicious, and even *I* was a bit suspicious of myself.

I walked into my office to find Di Anne on her mobile with a large family chocolate cake on her desk. 'Someone's birthday?'

She lifted her index finger to show she'd be off the phone shortly.

I left a pile of photocopying on her desk and sat with my back to her, trying to break the back of the next month's off duty. Staring at the spreadsheet, my mind returned to us sat in the paws of the lions in Trafalgar Square after going to Heaven.

I'd caught my bus, mesmerised by the street lights gradually turning off as I neared my home. I sat on the sofa with a cup of tea, stroking Princess, and a text message beeped on my phone. I immediately jumped on it, worried it would wake Luke, then remembered he was away for work. Otherwise I wouldn't have gone out with Gabe. *Oh yeah.*

It said: Amazing night. Sleep well. See you soon. G
x

A kiss on a text message has never had such significance in my life before that point.

I stared at the text message, warming my hands around the mug and his words rang around my head: 'I'm HIV positive. There's more... complications.'

Two weeks ago, I'd never seen this man, and then he told me this. It gave our friendship an immediate strength and candour, most take years to reach.

'I knew you'd be alright about it,' he had added.

'How?'

'You can smell these sort of things once you've done it a few times. Worst time was someone I met for a bit of extracurricular. We were down to our pants, and he'd been nibbling at my chest for a while, and I told him. He grabbed his clothes from the floor, shouted bye and left.'

'Just like that?'

Gabe nodded.

'But I'm not about to sleep with you, so it makes it easier, simpler.'

'Easier, but not simpler. If we're going to be friends and I hadn't told you, there would be all this *stuff* I couldn't tell you about. Stuff which I was finding hard, but without knowing, about *it*, you wouldn't be able to help, cos without knowing you'd just think, well it's nothing.'

'Otherwise we're starting off by lying, and that's not good for friendships.'

'Plus, if you freaked out, I've only just met you, so no big loss if you fuck off. And you're a nurse, so...'

'What, I'm caring and know all about it? I don't think so,' and I told him about when I was a student nurse, the taped off wards, being asked to put on a mask and gloves just to visit friends.

He looked back at me, shocked.

'It brings out the best and worst in people. Even nurses.'

'I can see that.'

We talked about how *it*, we didn't want to always use its full name in conversation, so we just said *it*, and his issues with *it* couldn't always trump my problems, otherwise I could never complain to him about anything in my life. We'd both experienced one sided friendships and knew that wasn't where we wanted us to end up.

After awkwardly referring to *it*, as I asked some questions, he proclaimed: 'I've got it, we'll call it Lernaean Hydra. We can say it publicly, no one will have a clue what we're talking about. It's a bit literary too, the labours of Hercules!'

I shrugged. 'The what Hydra?'

'Okay, we'll just say The Hydra. It's a multi-headed serpent thing which swims. Pretty apt I'd say.'

I tried to think of a better name, but The Hydra stuck. It was his Hydra and he could name it if he wanted to.

After *that* conversation almost all our texts to each other ended in kisses, like with an old friend. The way I saw it, we *were* old friends then, you can't share that and not be right into someone's life, whether you liked it or not. And I did, I embraced it. I loved it. I loved him. Could I say that? Had I fallen in love with him, but didn't yet love him? Were they different? I had definitely fallen in love with him. Of that much I was sure.

Now, I felt someone shaking my shoulder and I jolted back to reality.

'You were miles away,' Di Anne said. 'Anywhere nice?'

I smiled.

'It's my lunch.'

'What?'

'The cake, I can't afford to buy lunch in the canteen every day. We don't get paid for weeks and I'm on the bones of me arse already.'

'So you're eating a cake for lunch?'

She nodded. 'Cheaper than buying lunch.'

'You're not going to share it with anyone else?'

'Why would I? It's no one's birthday or anything special.'

'Why would you indeed,' I replied; who could argue with that logic?

'What's with this paperwork you left for me?'

I bit my tongue from saying, it's your job, and instead replied, 'I need some photocopying done, and after can you tell me who's on annual leave for the next off duty, so I can put it in the rota?'

'You must be joking, right?'

'Why?'

'I've not got time *for all that*, I'm only here till five today. I'm not staying late. I was here from seven, okay, in the car park, I had to sort something out for my car, but I was still here, so…'

I looked at the clock; it wasn't yet midday. 'Let's go through what else you've got today and see what can wait.'

'There's so much, I don't know where to start.'

'As Maria said in the *Sound of Music*, let's start at the very beginning…'

'I love having a gay boss. It's so much fun. I love the gays. You're all so funny, like that.' She smiled.

'We'll talk about that later; now get me a list of what you're doing today.'

She left to look for some paper, even though we were sat in an office with piles of paper all around. I took a deep breath and a sip of tea.

My phone beeped with a text from Luke asking when I was coming home and telling me it would be nice to see me. *Nice* to see me. From my husband, who I'd promised to stay with forever. An eternity with *nice* filled my heart with sadness.

I knew I'd have to tell Luke about Gabe at *some* point, but I just couldn't face it yet. He'd not asked me about Gabe, so I wasn't actually lying to him. He always asked me how my day was when I arrived home. The night I met Gabe I just told him I was tired and there was nothing to talk about.

After we went to Heaven together, Luke didn't ask about work, he was so full of stories from his travels, labouring to ensure Dior's brand image wasn't tarnished, and other stuff. He knew I wouldn't do anything of note without him, so didn't bother asking.

I will tell him later. Tonight, definitely tonight.

But I'm working tonight, 'Just a few extra shifts to save up for Christmas,' I told him a few weeks ago. The fact it was summer didn't strike him as odd, since I was renowned for my long-term saving capabilities.

'I feel like I haven't seen you in ages,' he added simply.

Couldn't argue with that. It was true, completely true and all my own decision.

I knew I had to tell him, but I didn't know where to start. How do you tell the person you've been in love with (and when I really thought about it, I did still love him) that you've fallen out of love with them, that it's more like brothers, or worse—neutered cats. Completely sexless. And that you don't want a sexless life until you die. There's not a card from Clintons you can buy that says that—I knew, I'd tried to find one.

I decided to leave it a bit longer, until I knew how I really felt about Gabe. Once I worked that out, I'd have something clear to tell Luke, even if it was 'I've fallen out of love with you and met someone else.' At least then, it would be clear. At this point it was anything but clear in my mind. Which is why I filled my time with work.

Now, Di Anne returned with a few sheets of paper, sat and tried to load them into the printer. 'IT need to have a look at this. It's not my job to service the printers. Got any other bits I can get on with, Dominic?'

'Any other admin you can do, which doesn't involve a computer or a printer?'

She nodded, fork in one hand, rest of the cake in the other.

I worked until I barely knew where I lived, sometimes only giving myself six hours between staying late to sort out admin, and the next shift. Luke and I communicated exclusively by text.

During the night, when I felt I was completely alone, I sat at the nurse desk, surrounded by care plans, wishing someone could write a care plan for my life.

I won't bore you with too many technicalities, but suffice it to say, a care plan is exactly that: a plan of the care a patient should receive, so any nurse can walk onto the ward, read the plan and look after that patient in the way best for them. It contained everything from whether they could stand or not, if they had false teeth, and whether they liked marmalade on their toast for breakfast.

If someone could write down what I needed to do about Gabe and Luke, now they were both in my life, it would all be so simple.

One moment I thought I'd worked it out: I'd be friends with Gabe—after all there was nothing more to it at the moment—and I'd tell Luke and we would live happily ever after. But, sadly I knew it wasn't nearly that simple. Now I'd had a taste for what Gabe would be like just as a friend, Luke as a boyfriend stood in sharp contrast to that. It was like eating a pavlova, then going back to the red wine you'd had with a steak. Your taste buds would always long for more of the pavlova. But without having a slice of pavlova, you'd have been happy sticking to red wine all night long.

But I didn't want to stop having the pavlova. I'd developed quite a taste for this particular brand of pavlova. I mean, I still liked red wine...or so I thought. I'd always liked red wine, who doesn't, nothing wrong with a good red wine. If only I'd left the pavlova alone...

Chapter Eight

I couldn't stop crying. I walked to the Tube on my way to work and tears streamed down my face. It wasn't normal winter blues, as it was bright sunny summer (well, as much as any British summer ever is).

Luke had tried to cheer me up; I sat picking at my dinner he made us, barely touching it. The only thing I'd eaten all day, having gone from morning to evening with only tea to keep me upright. I didn't tell him that; I kept taking the lunch boxes he packed for me, throwing the contents away at work. We watched TV together; even my favourite shows couldn't pierce the deep blackness I had descended into.

I started to dream about the supermarket of sadness again. Once again, people piled their packets of pure sadness into my trolley as I walked around the supermarket. I knew something was wrong. It was almost as bad as the first time. I knew what it was: I had let myself slip, I'd stopped my full-time hobby of being happy.

The thing is, it was hard to keep so happy while I had so many complex thoughts swirling around my head. Questions about my relationship with Luke, when I should tell him about Gabe, thoughts about if I really was falling for Gabe, all fought for space in my head.

Luke made my favourite dinner — toad in the hole with onion gravy — and put on one of my favourite films:

Death Becomes Her. I stared at the screen, my food cold, tears streaming down my face.

'What is it, babe?' Luke asked hopefully.

'There's nothing you can do. Nothing food, a film can do to help.' I tapped my head. 'Something's gone wrong here, and I'm wrong inside.'

He held me, rocking gently, while Goldie Hawn and Meryl Streep bitched at each other in the background. I didn't raise a smile. It only served to remind me of Gabe, and made me sadder.

He tried similar approaches over a few weeks, each evening baffled by my silence, compared to our usually chatty evenings together. He tried to start chipper conversations about the weather, if I wanted to go shopping together at the weekend, if I had any egregious stories from Mother we could laugh about together.

I met each question, each attempt at conversation with a shake of my head, or a 'No.'

'Has she said something?'

I stared at the TV.

'Your mum, I know how upset she can make you. She doesn't mean it, it just comes out. Is it that? She's not invited herself round again, has she?'

Memories of the previous Easter almost made me smile with horror. Who knew four days could pass so slowly, with so much happening? Alcoholic chocolate Easter eggs; an emergency to stock up on gin on Easter Sunday, taking in most of the supermarkets of the western Home Counties; or my personal favourite, taking us to a party thrown by one of her Chelsea friends where she introduced us as 'My son, and his special friend. It's such a shame he's gay, or I'd have introduced him to your daughter, but I suppose these are the crosses we have to bear. Children can be such a disappointment, don't you find? Now, Miffy darling, where's the champagne?'

To Luke, now, I shook my head.

I simply couldn't bear talking to him; it took all my strength to get up and go to work each day. I wasn't keen to let on at work anything was wrong, worried about being labelled a nutter. I knew all the rhetoric about 'mental health awareness' and how it's as serious as physical illness. I was supportive to the staff at work being signed off sick for depression, grief, including a couple who definitely had at least four grandmas, so unfortunate was their luck they seemed to regularly have a fortnight off after another died. I diligently put together sympathetic *return to work plans* when they appeared at the nurse station for their first shift back. I nominated my ward for a case study about mental health good practice for the staff newsletter. But for myself, I told no one, brushing it off with, 'I'm tired,' or 'just a headache,' when colleagues asked what was wrong as I returned from the toilet, eyes bloodshot from crying.

Gabe telling me about The Hydra had tripped something in my head. Despite my knowledge and experience, my mind fast-forwarded to one specific point: I imagined sitting beside Gabe's bed as he lay, covered in lesions, slowing drifting away.

I knew that wasn't going to happen any time soon; he was taking his meds, and since the eighties people were living much longer.

But there was still something which flicked my mind to that scene. I felt my trolley loaded up with sadness once again.

So when Luke asked what was wrong, I couldn't tell him everything. He hadn't yet met 'this angelic Gabe,' as he'd quipped once I took the coward's way out and dropped him into conversation one evening.

Soon I mentioned things we'd done together a while before, giving the impression they were recent events. At first it was, 'I'm going for lunch with my friend Gabe,' then 'we're having a drink after work... oh it's just me and Gabe,' and from that it was easy to drop in a few, 'Gabe likes that film too,' or 'He loves food, we should have Gabe and his *boyfriend* for dinner' making sure to emphasise the 'boyfriend.'

It was quite one thing introducing a new friend to Luke, or 'your new best friend Gabe,' as he like to refer to him, but it was quite another saying he was HIV positive, and that had caused me to have a revisit of My Depression, with an added side order of *do I fancy him more than you?*

Instead, I thought it best to just introduce Gabe as Gabe, rather than Gabe who is HIV positive. He'd been very explicit about how it didn't define him; it wasn't all of him, just a part of him. So I felt introducing both Gabe and The Hydra at the same time would somewhat undermine that wish.

So one evening, Gabe came round for dinner. *And then that happened.*

I wasn't sure how it did, but it did. His boyfriend, A, didn't come. Gabe apologised as Luke took his coat and explained that A wasn't very well, and didn't like travelling on the Tube much.

'How does he get to work?' Luke asked.

'He doesn't.' Gabe watched as Luke hung up his coat.

'Is he studying?' Luke walked towards the living room.

'In theory yes.' Gabe followed him.

'Right.'

Gabe looked at me and smiled weakly. 'He signed up for some A levels. Went to the first two weeks and hasn't been back since.'

I jumped in, leaning in to shake Gabe's hand. 'Have a seat.'

He looked at my hand, shook it awkwardly, handed me a bottle, and sat.

Gabe drank three vodka tonics before we ate, gradually becoming louder and more talkative as the evening progressed.

Luke offered red wine with the beef stew; Gabe drank three glasses before we had finished our first. By dessert—never pudding, according to Mum: 'So working class, pudding, makes me think of whippets and flat caps. Never darling, never'—he was arguing with Luke about

European politics and leaning out the window to smoke roll up cigarettes.

We both had to work the next day, so I tried to usher Gabe to the spare room where I'd made the bed and laid out a towel. I made a show of yawning and looking at my watch.

Gabe looked at his watch, drank the remains of his wine, followed me to the spare room where he immediately took his top off and lay on the bed, arms behind his head, revealing dark brown armpit hair. I tried to avert my eyes, but was fascinated by his chest, the little black trail of hair running from his belly button, disappearing inside his attractively filled jeans. A jolt shot to my groin.

'How did I do?' He smiled.

'Talk to you in the morning. What time you up?'

'I'm at Hillingdon Hospital for an early, at seven.'

'You can't drive, you'll still be pissed.'

'I'm just gonna call A, see if he's still up.' He winked.

'It's quite late.'

'Night.' He reached for his phone and stood to kick the door closed.

We cleared up the plates together. Luke liked him. Which made it all much worse. Or better, *something*, definitely harder. Anyway, it wasn't what I was expecting. Ideally they wouldn't have got on, hey presto, the perfect excuse for them not to see each other again.

'Makes sense now,' Luke said, drying a plate.

'What?'

'Why you wanted to be friends with him.'

I nodded, washed a saucepan and handed it to Luke.

'Mind you, he can drink, can't he?'

'Suppose so.'

'If I was with that A, I'd drink. What's he called, or is it just A?'

'Just, A to me. Doubt I'll meet him.'

'Why do you say that?'

'A feeling. I think he escapes from A with his friends.'

'I'm going to bed.' Luke kissed my cheek and threw the tea towel at the sink; it landed on the floor.

I stared at the damp tea towel, turned off the light, walked to our bedroom and fell into a deep sleep immediately, aware of Luke's back next to mine in bed.

Chapter Nine

1977-1982

I grew up with two parents—more than some can boast—who at first loved each other. I think the pressure of having me seriously affected their relationship.

Daddy would come in from work, take off his muddy boots and leave them by the front door, then sit in his chair smoking a roll up cigarette, while Mummy prepared dinner. Daddy was in and out of work as I grew up, and I knew when he had work, because we ate meat. When he didn't work, we lived on huge chunks of bread and soft overcooked vegetables in a thin 'soup'.

This was when Mummy—not Mother then—picked up work to help bring in the bacon (literally as well as figuratively). She cleaned at my primary school, much to my embarrassment when my friends realised the quiet lady, pushing the floor polisher and cleaning the toilets, was in fact my mummy. She cleaned early mornings at local pubs, getting up before I went to school and back after I'd left. As a consequence, I started getting myself ready for school from five years upwards.

Even when they both worked, they always watched every penny: there was always the threat and fear of it being the last pay cheque Daddy received for months. After school, Mummy took me to the discount shops to buy non-branded washing powder and soaps—Fairy and Ariel were unknown luxuries in our house. Then she walked me to the other side of town for the supermarket, scouring the reduced shelves for bargains. Dinners were unusual surprising concoctions, based on whatever the reduced shelves had thrown up earlier that day. Chilli, pudding rice and peas anyone?

During school holidays, I walked to the library to sit in the warm, reading books all day. The librarians used to ask where my mummy was and I told them she was shopping and would pick me up soon. Even then, I knew I couldn't tell them I was alone because she was cleaning an office round the corner. For lunch I went to the pick and mix at Woolworths and nicked some chocolate raisins, slowly nibbling them all afternoon among the books.

Sometimes Daddy came home later than normal, smelling of beer and more cigarettes than usual. Mummy spent the evening waiting for him, pacing up and down the hall, wringing her hands over the sink and washing them until they were red and sore. I asked if we could eat before he came home and she stared into the distance, leaning into space, stood next to the sink, tears streaming down her face, with the little make up she could afford smudging onto her cheeks. I gave her my hanky to clean herself up and she pushed me away. 'You don't have a clue; you don't know what it's like.' She continued to cry.

When he returned I was banished to my room and all I could hear was raised voices from the kitchen, and sometimes a smack. When called, I returned to the kitchen where Mummy was dishing up the food, cradling her face, while Daddy smoked in his chair in the lounge.

One Friday night, Mummy had prepared a special dinner to celebrate her job at the school—I didn't understand the details at the time, but she smiled when she mentioned hours, and I knew that meant more money, and meat, so I smiled back and hugged her. She prepared steak and kidney pudding, all from scratch, pastry and all, and it was ready to serve with veg and potatoes. Six pm came and went, so she dished it onto plates and left it in the oven to keep warm. Seven pm came and went and she washed her red hands again and darted between the kitchen and hall to see if he was approaching. Eight pm came and went, we sat at the kitchen table eating the dry remains of our meals. I tried to make conversation about my day at school and asked if I'd see more of her now her 'hours' had changed. She smiled weakly and chewed her food. I asked if I could watch some TV before bed and she told me I had to get to bed before Daddy arrived. I didn't fully understand the logic to this, but as a six-year-old I knew when Mummy was having one of her bad patches, so I pecked her on the cheek and disappeared to my room. She fell on the floor in a pile of tears and snot and I turned to help her: 'Leave me, nothing you can do, best go to bed. It'll all be okay in the morning.'

I woke at gone tem pm as the door slammed and heard them shouting from my bedroom. The voices became louder and louder so I crept from my bedroom and hid behind the kitchen door, watching through the crack in the door.

She told him she'd had enough (of what I wasn't sure at the time) and he promised he'd done nothing wrong. She grabbed his shirt and pointed at a red mark on the collar.

Daddy replied, 'What do you expect, when I've got you to come home to. Nothing wrong with it, all the boys on the site do it.'

'All of 'em, really.'

'Difference is, they look the other way, not like you. Always sticking your nose in where it's not wanted. Couldn't just leave it, could you, had to ask.'

'I wanted to celebrate, they gave me more hours at the school and now it's permanent. That's a second wage, coming in all year round.'

'What's that supposed to mean, all year round?' he spat.

'Nothing.' Mummy cowered from him.

'I'll give you nothing, you ungrateful cow.' He threw his dinner plate at Mummy, who fell to the floor. Mummy lay on the ground as he leant over her, kicking her chest before pouring leftover gravy onto her head and walking out. He bumped into me as he left the kitchen. 'Alright, Dominic? Mummy and Daddy are just having a little talk.' He left, slamming the front door.

'Mummy's just fallen over, can you be a good boy and get Mummy a towel?' she asked as I walked into the kitchen.

The next day she told me we were going on an adventure, 'Staying with Auntie Sharon for a bit. You like Auntie Sharon, don't you?'

I did like Auntie Sharon, she gave me spotted dick and custard, big plates of shepherd's pie and gravy. She was a dinner lady Mummy worked with at school. She even let me have my own mug of tea, once it was cool enough to hold. She wasn't a proper auntie, she wasn't Mummy's sister, no she was Mummy's best friend. But she was always Auntie Sharon to me.

Mummy packed a large wheeled suitcase with her clothes and makeup, and I took my favourite toys and clothes, squashed into a smaller wheeled suitcase.

'Is Daddy coming too?' I asked as we walked to catch the bus to take us to Auntie Sharon's house.

'It's a surprise for Daddy. Like your birthday was a surprise.' She smiled. 'Not long and we'll be at Auntie Sharon's. Be a big strong boy and pull the suitcase for Mummy.'

I started to work as soon as I was old enough, washing up in a pub. My friends spent their money like it hurt them to keep it: new trainers, singles from HMV and Our Price, sweets from Woolworths, clothes from C&A. I had always saved at least a third of my money since I started to work. Every time I spent it, it felt like a little bit of me was leaving forever; all I could think about was how hard I'd worked for that money, and what if the pub didn't need me next weekend?

When I was eleven or twelve, my school shoes fell apart and Mum could no longer repair them, as there was nothing to repair the shoe to, since the sole had completely worn off. I asked if I could buy myself some new trainers, knowing she wouldn't be able to afford them, but wanting to check it was okay all the same. She looked up from attempting to fix my school shoes with newspaper, smiled and told me it was my money and I could do what I wanted with it. I bought new school shoes instead and hid them until they were worn in, too late for Mum to object. Sometimes she borrowed from me to pay the bills, writing it on a bit of paper pinned to the cork board in the kitchen where we wrote who was doing dinner that night. I still visited the library, reading the young adult books by Sue Townsend, rather than picture books, but now to borrow music on CD and tape it at home.

Chapter Ten

September 1999

Matt sat opposite me, sipping his drink through a straw at the bar of the club in Portsmouth. A weekend at Matt's gave me an excuse for time away from Luke and my normal life.

I'd told Matt how I hadn't been well lately, how I needed someone to talk to.

'As long as we have a chance for some talent spotting, and can be *club kids together* again, I'm all yours,' he'd agreed to my spending the weekend at his. Strictly speaking it was at his parents' house, where he had recently moved back to live in his old bedroom between jobs.

I'd also hinted how I wasn't feeling too well, and so wouldn't be all laughs, and he'd just brushed it off, 'Nothing a few drinks won't sort out.'

Now, I took a deep breath and launched into the whole story of my life: meeting Gabe, how it affected my feelings for Luke, and how I felt bad recently.

'What, guilty bad, or what?' he asked, perplexed.

'No, just... confused, low.' I was keen to keep it vague. I wanted to ask him what I should do about Gabe.

'About what?'

'I just told you. Gabe, Luke. All that.'

'I don't understand what's to feel bad about. Just bin him, that's what I'd do.'

'Luke?'

'If you want.'

'But we've been together for years. And I don't know how I feel about Gabe.'

'If I was you, I'd know exactly how I felt about him by now.'

'Shagging isn't always the answer to everything.'

'Depends what the question is. You should try him out.'

'It's not that simple. There's other factors to consider too.'

'Boyfriend?'

I nodded.

'And?'

'It's not as simple as that.'

'When is it with you?' Matt replied. 'Look, I don't need to know it all, if you don't want to tell me something. Okay he's a tortured soul, so he has problems and his life's complicated. Big deal, Dominic, it's only as complicated as he lets it be. You just simplify how you look at things, and your life simplifies itself around you.'

I stared at him, open-mouthed.

'Trust me, I've done it.'

We danced in the club together, Matt looking around the whole time, 'talent spotting,' half-heartedly dancing, so he still looked cool. I really put my back into it, trying to recapture the abandon I'd felt as club kids all those years ago, and more recently with Gabe in Heaven.

I tried to broach the subject of why I needed time away from home, the great dilemma I found myself in, but

Matt half listened, scanning the room for men he could chat to. When he did pay attention, he could hardly hear me, the music was so loud. After a while I noticed how out of place I felt, wishing we'd stayed in with his parents, watching Saturday night TV, hunched over an Indian takeaway on our laps.

We left at two, the lights turned on, revealing the shocking state of most people, makeup smeared, tops tucked into back pockets, sweat dripping down naked torsos of varying attractiveness. As we walked to get a kebab (Matt insisted, I got chips, safer than the odd elephant's leg of kebab he ate), I stumbled about my words and said, 'I think I'm falling out of love with Luke.'

'Your Luke?' he asked, incredulous, mouth full of kebab.

'Course my Luke.'

'What's brought this on?'

'Weren't you listening earlier?'

'Oh yeah, this Gabe guy.' He paused, thinking about what to say. 'If you simplify how you look at it, it'll all become clear. Trust me.'

Was that it? Was that all he was going to give me? After I poured my heart out to him (admittedly not *all* my heart, I'd deliberately kept some back) that was the advice he gave. I looked down at my chips as Matt devoured his kebab and suddenly lost my appetite, dropping the chips in a nearby bin.

'Not hungry?'

I shook my head.

'Have you lost weight?'

'Yes. A couple of stone.'

'Lucky you,' he shrieked, devouring his kebab quickly. 'What did you do? Which diet did you go on? Not that you needed to lose it, though…'

I took a deep breath and began to tell him how I'd simply lost my appetite, lost the will to eat, got out of the habit of eating. He listened, eating his kebab until I finished.

'What's brought this on?'

'Gabe.'

'You really are in trouble aren't you? You've really fallen for him, haven't you?'

'That's the thing, Matt. I don't know if I have. All I do know is I've fallen out of love with Luke, and that Gabe's there. Sort of hanging in the background, moving closer to my foreground. That's the only way I can describe it.' I let the phrase hang there for a while as Matt chewed over both it and his kebab.

'And all this is from meeting this Gabe?'

'I have this sense of dread, this dark feeling which surrounds me too. You know how I get dark moods?'

He nodded.

'One of them.'

'What have you got to be low about? You've got everything you ever wanted: boyfriend, home, job, dog, everything. What's to be sad about?' He looked at me, tilting his head to one side, kebab juice dripping from his mouth. 'You need a holiday, that's what you need. Sort you out, get away from it all. We should go away somewhere, somewhere hot, just us two.'

I shrugged. 'We gonna get a taxi?'

'Well, we're not flying home if that's what you mean!' He wiped his hands on his trousers, stood opposite me and held my shoulders, looking into my eyes. 'The holiday — what do you reckon?'

I could have told him it wasn't about a holiday. I could have told him it wasn't that while meeting Gabe was one of the best things which had ever happened to me, it was also one of the worst. I could have said, I now didn't know which parts of my life really were right, and which were wrong. I could have explained I couldn't talk to Luke about this, 'Hey Luke, you know all this time we've been together, well let's call it all off. Why? Oh, I *think* (only think) I've fallen for someone else, who I've only just met.' I could have told Matt, I couldn't tell Gabe since he wasn't exactly an impartial adviser, he sort of, you know, had a stake in the whole situation. I could have told him all that.

But I didn't think I'd have to, I thought he'd get it. I thought he'd understand what I was struggling with, would see the low mood was bigger than both me, or my relationship with only Luke, it was *everything*. My whole life. That once again, something inside my head had tripped and sent me into the blackness — or one of my dark moods, as he thought of it. Somehow, I couldn't tell him about My Depression, because it would shatter his perfect view of me, which I felt duty bound to maintain.

So instead, I opened my mouth and said, 'Holiday sounds good.' I waved my arms as a taxi drove past. 'Our carriage awaits.' I got in the taxi, followed by Matt, and stared out the window all the way back to his parents' as he chattered about 'our holiday options,' at twenty to the dozen.

Chapter Eleven

Mother, keen to see me after too long, invited herself to ours for the weekend. Luke must have organised it with her, because I didn't remember any phone calls from Mother, and they normally stuck with me for a while afterwards.

Luke rushed about the house, fixing or removing everything my mother could possibly comment on or start an argument about.

The first night, I collected her from the station, something about her Mercedes being in for a service.

Luke prepared a meal, which Mother ate, with water, declining wine politely, and complemented him at the end: 'Such an inventive chef. You're so lucky Dominic.' She asked how work was for us.

I told her I was busy, lots of extra shifts.

'Saving up for Christmas, isn't it?' she asked, sipping her water.

'Yes.'

'Bit early for that isn't it, darling?'

I ignored her and started to explain about Luke's regional manager promotion, how it involved travel.

'I'm sure that's very interesting darling, but I want to hear about *you*. How *are* you?' I sensed the implied steepled fingers and tilted head, which came with the question.

'Isn't anything private?' I spat at Luke.

Mother stood to touch my shoulder, and I knew something was really wrong. She was rarely known to show excess physical affection for anyone. Once I'd introduced her to a friend from university and she'd pushed away as the greeting hug approached, preferring instead a light peck on the cheek. My friend thought it was so no one could linger behind her ears and spot the plastic surgery scars.

Now, she purred, 'Come now darling, he's worried about you.'

'I'm taking the new tablets, I'm fine.' Mother's *special* doctor had quickly put me back on medication as soon as I saw him. 'And I'm still seeing *her* too.'

Mother replied, 'Barbara?' She was my counsellor I'd seen since My Depression first struck. Mother waved her finger at me. 'It's money well spent, darling.'

I glared at her. '*Your* money well spent.'

'And it's up to me how I spend it, darling.'

'Yes. But it's not up to you to attach so many strings with it, is it?'

'Strings?' she replied innocently.

'You know what I mean.' I looked at Luke angrily.

He replied, 'Don't look at me. Nothing to do with me. I'm keeping well out of it.'

'I wish you had,' I replied. 'I'm going to bed. Tired, must be the tablets.' I left the room.

I heard Mother muttering, 'Strings, I have no idea what he's talking about,' before asking Luke to 'be a darling and make me a herbal tea.'

There was no way I could have told Mother the whole truth. Once I mentioned Gabe and The Hydra, she'd launch into full paranoid mum mode: 'You haven't kissed him have you? Has he been in your house? Which knife and fork did he use?'

I was livid, confused, embarrassed? At least all three of those, all at the same time. And I was also sure half of it would be assigned to my parents when discussing it with Mother-funded-Barbara the following week.

The next night Mother offered to take us out for a meal, which we jumped at. She chose a bottle of wine as soon as we sat, despite my protest. 'Oh darling, I can have one. It's not often I eat out with my two boys.'

I whispered in her ear, 'That's the point of AA. Once you stop, you stop. You know you can't just have one.'

'I've not got many of life's pleasures left. You can't begrudge me this small crutch can you? A little something to keep Mother going, before you throw her in a nursing home, thrown on the rubbish heap of life, while you spend my money.'

She'd drank two bottles by the middle of the main course. As was always the case, it was like she had left the room and another person walked in to replace her. She held her empty glass in the air, waiting for a waiter or one of us to refill it. She snapped her fingers to demand more bottles.

She told a story of going to the engagement party of one of her village friends, Helen Hennessey. 'Helen's daughter told me all about the huge white wedding she wanted, how excited she was to have finally met the love of her life. I noticed an awful lot of children rushing about at the party, so asked Helen's daughter (I forget her name) who they all *belonged* to. Two girls were hers, and two boys from her fiancé. I took a sip of my champagne (sparkling wine actually), took her hand, poor girl, and simply asked her if she didn't think a white wedding, down the aisle, with a church mightn't be a bit... vulgar... inappropriate for two people in their position. I mean, how many *loves of your life* does one person need? She walked away, didn't say anything. Next thing I'm in the middle of a family argument—I think they referred to it as a row.' She shuddered at the thought. 'All from what I'd said, nothing really. The fiancé was there with his parents and next thing Helen asked me to leave. I bumped into her in the village post office a while afterwards, asked how the wedding plans were, if I should save the date as they say now. She said she'd be in touch, which was lovely of her, simply lovely.'

Luke tried to explain delicately how what she'd said was inappropriate and upsetting.

In response, Mother finished her glass of wine in one go, ordered more, shouted, 'Excuse me, excuse me, excuse me,' until he stopped talking, chinked her glass with a fork and stood to make an announcement to the whole restaurant.

'This is my beautiful son and his gay partner and I'm so pleased they're gay. I always wanted to go to a gay wedding, and two years ago I did. And it was so lovely…'

The entire restaurant fell silent and I wanted to curl up into a little ball. I took hold of her arm and she shook it off.

'Don't interrupt me, I'm talking,' she shouted, shrew-like. 'When he told me he was gay, I thought what a shame, but now I have two and not one son, so that's good.'

I almost left, but for the fact we hadn't paid at that point, and a small part of me worried how she would get home without us.

I paid — she was barely capable of walking, let alone signing a credit card slip — we struggled home and I put her to bed, undressing her to underwear as her head lolled about and her hands tried to push me away. I left her on her side with a pint of water next to her, which after three attempts to get her to drink, I'd given up and thought, *Leave her to have a hangover.*

The next day, Luke prepared a roast dinner, all the trimmings. Mother sat at the head of the table like a ghost, picking at her food and running to the bathroom as her body rid itself of the alcohol poisoning.

'I'm so sorry darling; I just don't know what came over me.' She looked at us both and smiled weakly.

Luke made the effort I was unable to muster: 'That's okay, Carol Anne, no harm done. Next time, eh.'

'We'll go to a Michelin-starred restaurant in town, my treat. I promise.' She looked at me, reaching for my hand across the table and squeezing it earnestly. Her eyebrows completely still, unable to move, but I could tell if they could have moved, they would have formed into a concerned frown. 'You'd like that wouldn't you, Dominic? Your mother and your partner all getting on together. Nice meal out together, darling?'

I chewed a mouthful, stared at her, then looked at my plate. There was no answer to that, or her behaviour.

I drove her to Waterloo station for her train home. The clunk of her seatbelt reminded me of my earliest memory of a car journey: this time sat in the back, about five years old, my feet kicking the passenger's seat. While Daddy was driving, Mummy unbuckled her seatbelt and opened the door. Daddy grabbed her shoulder, held her back, slammed the door, saying, 'Don't be stupid, we can talk about it, what are you doing?' He leant across to lock her door and the car swerved.

Mummy had replied, scrabbling for the door handle, 'I can't believe you've done it again, you told me, you'd never do it again.' As I grew I gradually understood the significance of that scene, I played it over and over in my mind. Sat in the back of the car, my feet kicking the passengers' seat, I knew Mummy was sad, and Daddy was something to do with it. As we drove in silence after that, I noticed Mummy shaking slightly as she wiped her eyes with tissues from the glove compartment. I handed her my hankie, which I only used to tickle my top lip to comfort myself. She smiled as she took it from my small hand, only handing it back some time later, just before we arrived at our destination. I still couldn't remember where our destination had been, but even now, I could have drawn you a picture of Mummy's face as she took my hanky.

Now, on our way to Waterloo, she told me she wrote off her Mercedes when she drove it into a phone box on the way to post a letter. I stared straight ahead at the road, unable to quite process what she'd said.

'You see darling, I'd spent the whole afternoon in the pub drinking G and T's. I know what you're thinking darling, but I didn't *intend* to do that, I thought, I'll just have one, just a little one, as a reward for not drinking so long.'

No, she never *intended* to do anything, but it didn't stop it happening all the same.

'And as soon as it hit my taste buds I knew it was perfect, I knew I'd come home again. I sat at the bar telling the barman about my divorce from your father, how selfish he was and how I'd fought to get away from him. So he bought me the second drink. Before long I had quite a crowd, I knew I'd found *my people*, we laughed together, we cried together, I bought a few rounds, I bought a few more rounds. Don't remember them buying me anything, apart from the barman, but no matter. And I looked up at the time, and four hours had passed. I had a letter in my handbag I needed to post, I don't remember what it was now, something urgent, I knew that much. So I got in the car—walking through the car park I did feel a bit light-headed, but I thought, that's only the air, after being in the pub all that time. I only drove a few hundred yards, round a corner, but I suppose I missed it, and ended up in the phone box. Funny really, because I remember thinking, I could have used that to phone for an ambulance, if I'd not broken it. A kind man from the post office used my phone and called an ambulance, and the police, they were there too. Sitting in the police station made me realise, I had... *have* a problem so I went back to AA. Do you know how hard it is finding AA meetings you can walk to, in Hursley?'

'There must be some in Winchester!'

'I know, but, darling, it's getting there, that's the trouble you see, now I no longer have my darling little Mercedes Benz, I'm lost, practically abandoned you see without it.'

'Get taxis, you've got enough money.'

'Yes, I suppose I could do. What a clever boy you are.' She ruffled my hair, looking up as we approached Waterloo station. 'Is this me?'

'Yes, this is you.'

'Oh darling can you be a dear and fetch my suitcase from the boot. It's so heavy I can't lift it out, you wouldn't want me to hurt myself would you, darling?'

She leant to kiss me after I'd safely transferred the suitcase to the pavement. 'Bye darling, see you soon, it was all simply *so much fun*, it always is. Isn't it so super that we can have these little chats? You do know Mother cares very much for you, that's why she tells you. I'm so sorry.'

I jumped back into the car and asked out the window, 'For what?'

'What do you mean?'

'What are you sorry for, what *did* you do?'

'Oh, let's not go into that now, let's say goodbye and look forward to the next time darling.'

I wound up the window and drove off. *Yes, that is you, that's you all over.*

As I drove home in silence: *Is it possible to love someone but to hate them at the same time?* I never wanted any harm to come to Mother, not after her marriage to Dad. If anyone deserved some happiness, she did. And every time I saw her, I hoped, imagined, prayed it would be perfect, well, if not perfect, it would be better, different, simple, fun, easy. All the nice happy words everyone else used to describe time with their mums.

So yet again, we tried to make it perfect, tried so hard not to upset her, and before long she reverted to type. No matter how long she tried to maintain the Frauline Maria, she always descended into The Baroness. I half expected Luke to boo her each time she entered the living room.

I knew her comments about gay weddings and it being a shame weren't meant to be hurtful or tactless, she was — in her own grating style — just trying to tell everyone how okay she was about it, and how proud she was of me. It's just that unfortunately the way and where she expressed it meant it didn't always (ever really) come across like that.

I longed for a relationship with her where we were both adults. We'd done the version where she was the adult and I was the child — that was expected and normal. We'd also done the one where I was more of an adult and I looked after her as she rebuilt her life after leaving Dad. But now we were both adults and our lives were settled, why did it always have to be me who looked after her? It was worse than looking after a child. It was like looking after a full size, drinking, shouting, swearing baby who answered back and always knew the right way.

Isn't that a teenager?

Mother was a teenager. The last person to give up on her should be her son, who she'd given birth to, but she often drove me so close to giving up, so near to shouting at her to fuck off and leave me alone, I sometimes scared myself, so instead took a deep breath and walked away. Like I had just done at the station. I gave myself breaks, holidays if you like, from Mother, as she was only copeable in small doses, like the weekend. A night here, a weekend there. No more or the pressure cooker of it all would pop. And I knew who out of us two would burst, and it wouldn't be her.

Chapter Twelve

Gabe and I met in July and spent five months together: speaking most evenings, some lunchtimes; drinks after work; weekends away together.

Once he had met Luke, I felt less guilty about the secret. He wasn't a secret any longer; I'd got it out of the way. Ostensibly. Luke met Gabe, they got on, he had a face to put to the name I mentioned most evenings, someone he could attach to the voice on my mobile when he called most evenings and Luke asked who it was. 'Oh, him, another drama?' he would ask once I told him.

'I have a feeling we're going to be good friends, so we can fast forward through the getting to know you bit, and cry together now,' Gabe had said after telling me about the complications in his love life.

Soon we were finishing each other's sentences, having picked up our little verbal habits and tics, mocking each other in ways I only reserved for proper best friends. But with Gabe it felt right. It felt like we *were* proper best friends, even after only knowing him a couple of weeks.

I complained about Di Anne the administrator at the hospital, and having to do the off duty. Or rather, having to be the Keeper of the Off Duty. He listened intently, smoking his roll up cigarettes thoughtfully as I explained my mini battles with Di Anne, how it was two steps forward, one step back, as she'd mentioned stress when I pushed her (to actually do her job) one time.

'So you're Mister Male Matron Man, right?'

I nodded.

'And you earn quite a bit more than the other nurses on the ward.'

'Yes, and?'

'But you enjoy the nursing, because you're helping people. Same as me, I suppose. And you've got these people you have to manage who aren't all as perfect as you.'

'I'm not perfect.'

He raised his eyebrows.

'Suppose you could describe it like that. I wouldn't but you could.'

'I just have.' He dragged on his cigarette and stubbed it out in the ashtray between us on the pub table, surrounded by our glasses. 'Let me put it to you like this: IT'S YOUR JOB. YOU'RE PAID TO BE A MANAGER, AND THIS IS MANAGING. GET OVER IT. If you don't want all that, then work agency shifts. Turn up, look after people, get your timesheet signed, then leave. No commitment, nothing.'

'That's you all over, no commitment.' I laughed.

He shot me a look of thunder.

'Oh, I'm so sorry, I was only joking.' I reached to stroke his arm.

'Gotcha, I'm taking the piss,' he laughed. 'Fair comment though, for my work yes, I like to get in, get paid and get out. And there's no laws against that, that I'm aware of.'

Relieved, I said, 'None I know of.'

One morning, we sat in a café together, watching the world pass. Luke was away for work, something I pushed to the corner of my mind. You know those mornings, where you don't really have anywhere to be, anything to do, but you're just enjoying the day unfold in front of you with someone who makes the time pass so quickly? Well, it was one of *those* mornings.

Gabe pulled two tickets from his pocket. I looked up from my hot chocolate ('No point paying for tea at a café, it's just all water,' Gabe had said) and I started fanning my eyes quickly as they started to water.

'Calm down you, it's not An Audience With Goldie Hawn, not that she'd do that actually, because what would she say? She's just an actress, not funny on her own...'

'Watch it,' I shot back. 'So anyway, what are they for?'

'What, these?' He shook the tickets theatrically.

I nodded. 'Yes, those.'

'These little things here, well, in the absence of Goldie doing a show, you'll just have to make do with... tickets to see Erasure on the south coast!'

'Oh my God! I can't believe it. The south coast, where?'

'At the BIC, something about Bournemouth. Wembley had sold out, but I thought, we could make a night of it, stay in a hotel, see what the metropolis of Bournemouth has to offer. What do you reckon?' His eyes twinkled.

And then that happened. 'When is it, I can't wait?'

'Few weeks' time, midweek, we both need to make sure we're off work, can you sort it?'

'I am, as you know, the Keeper of the Off Duty, so I believe it will be possible.' I camped up the slightly gothic nature of my phrase, and Gabe laughed.

Obviously, I sorted my time off work, and I spent the next few weeks telling everyone about it. I couldn't believe that I was actually going to see one of my favourite artists in concert. Even people's cynical questions didn't dampen my enthusiasm, including a particularly killjoy comment from a work colleague: 'As it's all synthesisers — Erasure, how's that going to work live?'

'I'm sure they'll work it out,' I had replied casually.

Luke was harder to deal with, particularly since he pointed out that *we* could have gone to see it together, the implication being, without Gabe.

'I didn't know you liked Erasure,' I replied, trying to distract him from his original point.

'Well, I'm not as into them as you, but they're okay. Would have been a good night together,' he replied, persevering with his original point.

'We could go later in the tour, there are more dates after Bournemouth, Gabe said.'

'Did he?' Luke asked.

'I'll tell you all about it, so you can decide if you want to see it with me, or see something else together.'

'Sounds like a good idea.'

The important thing was, although, yes, we *could* have gone together, Luke and I, but *Luke* hadn't bought the tickets, *Luke* hadn't even suggested it to me, *Luke* had just sulked when Gabe had done all those things. I did tell him all about it, and he listened half intently, half bitterly, until at the end proclaimed maybe it wasn't for him, as it was quite a lot of money. So, I left it with him to suggest another concert for us to see together. As expected, he made no such suggestion, work was busy, he didn't have money, he just didn't get round to it, so we never did see anything together, just us two.

Conversely, with Gabe, although I was so excited I think a little bit of wee came out of me on the drive to Bournemouth, it felt slightly odd, slightly strange, since it was neither my birthday, nor Christmas, so his giving me the gift just stood out like a beacon in our friendship, flashing for all to see. The beacon announced something to everyone, only I wasn't yet clear what it was announcing.

Gabe had somehow managed to get places at the front of the venue, touching distance from the stage. I chatted to other fans, and as I revealed it was my first Erasure concert, their excitement mounted for me. 'Your first time? You'll be hooked after this!'

The concert was amazing; they put on an impressive show of lights, descending from the roof, sweeping across the stage suspended by cables, mixes of songs previously unheard, and also an Erasure version of the seventies song, *Come up and see me, and make me smile.* And it did.

Throughout the concert, I kept looking at Gabe dancing next to me, a huge smile plastered across my face. Periodically we held hands, dancing and swaying to the music, then took it up a notch for the classics, like 'Love to Hate You', where we, and the whole crowd went wild, jumping up and down in time to the music like we were in a nightclub.

It ended too soon, felt like it had just started, but I retained my grin and a light-headed feeling for hours afterwards.

Gabe looked at me as I started to come down from the high of the concert. 'Do you want to get some memorabilia tat to remember it by?'

I knew I'd remember it forever, but never one to turn down a bit of tat, we headed to the stall near the bar and I bought a T-shirt. I winced slightly at the price, but Gabe pointed out it was hardly a weekly occurrence.

Gabe had booked us into a hotel in Bournemouth, walking distance from the concert. Not wishing the night to end, we walked along the beach together, our ears ringing from the concert.

'Thanks, it was perfect,' I said as we heard the sea lapping on the beach.

'That's okay,' he replied, smiling.

'Why did you do it? I mean, it's not my birthday, or Christmas, so why?'

'Why not.'

'Suppose so.' I shrugged.

'Why wait for a special occasion to do something like that with someone you care for? Every day should be special.'

I thought about it for a moment, before he continued.

'I had an ex, right, and he just didn't *get* food. He lived on awful food, whatever there was in the freezer or fridge, didn't make any effort. It wasn't because he couldn't afford it, he just didn't see the point spending money on nice food, when you could have a night out, or a pair of jeans instead. I told him food's an everyday luxury. Not something you save for best, why waste a meal eating something you don't like? Why wait for a birthday before seeing a concert, going out for a meal, you get the picture?'

'But not all the time, you're not made of money, are you?'

'Course I'm not, you know what I earn; we do the same bloody job! But some of it can be on stuff like this, throughout the year. Well, that's what I think anyway, don't know about you.'

We walked back to the hotel, humming Erasure songs together.

Lying on twin beds, we compared notes on our favourite bits of the concert, sipping hot chocolate from the room's store. Gabe said he couldn't believe I'd never been to a concert before.

I said there were lots of things I've never done before. Gabe lay on his bed, arms behind his head, smiling at me.

'I wish I'd tried a few more things, a few more men, before Luke,' I said quietly. 'You did, you've got more than your fair share of men during your early twenties.'

'And before,' he replied.

'I can't shake this feeling I've missed out on so much. Missed something which, for so many gay guys, is such an important part of coming out, growing up gay.'

'You must have had your reasons why you didn't.'

'Course I did. I was scared, scared of all the people around me dying. And I'd met Luke, and he was nice to me, so…'

'…you stayed together.'

'Yeah, weeks became months, months years, and before I knew it, we'd been together a third of my life.'

'I didn't really think about it at the time, it wasn't an experience, I was just living my life, being me, meeting people, seeing what happened. Same as you I suppose, only none of the people I met, stuck, so I moved onto the next one. It's no better or worse, just different.'

'You would say that, though, wouldn't you?'

'I don't have anything to compare it to, so I don't know.'

'I just feel like I've missed out on so much, from being scared to try things.'

'But it doesn't matter if in the end, you're happy.' He paused. 'You are happy, aren't you?'

I picked up my book and started to read. Gabe sat on the bed next to me, stroking my arm slowly. I put the book down and lay on my side, tears making the pillow damp, I felt Gabe lay behind me, his arm around my waist; we lay like spoons, fully clothed as he turned the light off.

Chapter Thirteen

We went to his parents' house for the weekend, just us two, no boyfriends. I couldn't remember feeling so nervous since I'd met Luke's parents, years before. Gabe had suggested it, like he was saying, let's have a coffee. I wasn't used to friends meeting me halfway like this. With Matt it always felt like I was doing all the running around, I made the suggestions about what to do (most of which he didn't reply to, or declined). But with Gabe I sat back and the suggestions came thick and fast.

He met me at our house and I drove us to Hertfordshire. At first he was a bit embarrassed about where his parents lived, as I'd jumped up and down when he said it was Hertfordshire, imagining a pretty secluded village like a scene from a Jane Austen novel.

'Stevenage.'

He held my hands to stop them flapping. 'Or St Evenage as Mum says.' He pronounced it like collage for added effect.

We co-ordinated shifts, and both got Wednesday and Thursday off work. I felt so guilty spending time with him rather than Luke, as blocks of time like this were, as an unspoken rule, reserved for Luke and me.

When I gingerly announced my plans a few weeks before, Luke had barely registered, as it wasn't a weekend. 'Taking the car?' he had asked.

'If that's okay,' I replied.

'I've got meetings up town then, so it's fine.' He paused while processing what I'd told him. 'Meeting his parents, that's a bit… isn't it?'

'A bit what?' I asked, knowing what he meant, but keen to get him to express it, because I'd not yet managed to do so, even in my own head.

Shrugging, he replied, 'Boyfriendy?'

'That's not even a word.'

'You know what I mean. When was the last time your friends took you to meet *their* parents?'

'I met them all when I was younger. I've known Matt's since we were kids.'

'I see.' Luke nodded slowly, returning to his work diary.

We arrived at his parents' house in St Evenage (he told me the name of the actual village, now part of the new town, but I quickly forgot): a sprawling estate of modern detached Barratt homes, all slightly different, but basically the same from a distance. Off street parking for every house, and fake weatherboarding covered the first floor. It backed onto a Norman church: 'It's at the centre of the original village green,' his mum proudly told me over tea. 'Shame they added the video shop and recycling centre though,' she added, sipping her drink.

'Just call me Sheryl,' patted her brown permed hair and explained she'd made up the spare room for me, apologising for the not matching duvet and pillow cases. 'I've heard so much about you, Dominic. When we call

Gabriel on a Sunday, it's been Dominic this, Dominic that. We've hardly heard a word about A…'

Gabe replied, '…that's enough Mum, I don't want anyone saying anything about him. He's not here to defend himself so…'

'More tea?' Sheryl added. 'What you boys got planned while you're here? Bit of shopping? It's not as good as Hatfield, I love The Galleria, so good for shopping, but you don't have to drive far. It's all there. And there's the statue in the middle, about the New Town or something. St Evenage, we call it, did he say?'

'Call me Mike,' looked at his wife and noticed we were keen to do something other than sit in the living room with two parents. 'Sheryl, leave them alone.' He gestured to the door and we both left for the delights of the town centre.

I followed Gabe and asked, 'Thought you said you were half Spanish. Sheryl and Mike, that's not very Spanish, is it?'

'It's Michelangelo actually. He sticks with Mike cos no one can spell it otherwise.' He looked behind him as I struggled to catch up. 'Satisfied?' A smile and a wink.

I shrugged and followed his lead.

Gabe proudly showed me around the sights of Stevenage town centre, pointing out the statue of the town's planner, and explaining how it was all pedestrianised 'Way before town centres *were* pedestrianised.'

I know what you're thinking… I can see you rolling your eyes. And I agree, it should have been mind-numbingly boring, I should have wanted to leave immediately to see my boyfriend, but Gabe had a way of being enthusiastic about things that rubbed off on me. Soon I found myself asking if we could go to the museum and learn more about this wondrous creation known as The New Town of Stevenage. After saying it, I looked behind me to see if someone else had suggested it.

They hadn't. We learned and laughed together, just like I had with Luke when we first met. That made me feel worse than I already did, so I pushed that feeling deep down.

Over hot chocolates, at the one place in the town centre which served it actually — shock horror — made with milk, not instant, he told me how, during one reading week at uni, he'd had seven hours sleep and had gone clubbing every night. 'I knew the bouncers at the clubs I went, so never paid to get in. Just slept all day, partied at night.'

'Who with?'

'Some uni friends came along for some of it, clubbing friends, people who were there. You know how it is.' He smiled and my heart did that thing it used to do when Luke smiled at me. I instantly felt sick.

He also took me to the Jane Austen Hertfordshire, directing me along country lanes, stopping on proper village greens without recycling centres and video shops, looking across open fields that had remained the same for hundreds of years. We talked about previous relationships; he'd had three 'significant ones,' to my one. 'What about not significant ones?' he asked.

'One night stands?'

He nodded. 'If you want to call it that, although I prefer gentlemen friends for the night, but you say potato I say *potato*…'

I looked at the ground, embarrassed at my response, before I had even said it. 'One.'

'As well as Luke?'

'That's it, him.'

'Wow.' He leant back.

'I feel like I've led such a small life. Always worried about what might happen, I've not let anything really happen. What about you?'

'When I went travelling before uni, I was up to two to three a week at some points.'

'So how many?'

'And at uni, I suppose that was the same…'

I persevered. '*How* many?'

Gabe looked at the sky. 'Lost count after four hundred.'

This time, *I* leant back. 'Wow. Was it fun? Are you pleased you did it?'

'You've had sex, right? Course it was fun. I wouldn't do it again, don't think I could, I'm not nineteen anymore, if you know what I mean!'

'And I've just been with one person, no idea what it's like with anyone else.' I let that hang there in the air as I thought about all the experiences I'd missed. 'I've not even had a threesome. What about you?'

'Err, have we met? My first time was a threesome. Two big blond Swedish student nurses I met at a party.

Couldn't decide which one to try, and didn't have to in the end. They grabbed my hands as the party died, said something about "fun sexy times is good" in a comically Swedish accent, a bit like the chef from the *Muppets*, and that was it. I was fifteen. I woke up with a grin on my face, and a sore arse.'

'Please… you're such a slag.'

'Yes, but darling, I'm so good at it. Jealous much?'

'Maybe. I've always wanted to sleep with a proper muscle Mary, imagined it'd be like playing on a bouncy castle. Lovely.'

He stared at the village green we'd parked on. 'I went through a phase of them. Disappointing. So I stopped.'

'How?'

'I stopped picking them up in bars.'

'No, how was it disappointing?'

'So I pick them up in the bar, and they're all macho and I think this'll be fun. Get them home and it's helium heels, camp as Christmas. I mean, can you spell *power bottom*?'

'Yes I can, revolting.'

'You did ask.'

'And what about A?' I asked carefully.

'Next question! Let's go back,' he replied quickly.

We drove back to his parents' in silence. He wiped his face with his sleeve a few times. I turned on the radio and commented how I found myself listening to Radio Two as I teetered on the edge of my thirties. I explained how I listened to the radio, switching off the news, longing for my life to be like a Radio Two programme, as opposed to a Radio Four programme. If it could be filled with amusing frothy phone-ins about pets, interspersed with easy listening songs from the past three decades, rather than harrowing stories about the Middle East, bombings, unemployment, stories about 'a stretched to bursting point NHS,' no thanks!

He reached across the gear stick and held my left hand, smiling through slightly red eyes.

I looked to my left to make eye contact with him. 'I didn't mean to upset you, sorry.'

'As soon as I think about him, it all comes rushing back. The guilt, the regret, everything.'

I squeezed his hand.

He looked at me and forced a smile before looking straight ahead again.

And for that tiny moment I was as happy as I'd ever been in my life. We were together, no homes to return to, no boyfriends waiting for us, just us together against the world.

I felt like I'd met my perfect boyfriend, the opposite in all the right ways, but similar in others, but he happened to have a boyfriend, and so did I.

He lined up a Goldie Hawn marathon that evening, and we watched three films back to back, quoting the next lines at each other, until we introduced a moratorium for both our sanities. Between films, he started to tell me about A, and why he couldn't work, explaining that A's meds had much worse side effects than his, which made it hard to stay with a job, or anything it seemed. He started to cry, big splashes landing on his T-shirt. I wiped them with my hanky and he lay on my chest for the whole of *Private Benjamin*.

I dropped him home after our final day together. As soon as he closed the door I felt myself fill up with a mix of emotions, ranging from sadness our time was over, dread about returning home, via some worry about what I'd done had jeopardised my relationship, and a side order of guilt for good measure.

I cried all the way home, dreading returning to my real life, which made me feel so sad. As I reached home, I couldn't cry, only an empty croak came out, I was all cried out. I took a deep breath, gathered my things and opened our door, relieved Luke wasn't home. I used the time to make sure I was happy for his return.

When Luke returned, I plastered on my biggest teeth, tummy, tits smile, told him about Gabe's parents, how Stevenage wasn't 'as bad as people said' and that he should come next time. He leant his head on my chest while I gave him edited highlights, and all along all I could think about was how Gabe's head had been on my chest the night before.

Later that evening my mobile rang; I leant forward, pushing Luke's head off my chest, reaching for the phone.

He mouthed, 'Who is it?' while I answered.

'Gabe,' I mouthed back, listening as he told me about the mess A had left the flat in, how he couldn't face it much longer, and yet he couldn't think about how to get himself out.

Luke stood up. 'You've just spent two days together, what else he can have to tell you?' He stomped to our bedroom.

I calmed Gabe down, told him not to make any decisions now, as he was too emotional, and arranged to meet in a few days to talk properly.

He picked up that I couldn't talk, and simply asked, 'Is he in the room?'

'No… that's fine, I'll see you then, then…'

'Alright Mister, I know when I'm not wanted. Fuck off. And thanks. Love you.' He put the phone down and I followed Luke to our frosty bedroom.

'Alright?' I asked Luke as he read in bed.

'He okay?' he replied, not looking up from his book.

'He will be. What you reading?'

He put the book down and told me what it was about.

I listened, undressing as he continued talking.

He stopped talking, took a breath, then said, 'I've missed you. I do miss you, you know.'

'I know.' I climbed into bed next to him, willing him to kiss me, but he didn't.

Chapter Fourteen

1987

It was a full-time job being happy. I spent so much time rushing about keeping busy I didn't have time to be anything but happy.

Except when I wasn't. Except when I had episodes of My Depression, as those who knew referred to it. I didn't tell everyone, I always felt ashamed of it. I expected people to run away, or call me a nutter. It's not like having a broken arm, you can't see it, so it's got to be a bit made up hasn't it?

People say they're depressed all the time. 'I didn't get that job, I'm so depressed,' or 'He dumped me again, I'm depressed,' even 'I can't afford those shoes, I'm depressed.' Luke knew about My Depression, he couldn't really not know, having lived with me for so long.

Matt didn't know. There never seemed to have been the right time to broach the subject. I would gather myself together, repeat the phrase in my head, then he'd appear in tears over the latest love drama, and I'd (gratefully actually) pack away the words and leave it. He knew I had 'black periods' – times when I wasn't my usual self – he couldn't have missed them during the time we'd known each other. No, but he didn't know about the *details*, about the counselling or the tablets. I was a bit ashamed of it. I worried it would spoil his perfect view of me. If *I* wasn't perfect, where would that leave him in the grand scheme of things?

All people get depressed, it's part of the up and down of life. Without sadness, you can't appreciate happiness. Your cat dies, you lose a parent, you lose your job, all perfectly good reasons for a bit of depression. But I was special, I didn't just get depression, I got *My Depression*. My own special, solid gold, premium version of depression.

The first time I got it was the worst. I was sixteen and walking back from school, I saw a cat by the side of the road *dead*. It was a quiet night when my mum just sat silently watching TV, exhausted from cleaning and dishing up school dinners all day.

I recognised the cat; it was the large ginger tom I used to stroke whenever I passed. I'd seen it grow up from a kitten, when the owners — a friendly couple a few doors down — had brought it back from the cat sanctuary in a little box, meowing loudly. I had gone round to see it and I'd never seen anything so small and cute; it sat on my lap purring loudly and as soon as I returned home, I asked if we could have one. We never got a cat, but it didn't stop me popping round a few doors down to make a fuss of it, or stopping on my way to school, stroking it as it walked along the wall.

It was hit by a car which didn't even stop; they'd just left it by the side of the road. I knocked on the neighbour's house and told the woman what I'd seen. She quickly followed me to the scene, and screamed, recognising it was her cat. I waited by the road while she went indoors to collect an old towel to wrap the cat's body in.

'But he never crossed the road,' she wailed as she carried his little body home.

I followed her, arriving at her kitchen and suddenly feeling of no use whatsoever. 'Do you want me to call a vet?' I offered feebly.

'He's cold. Been dead for hours,' she cried. 'I'll wait until Tony gets home and we'll bury him.'

I stood in the kitchen watching her lean against the work surface, staring at the little wrapped bundle on the floor, wiping her eyes.

I made my excuses and walked home, dragging my feet on the way. I went straight to my room where I stared at the road, at the exact spot where I'd found the cat. Tears streamed down my face and I sobbed slowly. Big globules of tears just continued to leak from my eyes.

That night, I couldn't eat any tea and when Mum asked what was wrong, I tried to explain, but got as far as 'Cat, road,' and broke down again.

And then it wasn't just about the cat, it was about everything. The whole world was an unfair, cruel place, full of sadness. I watched the news, every story pierced my heart with pain. Wars in the Middle East (and I didn't even know where that was, but I knew it was *awful*), children missing in the West Midlands (I didn't really know where that was either, but I knew it would be ripping their parents apart), and I felt their pain, every single moment of it until I could hardly breathe.

The sadness was so overwhelming that eating just seemed like an insult to the memories of the lost children, the dead cat, anything sad. So why bother eating? And I didn't. I skipped breakfast, threw the contents of my lunch box in the bin at school. Every evening I would pick at my dinner, pushing peas around my plate as Mum encouraged me to eat.

I had recurring dreams of walking around the supermarket with a trolley. On the shelves were cans, packets and jars all labelled with different types of sadness: mourning, regret, guilt, pain, all with the number of grams or millilitres next to the description, followed by 'pure sadness.' I walked around the supermarket and other customers slowly filled my trolley with the containers of sadness, until it was full, and I could barely push it. I took it to the checkout and the lady rang up the items, every time a different sort of sadness, my heart filled with blackness. I paid and left. The dream ended and I woke with more tears streaming down my face, wishing, hoping it would all just end.

I walked past a scrap yard on my way to school and stopped to peek through the gaps in the fence. I saw the cars piled on top of each other, slowly rusting and decaying together. Their headlights seemed to implore me to rescue them. That was the thanks they got for faithfully serving families for years, taking them on the school run, to work every day, to the supermarket, and now they were just thrown away. I felt my body shaking as I sobbed next to the fence. *I cried for the souls of dead cars.*

I stopped leaving the house; it was near the summer holidays, but I'd arranged an interview for a summer job. I just couldn't face it; what if they said no to me. What if I got hit by a car on the way?

Then I stopped leaving my bed. I slept most of the day, emerging from the covers only when Mum fed me soup and water. I lost over two stone; my lowest weight was just under eight stone. I stopped washing and Mum had to strip wash me (not the sort of thing I would have ever agreed to had I been of even half a mind) with a flannel and a bowl of hot water. She noticed how much weight I'd lost and called the doctor.

The doctor took one look at me, asked some questions about how I felt. I don't remember what I said in reply but quickly he diagnosed depression, prescribing antidepressants.

'Why?' Mum asked.

The doctor put away his stethoscope. 'Did something happen, it can trigger it, or it can just happen. It's chemical, in the brain. Some people just get it. Nothing to do with what's happening around them, it just happens.'

'Next door's cat died.'

'Maybe. How old is he?' he asked, like I wasn't in the room. In fairness, at the time, I didn't feel like I was anywhere near them both.

'Sixteen.'

'Puberty can trigger it, hormones.' And he left, handing Mum a green piece of paper.

Mum forced me to take the tablets. I thought they were pointless. 'Will they bring back the cat? What about the children in the West Midlands? I want to go to the scrap yard!'

After a while I still felt the world was sad, and still worried about the Middle East, but it became more of a background sadness—like you know it's there, but it's not all consuming, pervasive all around you like before. I started to wash myself again (Mum's flannel washes became worse than the effort it took to do it myself). I got out of bed and ate some chocolate from the fridge. Mum asked if I wanted more, so bought me kilos and kilos of Cadbury's Dairy Milk.

I put on weight and started to venture out of the house. We took little trips together at first, gradually venturing further and further from home. 'Let's go to the park!' she would say brightly (not that I was even aware there was a park nearby). We would walk just round the corner, and I'd sit on the swings before returning home. Then, 'How about we get some bits for tea? Fish fingers and chips.' My heart nearly jumped out of my chest at the thought of *other people, talking, in the shop*. But she took my hand as we left the house, and we made it back home, safe and sound, with my reward for tea. Then she started sending me out alone. 'I'm peeling the potatoes, nip out and get some milk, will you?' After a few aborted attempts at that, I did eventually leave alone, clutching my list, which read: shop, milk, home. Before leaving, every time I worried about what might happen: might I get run over, would I see another dead cat? Each time, I took a deep breath, waited for the thoughts to go, and left. If the thoughts stayed, that was a bad day and I returned to my bedroom. As I started leaving more on my own, to visit friends, I thought of the people I had to see, who were relying on me ('Dominic, they'll be so sad if you don't come, imagine their faces,' Mum would say). So I quit the warm comforting cocoon of my bedroom and left, facing the cruel, sad world.

I gradually came off the tablets; we held our breath, fearing I'd plunge straight back into the supermarket of sadness. I didn't, because the doctor had another trick up his sleeve, another trick called Barbara.

I was studying my A levels then, which kept me busy. I got the idea into my head that I wanted to do something to help and sooth people, so being a nurse seemed to fit that. Every day I went to college, worried what I'd find on my way, I imagined healing everyone's ills, curing everyone's pain, and it spurred me on to go to college, and not just return to bed and the TV.

Since coming off the antidepressants, I'd made it my secret hobby to keep *My Depression* at bay. It felt like it was creeping up to me when my back was turned, like the children's game grandmother's footsteps. Every morning I expected to wake and find it lurking in my image in the mirror when I did my weekly shave, or brushed my teeth. Keeping it at bay was a full-time occupation as I always tried to keep busy: meeting friends, working hard, being happy. Always the being happy. I kept a smile firmly plastered on my face and rushed to the next activity, keeping any nagging clouds of blackness or sadness pushed away.

When friends complained they didn't have a hobby, as they so often did, I smiled to myself, pleased about my little secret. It appeared to everyone that I was a busy outgoing happy person, but what they didn't know was all of that was actually under the heading of Keeping My Depression at Bay, sub section Busyness. Amid all the activity, I hardly gave myself chance to notice the scrap yards, the news, or think about any dead cats. I coped with the little mini depressions life threw at me, but what really scared the living daylights out of me, was the fear of becoming depressed again, not for anything happening to me, but just *because of life*. That's the hardest type of depression, where you look around at your life and overall it seems pretty good, you've got quite a lot to be happy about, and yet no matter how hard you try you can't stop crying, can't get up, can't wash yourself.

Although the dead cat may have triggered it, I felt it was always lurking inside me, waiting to fill my trolley with sadness. The cat was just a catalyst (sorry), it could have just as easily been a news story, because the sadness was, and always is, inside me. No matter how perfect my life was, I always knew it was there and could return any time.

Chapter Fifteen

September 1999

I answered my mobile in my office to Gabe's voice: 'Guess who's got an interview as a senior charge nurse at Guy's Hospital?'

'If it's not you, this is a really boring call,' I replied.

'Drink tonight to celebrate?'

'You've not got it yet, isn't it a bit early to celebrate?'

'Who's shat in your handbag today? If I get it, we can celebrate again. Come on, I need someone to be happy with me.'

I noticed Di Anne had stopped typing and was listening to my conversation. I said, 'Finished typing my training notes?'

Gabe replied, 'What?'

'Not you. Have you, Di Anne?'

Di Anne replied, 'I'm giving my fingers a rest. Health and safety said you can't do more than three hours at a computer without a break. This is my break.'

'Why don't you have a proper break and get a tea and some fresh air?'

'I'm fine here thanks.'

'If you go now, you can have fifteen minutes, paid, but only if you take it now.'

She left instantly.

'And bring me a tea on your way back,' I shouted after her. 'Right, where were we?'

Gabe said, 'Get you, mister manager man?'

'You'll have all that to come if you get the job. So where tonight?'

We met at the Oyster Bar in Harvey Nichols. 'To fortify ourselves before buying me an interview outfit,' Gabe explained, sipping his champagne.

Three hours and four bars later, we were still drinking in Harvey Nicks. As part of his fortification programme, Gabe had opened a packet of Tic Tacs, popped one first in his mouth, then mine.

'These aren't Tic Tacs, are they?' I asked, knowing the answer.

We were asked to leave a while later as he lay across my lap, playing with my chest in my opened shirt. 'This is not the position, gentlemen,' the barman advised, gesturing to the rest of the bar, where everyone else sat, open-mouthed.

Somehow, we got back to Gabe's house and stayed up most of the night, talking about sex. Not just scratching the surface, like I'd done with other friends, but proper no holds barred what do you really like to do in bed, talking. At first, it felt odd, but soon we got into our stride and there was no stopping us, shrieking with laughter as the other revealed another fantasy. I hadn't even told *Luke* about this, and I felt so disloyal, like I was really cheating on him.

The next morning, once we'd both called in sick (me for the first time ever) as he made us tea and I packed up the sofa bed where I'd slept, alone of course, I gathered my thoughts and told him. 'I think I'm falling for you.'

'Right...' he replied.

'I don't want to sleep with you. I couldn't bear the guilt of cheating on Luke. This is enough, emotionally cheating on him, but physically, no way. But I have to tell you, there's no other way to describe it. I want to be around you, I want to talk to you, I enjoy laughing with you. The more time we spend together, it's never enough. Every time you suggest we do something I say yes, and the same if I suggest something. It's so easy.'

'Okay.'

'That's it, I pour my heart to you and you say okay?'

'What do you want me to say? Yes, let's run away together and open a B&B in Surrey?'

'What?'

'I'm being dramatic. You know what I mean. I can't, you can't. I'm with A, you're with Luke, we don't want to ruin that. I feel guilty enough as it is, having fun with you. I'm not used to having a relationship with someone who's an adult. All this fun we have together, when all I get from A is problems. I'm so used to looking after him, always being the adult to his child, that I forgot what it was like, until you. And sleeping together would change what we have now. It always does. Trust me, I've done it enough times with other friends. It's never the same after you've seen someone naked.'

'I suppose.' I shrugged.

'I don't want to risk what we have on a five-minute fumble. It's complicated enough without adding *that*, don't you think?'

'Five minutes, I don't think so.' I looked at him, smiling.

'Well, I'll never find out, hopefully.'

'Okay.'

'Friends?' He held out his hand for me to shake.

'I feel like such a twat, telling you that.' I shook his hand.

'You didn't have to tell me, I knew. I felt it too. It's the same for me.'

'But we can't do anything about it?'

'You know we can't. In another lifetime, we should be together, like that, but not this one, not this lifetime.' He paused, looking around his flat. 'Did we get anything for me to wear at my interview?'

'Are there any bags?'

'That's what I'm looking for.' He walked around the flat, searching for Harvey Nicks bags. 'I suppose we'll have to go back again, what a shame.' He laughed.

A few days later we went back and I helped him choose a 'responsible and eye-catching outfit,' for his interview, as Gabe had described it. We settled on a charcoal grey suit, shiny black shoes with wedge fronts, a white shirt with red flowers and a black tie.

'You've got to look responsible, but not like a stuffed grey suit. You don't have to check in your personality at the door. If they want you, they'll want *all of you*,' I explained, having been to a few interviews where my shirt style and obvious *personality* (a diplomatic way of saying *gayness*) had put them off me. At first I'd felt mortally wounded, then on reflection I realised anyone who didn't want to work with me, wouldn't be that accepting to work for anyway, so moved on until I found somewhere I could be myself.

'The old gays didn't fight for us chickens to be ourselves for nothing you know,' I explained as he wavered over two shirts—one was like an advert for the Chelsea Flower Show, the other wouldn't have looked out of place in a DIY shop. 'Go on, be a man, pick the flowery one,' I added.

'And real men take it up the arse, right?' He looked down at the shirt.

We ate oysters and bar nibbles, and sipped one glass of champagne each in the Oyster Bar at Harvey Nicks, surrounded by shopping bags. We surveyed our purchases; he had helped me with some purchasing decisions too: I was the proud owner of a pair of shoes made of such soft leather I feared they could have been from small puppies (they weren't, I did ask what sort of leather they were from and was reliably informed it was calves leather) and a waist coat, 'So versatile, you can wear it with a T-shirt, or at work on management days, and it goes with everything as it's black, Mister,' Gabe said as I had dithered over it.

Soon after he called to tell me, he'd been offered the job. 'They loved me, said I'd bring something to the ward, which was really lacking.' He babbled on excitedly about how much he was looking forward to it, and how he had hundreds of things to ask me about managing a ward, and when could he ask me?

'Dinner?' I suggested.

'And drinks…'

'Of course.' We agreed a date a few nights away and I put the phone down. Luke frowned at me and asked if that was Gabe.

'He's just got a new job. We're going out to celebrate, and talk tips.'

Luke said, 'I heard. When?'

I told him and Luke pointed out we had agreed to have a quiet night in together then, as we'd hardly seen each other over the past few weeks.

'It's one night, he's happy, we can have some time next week, I think I've got two days off together. We could go back to your parents' place?'

'You've *just* seen him. What else can you talk about? What about your other friends, what about *me*?'

'I thought you'd be happy I wasn't such a workaholic, have some interests outside work, you said.'

'Yes I did, didn't I.' He walked out the living room into the kitchen and started banging pots and pans.

Gabe noticed I was finding the trials and tribulations of work more than usually challenging; our last few phone calls had been dominated by almost non stop Di Anne, with a side order of The Off Duty, and some performance issues with one of the senior staff nurses.

'Let's get away from it all, pretend we're students during summer holidays, what things did you used to do when you were a student?' he suggested one evening after a particularly fraught call from me.

'Study for the autumn term?' I shrugged my shoulders.

'You didn't?'

'I did.'

'Okay, let's put that to one side for the moment. What you need is a break, a complete break from all things hospital, responsibility, everything. Back to simpler times, when we were students. I know we didn't know each other then, but go with me on this one.'

'So what are you suggesting?' I struggled to grasp the point at this juncture.

'Let's stuff ourselves with ice cream, go swimming, and ice skating. All in one day.'

'In that order? Cos I think I'd be sick.'

'Not necessarily in that order. So, what do you reckon?'

'When?'

'When can you get a day off in the week, quieter then?'

We co-ordinated diaries, and the date was set for the following week.

Gabe arrived at mine at ten past eight (ten minutes late, but I didn't mention it as he looked pretty delicate) on the agreed morning, eyes barely open, smoking a cigarette on my doorstep in jeans and a hoodie.

I'd insisted if we were doing it, we'd do it right and make a full day of it. Gabe's protestations about not being a morning person were ignored, as I wanted enough time to do everything and not feel rushed.

The sun shone; we played tapes of groups from our student days, so on the way we had Dario G, Blur, and an album by Kate Bush called The Red Shoes. This was part of the *total immersion approach* we'd agreed, part of *the rules for the day*: Gabe said, to get the full benefit from the day, we had to pretend we were still students, not adults with boyfriends, mortgages and jobs. So we weren't allowed to talk about any of that adult stuff, just music, money (the main difference being that now, we had money rather than then, we didn't) or boys we fancy.

We went swimming on the flumes first, which was quite an awkward introduction to the day, getting changed with Gabe. So, I did what every gay man does when faced with a similar situation: hid my modesty with a towel, while looking out the corner of my eye at his body — purely for comparative purposes obviously. Once both safely trunked up, I got used to seeing Gabe in that state of undress (it was, after all, only as naked as all the other men around him, so the novelty quickly wore off). We rushed about the complex, trying all the different types of flume, ranging from a small black one with an almost vertical drop called the black hole of death, or something suitably dramatic, to the meandering white water rafting one, called something about the Zambezi river, where we had to hang onto an inflatable as it threw us from deep to shallow water, in warm water, rather than the all too realistic cold water of real rapids.

Afterwards, dripping on plastic chairs, we had an ice cream and Mars bar for lunch. As I started to object, Gabe asked what I used to eat as a student, so I agreed it was a fair comment and tucked into my lunch, surrounded by people's shouts as they explored the flumes as we had done earlier.

Ice skating proved to be much more tiring than either of us had remembered. We whizzed around the edge of the rink; quietly enjoyed the spectacle when the cool guys slipped onto their arses and tried to pass it off as a deliberate move, each time standing up and looking around to see if anyone had seen them. We played *It*, chasing each other around the rink until, both completely out of breath and legs aching more than we could ever remember, we collapsed at the rink-side café, surrounded by others wearing ice skates.

I started to comment how Luke would enjoy this, until Gabe silenced me, reminding me of *the rules of the day*.

It was true, he would have enjoyed ice skating, if he'd thought about going there, but I equally enjoyed it as it was, in my little early nineties bubble with Gabe.

We ate dinner in an Italian restaurant in the complex, without ice skates obviously, talking about what we hoped for after finishing our degrees. Gabe was very broad, said he wanted to be happy, 'As happy as I am now,' he ended with, smiling and taking a bite of his pizza. 'What about you?'

'A job I care about, a house of my own, and someone to love me—a boyfriend,' I replied.

He smiled back at me.

We spoke nearly every day. He called me, I called him, there was no set pattern, it just happened. He rang me as he walked to the Tube some mornings, asking me what I thought I'd face with Di Anne that day. I asked how he was getting on with his new job, gave him tips and listened when he needed to share about a challenging patient or family member.

Not only did we have our own work shorthand between us, for obvious reasons, but we had a life shorthand too. Our phone calls could be five minutes or two hours, stretching to accommodate whatever life threw at us that week. He listened without interrupting as I talked about work, Luke, anything.

I sometimes complained about Luke not tidying up, or having to walk Princess as he was out.

Gabe replied, 'I've been at work all day, and A just texted, saying we're out of loo roll, and can I get something for dinner. He's been at home all day, and has done nothing. Probably didn't get up till midday again. He won't have even stacked the dishwasher.'

'Okay, you win,' I replied.

'It's not about winning, I hear what you're saying about Luke, I wanted to put it in context. I'm not complaining, he's my bed so I lie in him, or whatever it is...'

Chapter Sixteen

Gabe called after work and I prepared myself for an onslaught of ward politics and bureaucracy. I started making myself a tea.

'I've done a bad thing.' I could hear the anxiety in his voice.

'It can't be that bad,' I replied, putting sugar in the cup.

'I think I'm cheating on A.'

'Either you are or you're not. Anyway, I thought it was allowed, within your agreement.'

'It is, not at the flat, not with friends, and not more than once. Otherwise it becomes a relationship, and that's proper cheating, not just a bit of rumpy pumpy as you'd describe it.'

'Go on.' My stomach lurched, my heart sank.

'I met him in a bar, we went back to his, I didn't tell A, but he didn't ask, so that's allowed with our agreement. Anyway, after we... you know... which was amazing by the way...'

'Thanks, I don't need a diagram, get to the point please.' I sipped my tea.

'Okay, so afterwards, basking in the glory of our sex together, he offers to make me a drink. I thought, this is nice, normally once it's over most blokes want to just go. So he makes me a tea, and comes back to bed. And we just sit in bed for the rest of the morning talking.'

'What about?' I took my drink to our bedroom. I didn't want to have this conversation in the living room in case Luke came home.

'Can't remember everything, but just, stuff, life. Favourite films, jokes, funny things about our families, quotes from TV shows. Politics, pets, cooking. Everything.'

'Then what?'

'I'm getting there, don't rush me.' I heard him rolling himself a cigarette and lighting it. 'Then he gives me his number, asks me to call it. Then, this is the really weird bit, he kisses me, on the lips, really slowly, holding my face. Then showers while I dress.'

'Why's that weird?'

'Normally there's this awkward moment where you pretend to care about seeing each other again, and you scrabble about for paper to write the number on. Once you've had the sex, you don't normally kiss. In fact quite a few guys won't kiss on the lips during sex.'

'Why?' This was a whole new world to me.

'In *Pretty Woman*, Julia Roberts says she doesn't kiss on the lips, right?'

I nodded, then realising he couldn't see me, replied, 'Okay.'

'Too intimate. If it's just sex, it's sex, but kissing on the lips is too intimate.'

I spluttered down the phone.

'I know it's weird. One moment I'm bent over and he's licking my…'

'…enough, I get the picture…'

'But this time, he was *all about the kissing*. In fact, we almost started again cos it was so good, but he had to be somewhere.'

'And since then?'

'I saw him last night. And I'm seeing him tonight.'

'Dating?'

'If that's what you want to call it. I don't think it's quite that clear cut. He was a gentlemen friend for the night, and another night actually, and now we're seeing what else there could be.'

'But that's not in your agreement with A, is it?'

'Strictly speaking, no.'

'Well is it or not?'

'No.' He paused as he took a drag on his cigarette. 'So you see why it's a bad thing.'

'What are you going to do?'

'Dunno, strangely he already feels like more of a boyfriend than A, after four years.'

'Shit, Gabe, you really are in trouble, aren't you?'

He mumbled in the affirmative.

'Be careful. I'm on your side, but be careful, okay? You know what I mean.'

'Yes Mother, I know *exactly* what you mean.'

'Err, have fun on the date? Is that what you want me to say?'

'Perfect, more later. You can fuck off now. You're amazing, love you.' And he was gone.

After telling him I was falling for him, this was the last thing I expected. Literally the last thing. First, I thought he would split up with A. Then I thought he would say he felt the same about me. Then we would fly away over a hill and live happily ever after.

Instead, all I could imagine was Gabe and this gentleman friend for a series of nights, kissing, hugging, fondling and then I wished it would fade to black, but it didn't. Despite not having a clue what this man looked like, my mind's eye managed to conjure up an image of a perfect Greek Adonis, all bulging muscles and tiny leather shorts—isn't that what they wore then? This wasn't helped by Gabe's insistence that *we* refer to this guy as Hercules—he explained how one of Hercules' labours was to kill The Hydra—but all this did was increase the little leather shorts count tenfold. Each time my mind imagined that, rather than feeling pleased for Gabe, pleased he'd found someone to have fun with, instead I noticed a knot in my stomach, growing and growing.

Actually, that wasn't what I expected, that was what I'd dreamt of a few times. Having confessed my undying love for Gabe already, I decided to keep these dreams to myself as a secret. Because once you tell someone a secret, it's no longer a secret.

Gabe and I still spoke and saw each other *almost* as often as before Hercules came into his life.

Gabe was happy in his relationship with Hercules, for it was soon exactly that, *a relationship*—and so I was happy for him. I was happy for them both.

I wasn't a fan of A, but I didn't condone lying to him, and I made this clear to Gabe, saying it was all bound to end in tears.

For a few weeks I noticed I was taking second place to Hercules. At first I felt angry and upset, like I'd been snubbed, then standing back from the situation, I realised he wasn't my boyfriend, so why should he behave like one?

Gabe's calls focused more on what he'd been doing with his Hercules than work, or A. I listened with interest as he described meals out, day trips and even tentative discussions about meeting his parents.

'How are you going to explain him?' I asked.

'I'll tell them he's a friend,' he brushed off easily.

'But you're all over each other, you can't say that then share a room at your parents' place. It doesn't make sense.'

For a while, as he was in the early days of a relationship, it was all he spoke about, and I had less opportunity to talk, as by the time he'd finished telling me happily about his latest escapades with Hercules, he had to go. I didn't mind, as I saw how happy Gabe was, compared with his deep, permeating sadness from how much A used to drain his energy.

Hercules didn't meet Gabe's parents.

Late one night I received a call from a hysterically crying Gabe, struggling for breath between tears.

'Take a deep breath, what happened?'

'He dumped me,' he spluttered.

And then that happened. 'Were you properly going out with him then? I thought you were keeping it casual.'

'We *were* seeing each other. Yes I'm a bad person, yes I'm going to hell, I know I know, I can't help myself. He's the only happiness I've had in so long.'

'Oh thanks.'

'Apart from you, sorry. He was different, sex too, and not just sex, but the good sex where you have feelings as well. He hadn't had a proper relationship before. He said it was quite kinky, this monogamy lark.'

'You were going to do monogamy with him?' All this was news to me.

'Why not?'

I hesitated, not wanting to point out he'd just been two timing his previous boyfriend, of which he wasn't in a monogamous relationship. Instead I plumped for, 'Just didn't think it was for you. That's all.'

'Doesn't matter, cos he's dumped me.'

'Why?'

'I told him about The Hydra and he was angry I hadn't told him before. I asked if he'd have slept with me if I'd told him. He didn't reply.'

I listened as he told me more. I had assumed he'd told Hercules about The Hydra ages ago, hence the name — Hercules slew The Hydra, or so the Greeks said. I hadn't actually asked Gabe if he'd had *that* conversation with Hercules, I didn't think I needed to, until now.

I thought about what to say, assembling all the bits of the jigsaw in my head. 'If he can't accept it, you're better off without him. Other people accept it — I did.'

'But you're not sleeping with me. It's much easier to accept if you're not sleeping with someone who's HIV positive.'

There was no answer to that, so I said nothing.

'He *was* perfect...' Gabe said, taking a breath between crying.

'...until he wasn't.'

'Easy for you to say, in your house, with your dog and boyfriend. All easy for you.'

'That's unfair, you know it's not that simple. And we talked about this, The Hydra can't always trump my problems, or it means I don't have any problems worth talking to you about.'

He sniffed and replied, 'I'm angry, I shouldn't take it out on you. Sorry. What am I going to do? Who's going to want to be with me now?'

'You'll find someone. It's not all you are; it's a part of you. People will see that. I did.'

'Boyfriends?'

'Yes. And let's not forget, A. What are you going to do about him?'

'Another day, another phone call, another conversation.' He started to cry again.

I stayed on the phone until my tea was cold, listening to him cry about losing Hercules.

Gabe took it really hard: when we didn't see each other, he rang telling me how much he missed Hercules, how he was never going to find anyone, and how he still didn't know what to do about A.

I went round to his flat; the floor was covered with pizza boxes, clothes hung on airers, the kitchen work surface buried under layers of grease and washing up.

He hugged me, his breath and body odour hit me before we touched, his features hung from his thinner face. We sat in the living room. 'Oh yeah, sorry, it's been a bit much lately. I suppose I just let this slip.' He gestured around the room.

I asked where A was, and he explained he had finally got it together and started attending his access course.

'Makes me feel worse.' He looked me in the eyes, and I noticed how red his were.

'Why?'

'Because now, he's less useless than he was, so why should I leave him?'

'It's more than the access course surely?'

He nodded slowly, scratching a week of stubble on his chin.

'How are you?' I asked, the answer plainly obvious, but I wanted to hear it in his words.

'Everything feels a bit pointless. Without him, I look at my life and it just makes me feel... nothing. A hole, dark, empty.' He stared at the floor at a six-inch pile of pizza boxes.

'Have you seen someone? Your doctor?'

'Why?'

'I think you might be suffering from depression, grief, loss, coming to terms with The Hydra, and how it impacts on other things.'

'Are you a doctor, then?' he spat.

'No, but I've been depressed enough to recognise it. I'm trying to help. Promise me you'll see someone.'

'There's a counsellor at the clinic.'

'Clinic?'

'The *Hydra* clinic—if we're sticking with that.'

I nodded. '*You* called it that.'

'Part of getting used to having it, is getting used to relationships with it, or not. Maybe I could talk to her about that, I suppose.'

'Can't do any harm. It's helped me.'

'Barbara, wasn't it?'

I nodded. We'd had the 'my counsellor Barbara' conversation some months before, as part of our full disclosure friendship. The only people who knew about what Barbara and I spoke about in that sad little room were Barbara and I, and Gabe. I didn't even tell Luke about it most of the time, not least because quite a bit was about him. Sometimes we'd meet after my session and Gabe would help put me back together again after a difficult session. Other times Gabe and I would bounce Barbara's theories around, trying them out for size, sometimes agreeing, other times throwing them out with a laugh. Or I would call Gabe on my way to an appointment, rolling off reasons for bracing myself for the session. He always listened, without interrupting, keen to understand how it helped keep me on an even keel.

'I brought something.' I reached into my bag and handed him a box of muffins. 'Make sure you eat. And wash.'

'Okay. I know.' He sniffed his armpits. 'I just haven't been bothered, it's not like I'm going anywhere.' He shrugged.

'Depression. How long you been off work?'

'A week.'

I suggested he try to return in the next few days. Experience had taught me, the longer you left it, the less likely you were to return to normality at all.

'Okay, Okay, I'll call them tomorrow.'

'Get in the shower and get rid of that facial foliage, it's aged you by about ten years. I'm not leaving until you do.'

He reappeared, smooth faced and smelling of shower gel, with a towel wrapped round his waist.

The next day, I sat with him while he phoned work and agreed a return date. I didn't leave until he wrote an appointment in his diary with the clinic's counsellor. Dressed and showered, two days running, Gabe reluctantly came with me to the park, and afterwards ate the home made muffins I had brought.

We talked every day, scheduling phone calls during the day and seeing each other when we could fit it in between work. He told work it was flu—I told him not to mention depression or they think you're a nutter and your career's fucked.

I knew if there was a time when he needed me, it was now.

One lunchtime, I sat in my office, having banished Di Anne, while Gabe explained: 'So, I started seeing the woman, all tie dye and beads, but she knows what she's talking about. With her, we cut through the crap and cover a lot in the sessions. I come out of them like I've been in a fight with a boxer. Who knew thinking and talking could be so tiring?'

I smiled, that was my speciality — thinking.

'The guilt's not just about cheating on him, it's everything. It's too big to think about, so I'm not at the moment. What's up with you?'

'Oh, it's me now, is it?'

'Fuck off.'

'I'm taking the piss. I'm fine. Well, work's annoying, this Di Anne keeps changing what she does. One minute it's performance, then it's conduct. So I try to manage one, then another thing pops up where I wasn't looking for it.'

'What like?'

'One day, she read a paperback. One of the nurses asked for a care plan to be printed, as she needed it for a review with a social worker. An elderly woman who couldn't be discharged until we sorted out carers coming to her house. She looked at the nurse, one of the senior staff nurses, and said "I'm in the middle of something at the moment, can you come back in a bit?" And turned back to her book. I reminded her that was her job, what we actually paid her for, and she threw her hands in the air, said I was bullying her, and went home.'

'Brilliant, so now what?'

'She's signed off sick for a month, I've been advised to take a more caring, sharing approach when she comes back, and I'm doing my own admin.'

'What about your parents?'

'Mother, the same. Dad, haven't heard from him in a while. Which makes me worry he's lost his job again and he'll come round asking for somewhere to live.'

'Is that likely?'

'He's done it before.'

'Luke?'

'Next question,' I was too embarrassed to tell Gabe how long I'd been avoiding having the conversation with him. The conversation about our love life, or rather our lack of love life. When I'd told Gabe how long it had been, he thought I was joking.

'Ten months? You are joking, aren't you?' was his response, both of us a bit drunk, in mid-conversation about sex.

So, now, with no alcohol, the fact I'd not talked to my own boyfriend about it wasn't my best achievement. I wondered if I was avoiding talking to him about it, as I didn't *want* it resolved. Unresolved, it would give me a perfect excuse to pick a fight and see where that led to.

A month (twenty-nine days, but who's counting—I was actually) after Gabe called me about Hercules's rejection, he told me they were 'Giving it another go, taking it slow this time.'

'Alongside A, or instead of A?'

'Next question.'

I was relieved I hadn't rubbished the mighty Hercules too much, for exactly this eventuality. Maybe in the back of my mind, I always knew they'd get back together. Naturally pessimistic, or cynical, call it what you like. Once you declare how much you'd always hated a friend's ex, there's no climbing down from that. It's been said, you can't un-know your friends hate your boyfriend.

He told me how Hercules had researched The Hydra (he didn't call it that, but Gabe did); he'd gone to the library, spoken to a doctor, looked at treatments, combination therapy, risks, being in a relationship with someone who is HIV positive, and after talking to his friends, he'd decided he could give it a go. He said they'd agreed certain rules in the bedroom, I didn't want any more detail than that. There was one bit of his story which I queried: 'He told his friends?'

'Yes,' Gabe replied, matter of fact.

'Did you say he could tell them?'

'No, why?'

'I haven't even told Luke, not even when My Depression came back.'

'It's different.'

'How?'

'He needed to talk to friends about being in a relationship with me. And The Hydra. You're not in a relationship with me.'

Got me there. 'I thought it was about respecting privacy.'

'You could have told Luke, I didn't say you couldn't tell him.'

'Different ways of coping I suppose.'

'He did some research and talked to his friends and thought, yes I can do this. You thought it was all so sad, which made you depressed.'

'What did you say?' I felt all the air leave my lungs and a sickness in my stomach, all at the same instant.

'I didn't mean it like that.'

'I've got to go, HR is coming, to talk about Di Anne. Bye.' I put the phone down.

We didn't talk for a week.

It felt like someone had cut my arms off. Every time something funny happened at work, I thought, I'll have to tell Gabe. Every interesting patient, or rude doctor, I knew he'd understand and be interested.

I didn't want to tell Barbara about it, but when I sat in the sad brown room, I didn't have anything else to talk about. My whole mind was consumed by what he'd said, and how angry and hurt I felt. *He did some research and talked to his friends and thought, yes I can do this. You thought it was all so sad, which made you depressed.* The words rang in my head.

Up to then, I'd only told her bits about Gabe: he was a friend, we spent a lot of time together—edited highlights. Now I could only tell her everything; without the whole story it wouldn't make sense.

Barbara smiled, steepled her fingers and said, 'What's happening with you at the moment?'

'Nothing.' Then I started to cry, staring at the carpet, not making eye contact with her.

'What's going on there for you?'

So, I told her everything, how I'd fallen for him, told him, and he'd said nothing. How Hercules had arrived, and then left, then came back. About The Hydra. She liked that, it was like a new challenge. She seized on that like a cat on a mouse.

'Is there significance of the name, The Hydra?'

'He picked it.'

Not to be deterred, she continued, 'What about now?'

'I'm not calling him, not after what he said. It was so hurtful.' I'd replayed his words in my head countless times, not quite believing he'd actually said them.

'I thought you were going to have an affair. When you first told me about this new friend, that's what I thought.'

Shocked, I replied, 'Why didn't you tell me?'

'I didn't want to influence your behaviour. It was for you to make your choice, not me.'

Typical tie-dyed-with-beads counsellor response. 'What am I supposed to do with that, now you've told me?'

'It's time now.' She looked at the clock on the wall above my head. 'We can discuss *that* next time.' She folded her note pad on her lap and smiled.

Fuck fuck fuck fuck fuck.

A few weeks later, I opened a letter, hand addressed to me, I knew it wasn't a bill.

Inside the card it read, in his swirly handwriting: *I'm sorry. Didn't mean to hurt you. Lots of shit in my head at the moment. Shouldn't have let any spill out at you. Special dinner at mine? Gabe x*

Chapter Seventeen

I arrived at Gabe's flat, packed for the weekend, pleased how close I parked to his flat. A was away, he gave no more detail than that. I told Luke, Gabe was going through a hard time with his boyfriend and needed his friends. I don't want to say Luke *let* me go, because he didn't own me, but he didn't put up much of a fight. I told him I would be away for the weekend, clubbing with Gabe (I knew Luke hated that now), he asked if there was anything he could do, said, 'Have fun, what time will you be back? Love you.' And I was gone.

Now, Gabe greeted me at the door, hugging me tight. He smelt of CK One, he kissed me, his cheeks were smooth. He carried my bag to the spare room, which was made up like a hotel bedroom: towel and chocolate lay on the bed, with a selection of toiletries on the bedside cabinet. 'Drink?'

'What are we eating?' I asked awkwardly, a bit overwhelmed by it all.

'Surprise.'

'No, red or white?'

'I've got gin, vodka, Scotch, everything. You can behave like Goldie in *Overboard*.'

'Before she lives with Kurt Russell and his kids, or after?'

He smiled. 'Before, after, whatever you want.'

And we were back.

We ate, sat opposite each other at his dining table, lit only by candles.

He brought each of the four courses out like a waiter, with a napkin draped over his arm, checking if it was all to my satisfaction, then sitting opposite me again.

During the smoked salmon and cream cheese, we made small talk. By the duck in orange sauce with veg we broached the topic. I explained I was only trying to protect him from being hurt again, now Hercules was back, and he said he had so many things to think about, it was all too much, so he had lashed out at me.

Gabe finished a mouthful. 'I'm better now, the woman at the clinic is great. They gave me some tablets too. Some of them can interact with the other meds, so...'

'But the clinic knew which ones would work with your other meds?'

He nodded, his mouth full of duck.

'How awful are her tie-dyed clothes?'

'Why?'

'How bad though?'

'I hadn't thought about it before, but now you mention it, there is a lot of multi-coloured action going on.'

'Beads on necklaces?'

He nodded. 'Oh yes.'

Where did they all come from, these counsellors? Did they all go to some school in Birmingham for classes on finger steepling, and workshops on 'how does it make you feel?' where they also got a discount on hippie clothes left over from the seventies?

Gabe continued, snapping me out of my own thoughts. 'I didn't think you'd want to go out, so I've got enough food for the whole weekend, we don't have to leave unless we want to.'

'I told Luke we were going clubbing to cheer you up.'

'But we don't have to, do we? He'll never know. We're not doing anything wrong.'

We ate and talked — not just surfacey small talk, but proper talk: hopes and dreams for the future, him 'Being whatever they call male matrons,' me 'A director of nursing, on the trust board', fears him about being alone, me about whether I still loved Luke, favourite pets, both of us, dogs, which made us laugh, then he started taking the piss out of my dog's name.

Between talking, we dipped into some of the films in his collection, which seemed to include, I noticed, a particular penchant for eighties high school romances: *The Breakfast Club; Pretty in Pink; Some Kind of Wonderful; Adventures in Babysitting; St Elmo's Fire.* At first I resisted, but once I got used to their style I found myself revelling in the period incidental music, and clothes, always rooting for the cute guy to get the cute girl (secretly hoping he'd get the other cute guy, but always being disappointed). After a few, I looked at Gabe sideways and said, 'You're quite an old romantic, aren't you?'

'What makes you say that?' He looked at me.

'They're hardly action films.'

He pursed his lips, bit off a chunk of chocolate from the huge slab on the table in front of us, and replied, 'Maybe I'm always looking for the happily ever after. Anything wrong with that?'

'No.' I shook my head, smiled and returned to the film. In one of the films, I think it was *St Elmo's Fire*, Demi Moore was rescued by Emilio Estevez from a cocaine induced paranoia frenzy, rocking back and forth in her empty flat.

Gabe pointed to the screen. 'I love this bit.'

I nodded.

'I can't feel my legs. Walk, fresh air?' Gabe suggested after spending what seemed like forever in our own personal bubble together.

I enjoyed it so much, part of me was reluctant to step outside the bubble, but my legs had gone numb too and I had started believing I was part of The Brat Pack, half expected to see my name in the credits of the next film.

I grabbed my coat and I noticed Gabe quickly making a larger than usual roll up cigarette. He looked up. 'Ready?'

'I've got mine too if you want.' I patted my cigarettes in my pocket.

We left his flat and he directed us across the green. 'Not that way, even *I* don't go that way, and I've lived here for years. Come on, follow me.'

We sat on a bench, overlooking the green. It wasn't quite a park, it didn't have fences around it, and it wasn't a common, so I guessed it was a green. He lit the newly rolled cigarette and took a deep drag, before handing it to me.

'I've got my own.'

'Not like this you haven't. Go on, just a little bit.'

I took the cigarette from him and inhaled gently, filling my lungs with the smoke, closing my eyes as I felt slightly dizzy. I coughed so hard, I thought I was going to cough up my lungs.

'A little bit, I said,' he replied, taking it off me.

I leant my head back against the bench and closed my eyes, the green tilted to one side. I regained my composure, sipped a bottle of water Gabe handed me, opened my eyes and smiled at him.

'Okay now?' He rubbed my back.

I nodded, still smiling.

'Wanna walk a bit?' He took my hand, I looked around in case the world came to an end as two men held hands in west London. It didn't. We stood, walking around the edge of the green and into what must have been Acton's town centre.

All the colours appeared as if someone had turned up the colour and contrast dials on my personal TV set. I walked slowly, noticing a slightly floaty feeling throughout my body, following Gabe as we drank in the fresh air and food smells drifting from the fast food outlets.

'Can we get something to eat?' I asked.

'What do you fancy?'

'What is there?'

He gestured to a row of brightly lit fast food shops ranging from pizza, kebabs, Chinese and burgers.

'Let's get something we can take back to the flat. Unless it's too far.' It felt like we'd been walking for hours, so I wasn't sure how far we were from his flat.

'Five minutes, that way.' He pointed back to where we'd walked. 'Other side of Acton Green.'

'So it is a green?' I asked, pleased with my powers of deduction.

'What?'

'Nothing. Pizza?'

He led me into the shop, steadying me as I wobbled slightly up the step.

We lay on his sofa, greedily shoving slices of greasy pizza into our mouths, picking up the cheese and tomato as it trailed back to the boxes. Full, and feeling completely content, I lay my head against the sofa, my legs resting on Gabe's lap as he stroked them slowly.

We lay there in happy, companionable silence for a while, listening to our breathing.

I opened my eyes, Gabe's face was inches from mine, smiling. I smiled back, he continued to stroke my legs and I felt my groin stir. He leant in and kissed me. I felt his lips against mine, his tongue exploring my mouth with little darting motions as it flicked in and out. My head knew it was wrong, but my body wanted more. I kissed him back, this time my tongue exploring his mouth, our hands behind each other's heads, gently stroking.

He put his hands under my T-shirt and explored my chest, gently tweaking my nipples as they immediately became hard. His hands gently stroked my chest in a circular motion. He turned to sit opposite me and sat on my lap, his legs either side of my chest, wrapped around my body. I followed his example and reached under his top, reaching greedily for his nipples, kissing his throat, gently biting his chin.

He leant back and pulled off his T-shirt, revealing his chest. I nibbled his left then right nipple as he arched his back, pushing his chest towards me. I reached inside the waistband of his jeans, his belly button inches from my mouth.

He grabbed my wrists, stepped off my lap and held my wrists against my hips.

'What?' I asked, confused.

'Stop,' he said firmly, staring me straight in the eyes.

'I thought...'

'I do, but this isn't you. It's the pot. Think of Luke. Think of how you'll feel afterwards.'

'Fuck him, I want you.'

'Now I know it's definitely not you talking.' He let go of my wrists, picked up his T-shirt from the floor, and walked to the kitchen, rearranging himself in his trousers. 'Herbal tea?'

I looked at myself on the sofa: legs apart, tenting my jeans, T-shirt crumpled on the floor, and I held my face in my hands and squeezed my eyes shut. Anything to not be here, now, at this moment, I implored to myself.

Gabe appeared with two mugs of herbal tea, put them on the table in front of us, and handed me my T-shirt. I put it on and took a sip of the tea. 'What's this? It's vile.'

'Herbal tea, meant to help you sleep, calm you down. Try it, you'll get used to it.'

I took another sip and my taste buds, now prepared for it, didn't immediately reject it like last time. We sat in silence, sipping the tea.

I broke the silence. 'I don't understand.'

'It's not what you want. It's not what I want. I know it's not what I want, what I really want.'

'How do you know it's not what *I* want? I could have been dreaming about that since we met. Everything I've done up to this point could be because I wanted to get you into bed.'

'It could be. But it's not,' he replied.

'How do you know?' I sipped the tea again, by now starting to actually like its taste.

'Because I know what it looks like to just want to get someone in bed. I'm an expert at it. And what you've done isn't it.'

Busted. I couldn't argue with that, so instead I sipped the tea quietly. 'You drink this a lot, do you?'

'Sometimes. If I need to relax and sleep.'

'I feel like a sex ball, a ball of sex, all bunched up inside me. If I don't do something I'm going to explode. I ache.'

'Me too, it's called being a man. Doesn't mean we should just shag.'

'Doesn't it?' I said, looking into my mug.

'You're not one of my gentlemen friends for the night. I'm going to see you after this.'

'Doesn't mean we can't see each other afterwards,' I threw at him.

'Trust me, it does. No way we could carry on like we used to be once we've seen each other's cocks.'

'Sure?'

'Sure.'

There was a pause while we thought about what had almost just happened.

I began, 'My counsellor thought we were going to have an affair.'

'She said that?'

'Yep, just came out and said it.'

'And why didn't we?'

'She said, something to do with not wanting to jeopardise our friendship. But I'm not convinced.'

'Of what?'

'That it'll jeopardise it. Also I suppose I wasn't sure you fancied me. It's been so long since I've made someone excited, just by, you know, being there.'

'Do you believe it now?'

'Suppose.'

We talked for hours, well into the night, about how we both had to sort out what we felt for our current boyfriends before we thought about how we felt for each other. Eventually we agreed it would be hard to make a decision about A and Luke if we were still friends. Tonight's Pandora's Box having been opened, we weren't really able to completely close it once again.

I found this the hardest part to agree with: 'So we might as well have just shagged, if we can't be friends?'

'We can still come back from this, if we'd gone further there would be no going back.'

So we agreed to not see each other. We didn't set a time limit on this, and when I asked, Gabe replied, 'How long do you think it'll take to work out whether you love him? Cos I don't know how long it's gonna take me.'

Reluctantly, I agreed it was hardly something you could put a deadline on, so I packed my things, took one last look around the flat and hugged him very hard, whispering in his ear, 'I love you.'

I felt his head nodding as he replied, 'I love you too.'

And I was gone, into the cold light. I looked at Acton Green, where a few hours ago, everything had seemed so idyllic, so perfect. I had my perfect friend, we were in our perfect bubble together, and nothing could burst that. Only we'd burst it all by ourselves, by thinking with our penises, like most men so often do. And I thought I wasn't one of those people, and yet I'd almost become one. *And then that happened.*

I drove home, crossing west London suburbs, each high street merging into the next, remembering conversations we'd had that weekend, and since knowing him. I pictured the first time I saw him, his smile, those deep brown eyes. I laughed to myself, remembering the trip to Harvey Nichols for clothes. All the new experiences he'd shown me.

I thought about Luke, waiting for me in our house, with our dog, Princess, sitting on our sofa. Innocently waiting for me to return, after my weekend of being a good friend to Gabe. After my little mercy mission, because I was such a great friend and boyfriend, Luke would be waiting at home, ready to hear about my mercy mission. *If he asked me.* Which, when I thought about it, was pretty unlikely. He'd recently developed a habit of not asking anything when I came home after seeing Gabe. He couldn't have been less interested.

Just in case, hoping he asked me, I started to think about what to tell Luke when I arrived in the middle of the night, supposedly back from clubbing with Gabe.

I'll ask Gabe, he'll know what to say.

No.

Meeting Gabe, who was in so many ways my perfect man, made me re-evaluate my life so far. I thought about every little choice that had led to that house, that car, that dog, that boyfriend. Were they the right choices, the safe choices, had I even made those choices or had I just not disagreed with the choices being made around me? If you do a few of those along the way, getting swept along in the wash of your own life, you suddenly find yourself looking around thinking 'is this my life? Is this what I asked for?'

I turned my key in the door quietly then crept into the hall. Luke was asleep, Princess ran to greet me. I sat in the living room, looking at the pictures and ornaments we'd chosen together (some I hated, others I loved), remembering each trip to Ikea together, and was back into my small life once more.

Chapter Eighteen

We sat in Matt's parents' kitchen, dancing around the real issues (his relationship with Marcus and my loss of Gabe), instead talking about the weather, work, before settling on music.

'Have you got the new Erasure?' Matt asked.

'Yep.'

'They're touring. Do you want to see them in concert? Wembley's probably easiest for us both.'

'I've seen them.'

'When? Who with?'

'A while ago, with Gabe. It was great.'

'I'm sure it was. How did he know you liked them?'

'I told him.'

'Would you see them again? With me?'

'Definitely. You don't only listen to an album once, do you, so yeah, definitely with you.'

'I'll give you some dates. Marcus wants to go away so we'll have to work around that, but I'm sure we can sort something. Says he wants to woo me, mentioned Paris or something.'

'I'm sure we can fit around Paris.'

We spent an amiable day together. We picked through sale rails in Portsmouth's shops; him slightly dismissive of the mainstream shops I favoured, me baffled why anyone would pay thirty-five pounds for a T-shirt in the sale while in his shops.

He asked me about Gabe, I gave him edited highlights, deliberately omitting The Hydra and our decision to stop seeing each other. I knew how judgemental he would be about The Hydra, despite his 'little mishaps' of the past. I wasn't ready to tell him Gabe was out of my life, he'd only just caught up with him being in my life, and I wasn't ready to share how I felt with everyone.

He listened, then, chewing on the information, replied slowly, 'And this boyfriend of his, A?' I nodded, Matt continued, 'He's okay with this open relationship, gentlemen friends for the night business?'

'They both are, there's rules—their own rules, but rules to stick to, yeah.'

'And remind me why you didn't clutch your pearls and run away in disgust when he told you this?' He held up a plain white T-shirt with a small and, I gathered, much sought after logo over the area where the left nipple was.

'Because I'm not twelve.'

'But really, you must think it's wrong, a bit disgusting, a bit seedy. No?'

'It's not for me, but if it works for him, what's to run away for?'

'I know that I wouldn't run away. In fact I'm quite interested in these rules, might suggest it to Marcus, as it goes, but you, no.'

'It's good I can surprise you after all these years.' I smiled back. 'You trying that on?'

'Wait here, I'm going to the changing rooms.' He left.

A while later, sipping smoothies through straws, surrounded by shopping, he asked me why all of a sudden I was spending so much time with 'this Gabe?'

I'd been waiting for this to come up, and was surprised he'd held onto it for this long. All the way through River Island, Top Man and Boots he'd held off, but here it had reared its head, imbuing the smoothies with an awkward tang.

'It sort of happened. We see each other, he calls to arrange something. I call him, and we arrange something else. Between that, and speaking so often, it just rolled on.' To me, that showed it was in the past, it rolled on, not it rolls on, but Matt didn't pick it up.

'Sounds like it does.'

'Why do you ask?'

'No reason. Seemed to me, he'd come from nowhere, and now I know.'

We sat in a bar we used to practically live in during our teenaged years. Matt described the night as 'Us club kids together again.' We were reminiscing over old times, and both reflected that it wasn't the same as we'd remembered. A man walked over to us and said his table included two single guys, were we interested in joining? I explained we both had boyfriends, thanks, and the man left with a smile and a 'no worries.' Matt became really stroppy, he told me off for speaking for him. I couldn't understand what the issue was, we *were* both in couples, and the men on the other table were clearly after only one thing. 'What if I wanted that?' Matt asked, playing with his coaster angrily.

'But you're with Marcus, so why would you?' I asked, confused.

'Just a snog. Something to make me feel better.'

'What about Marcus?'

'He's not here. It's harmless. I knew they were interested, it would have been easy, but you spoilt it.'

'Snogging someone else, how's that going to make you feel better about your relationship with Marcus?'

'Take my mind off it.'

'You talk about the relationship like it's something bad, like cancer or something.'

'That's how it feels at the moment.' He stared at his drink and continued to tear apart drinks coasters.

'He doesn't hit you, does he?'

'Course not. He… it's everything…' and he explained how Marcus had a new friend, a young lad a few years younger than Matt, who he spoke to, texted or saw every day. He told me how Marcus insisted it was nothing more than friendship, but his gut didn't believe him. How he'd suggested to Marcus they get a place together as he didn't want to live with his parents any longer, but Marcus had bought a one bedroom flat on his own, without consulting Matt, and said he could stay round whenever he wanted. How he'd asked Marcus to help him apply for jobs as he finally realised he didn't want to work in a call centre approaching his thirties, and Marcus said they'd look at his CV that weekend, which became next weekend, next month, and then never.

'Did you tell him?'

Matt nodded. 'But it doesn't make any difference.'

'You can't *make* someone love you, either they want to do boyfriend things, because they want to, or they don't want to.' I paused. 'You deserve better you know.'

He didn't reply. We both sipped our drinks in silence. After a short while, we started to talk about what to do the following day. I said I wasn't bothered, just seeing Matt was enough; he suggested ice skating.

'Do you *like* ice skating?' I asked, bemused at where it had come from.

'Course. Always have done. Haven't I mentioned it before?'

'Not that I can remember, no.'

Matt said, 'We used to go when we were younger, our parents sent us there during the summer holidays, supervised with play leaders.'

I looked blankly at him, with absolutely no memory of this whatsoever.

'You fell over, I wanted to wear my own shoes when we went bowling, I threw a strop about wearing communal shoes.'

This sounded familiar, or at least typical Matt, but I still had no memory of it. 'We definitely did it together?'

'The summer before we started our GCSEs. I didn't know what to study, you chose ages before.'

'We didn't meet till we were sixteen.'

'Well who was that, then?'

'I don't mind going, I'm quite good now.'

'I wonder who I went with…' Matt looked at me, frowning. 'What did you say?'

'I don't mind going?'

'Before that.'

'I'm quite good now?'

He nodded. 'So you *have* been before, even if it wasn't with me, as we've just established?'

'Yep.'

'Oh, hang on, no, don't tell me. I can guess who it was with… Gabe by any chance?'

'Don't be like that. No need to get funny.'

'Funny? Funny? I'll give you funny: how about I've known you for years, it's always just been us, I know we've had our ups and downs, but it's us two. Then suddenly this Gabe turns up and you're doing all this stuff with him. What does Luke think about this?'

I looked around, worried someone local would notice the histrionics on table thirty-three: 'Nothing.' I didn't want to give too much away. Strictly speaking that was almost true: he'd not as such told me what he thought, although I knew he thought something was going on. But I wasn't going to give Matt the satisfaction of knowing that.

'Nothing?'

I nodded.

'Really, he's not jealous, doesn't ask to meet him, doesn't want to know what's so great about this Gabe?'

'He met him, I never said he'd not met him.'

'So we'll go ice skating tomorrow. That's okay is it? You don't mind repeating it all again, this time with me, a pale impersonation of Gabe?'

'Don't be like that.'

'Like what?'

'Funny about me being friends with Gabe,' I replied. 'Doesn't matter anymore, cos we're not seeing each other.'

'Since when?'

'Few weeks ago.'

The next day, we went ice skating, and while avoiding young children's fingers on the ground as they scrabbled to stand, we continued the long conversation about Matt and Marcus: how they got back together, but Matt still suspected him of cheating, which led to Matt cheating, 'To even things up a bit,' he explained. But they were now spending less and less time together, both pursuing their 'extracurricular relationships' as Matt termed them, to the extent he didn't even know what Marcus was doing one week to the next.

Now, he swerved in front of me, grabbed the handrail and stopped, panting. 'So I don't know whether to stick with Marcus, or one of the others. What do you think?'

Incredulous, I replied, 'How many others are there?'

He counted names on his fingers. 'Three.' He smiled. 'I think I got a bit carried away with evening things up.'

'I'm not even going to ask if you're taking care of yourself with these three…'

'…no, you're not going to ask that are you, Dominic. So, advice please?'

Although I had a strong sense of déjà vu, since Matt regularly found himself (got himself more accurately) in situations like this. I did find it a welcome a break from my continued anguish and repeated thoughts about how *I* felt about Gabe and Luke. In situations like that, someone else's problems provide a nice diversion. Of course, I didn't tell Matt that, as it was deadly serious, this latest situation he'd got himself into.

He snapped his fingers in front of my eyes. 'Hello, anyone there?'

Someone bumped into the back of me as I held onto the rail, and I nearly landed on my bum. 'I think this calls for a proper seat, and some form of sweet comestible.' I pushed away from the edge and glided to the café.

Two muffins and a millionaire shortbread later and I'd just about established Matt was 'kind of used to having Marcus around.' Unclear whether this *was* or was *not* in fact what others called love, we parked that and moved on to other matters. I asked if he suspected who Marcus may be cheating with. Matt said it was likely to be the young friend Marcus was texting and speaking to recently, so I suggested Matt make friends with said young lad, give him a particularly distinctive brand of soap as a present, and if Marcus returned home smelling of this soap, he'd know he was cheating. Failing that, I suggested he check Matt's phone and pockets for actual evidence of cheating. I also pointed out it would be much easier for him to retain the moral high ground if he stopped seeing all the other men.

Matt nodded. 'It's exhausting, I tell you. Exhausting. I don't really like any of them, it's just to pass the time, and make a point I suppose.'

'So stop.'

Matt wrote it all down on his napkin. 'It's so sneaky. I love it.'

Not being personally familiar with this sort of subterfuge, I was grateful for Gabe's recent revelations about what lengths his ex had once gone to, trying to find out if he was cheating or not.

That evening, our legs sore and aching from ice skating, he hugged me after I shut my car's boot, packed to return home. 'I'll let you know how it goes with the soap,' he said.

'Definitely.' I got in the car and waved.

'Thanks for a lovely weekend.' He waved me away.

Chapter Nineteen

1987

She was called Barbara. She wore baggy jumpers, stone washed jeans and walking boots. I met her every week in a small brown room with chairs in opposite corners, a low table with a spider plant and a box of tissues.

I didn't want to see her, but the doctor insisted, if I stopped the medication, I would need something 'to cushion the blow.'

The blow of what, I wanted to scream? The blow of life, its unjust nature, its inherent cruelty, which the medication had cushioned me from?

Even I, a complete cynic, could see the benefits of medication, but after a while I couldn't live with the removed from reality, remote, wrapped in mental cotton wool feeling it gave me. A part of me knew I wanted to get on with my life, to be a nurse, but the medication, while stopping me worrying about the Middle East, the lost children in the West Midlands, and the cars in the scrap yard, also stopped me caring about moving myself forward.

So I agreed to see Barbara. She asked me questions about my childhood, starting with whether I wished I had a brother or sister.

'I've never had one, so I don't know what it's like. A bit like a tail,' I offered, slightly perplexed.

'A tail. Interesting you say that.' She steepled her fingers and leant towards me.

I knew I was in trouble when she did that. I'd spoken to enough doctors to know what came next. It was full on, all guns a-blazing concerned mode. I knew what was coming next, and braced myself.

'So, how did that make you feel?' she asked softly.

I knew it, I'd have bet money on it. 'Nothing, I don't miss it. Nothing.'

She leant back and asked me about my parents. I didn't know why she was asking about them, it was *me* with the depression. Dad thought it was all made up, I had stopped seeing him when I was in the supermarket of sadness, and when I resumed visiting all he said was, 'Just pull yourself together lad,' and offered me a cup of tea. Mum sympathised — she would often 'take to bed, it's my nerves' periodically, sometimes staying there all weekend, while I cleaned the flat and tried to get her to drink tomato soup, fed to her one spoon at a time. But I didn't want to tell Barbara that, it was none of her business.

'Your dad, do you feel loved by him?' Barbara asked, making uncomfortable amounts of eye contact.

'He never said so. But I wouldn't expect him to.'

She stared at me. So I continued, crafty people these councillors.

'He was just Dad, working, when he worked I suppose. Otherwise he was around the house.'

'Tell me about when he didn't work?'

I didn't want to tell her about what it was like when he didn't work: Mum and Dad arguing about food,

Mum working at anything she could, while he sat in his chair in a vest and trousers. That was none of her business, and it was nothing to do with My Depression. We were here to talk about My Depression, not My Dad's Unemployment, which made me feel disloyal, so instead I said, 'It didn't happen much.'

Barbara looked disappointed. 'Tell me about happy times with your parents.'

I told her how we went on day trips (omitting the fact that we didn't when Dad wasn't working) and how we often went to the pub together.

With a glint in her eye, Barbara seized on this and said, 'Tell me about your parents' drinking.'

'They have a drink in the pub, same as anyone else.'

She leant in and did the fingers steepling thing. I braced myself. 'How does that make you feel?'

'Fine.' I didn't want to talk about Mum drinking to take the pain away after Dad hit her. If Mum was depressed, she should talk to her own Barbara, and I wasn't going to talk about it, as it was supposed to be about My Depression.

'How is your parents' relationship now?'

Bloody hell, it was like a job interview! 'They don't see each other.'

She nodded.

I braced myself for the fingers again…

'Are they *separated*, Dominic?'

What's with the names all the time, does she want a prize? I nodded. She asked when it had happened, and I told her how Mum left him. I explained how I still saw them both, just never together.

'That's a lot to see when you're only six or seven.'

I shrugged.

'And does it feel like it's your fault they separated, Dominic?'

Again with the name. 'Yes, I knew it wasn't my fault, but it made birthdays and Christmases difficult, and I wished I could split myself in half.'

Her eyes glinted at that, so before she could dive in, I continued with: 'Not physically, but maybe clone myself. Or if they could just bear to be in the same room together. It would make things easier.'

She nodded, and somehow I started crying. I'd no idea what about, nothing unusual, but the tears streamed down my face, huge drops, splashed on my jeans, leaving a dark patch in my lap. She handed me a box of tissues, making eye contact and nodding slowly, before writing something on her clipboard.

'And I'm afraid that's time, Dominic. We can pick this up next week. Have another tissue. I'll leave you to tidy yourself up. It's ten minutes before my next client so…' And she was gone.

Tidy yourself up? I felt like my guts had been spilled across the floor and this was meant to make me feel better?

So at first I avoided these difficult questions, but eventually the answers just slipped out. And once they were slipping out, they came thick and fast, one after another. Dad not getting a job, how hard it was for us.

Mum drinking to self-medicate, disappearing to take to her bed for days. Me wishing they were still together and feeling the pain every time one slagged off the other to me.

Because seeing Barbara was all under the heading: Keeping My Depression at Bay, and I wasn't sure if I stopped seeing her, as well as stopping the tablets, I would return to the supermarket of sadness, I returned each week to talk to her.

In the sad little room, she handed me tissues when I cried, moved the bin nearer so I didn't miss when I threw them away, and leant in steepling her fingers to ask how it made me feel. In *that* sad little room, I gradually opened up to Barbara, realised that My Depression wasn't all down to me and it wasn't down to my life now. She said I had an awful lot of emotional baggage to carry, as a young boy. Gradually I began to understand what that meant.

Sometimes I left feeling a huge weight had been lifted. I told her things I'd not even talked to my parents about. Most of the time it was hard work, going back to memories, which were still painful, which I'd put in a box and hidden away.

With Barbara, I got used to opening up the boxes, playing with them in my hands to see how they felt all these years later. Mostly they still hurt me very much. So I left feeling like I'd been run over by a truck and needed a lie down. But afterwards, I felt better, lighter, more free as I realised the boxes could be opened without the world coming to an end.

And after a while, once I had returned to a more even keel, it seemed a bit... *self-indulgent*, all that talking about myself, my problems, every week. So between Barbara, Mother and my doctor, they agreed to 'titrate' (a new word for me then) me down from weekly, every other week, to monthly. I still dreaded seeing her: what horrors would I share with her this time? But after each session, I left feeling better. Mother remained in the background, discussing my progress with my doctor and trying to get as much out of Barbara as her 'client confidentiality' clause permitted, regularly handing out cheques to Barbara's office.

Chapter Twenty

November 1999

I had hoped space from Gabe would reinvigorate my relationship with Luke. I had hoped it would allow me to focus on Luke, rather than avoiding him through escapism with Gabe.

Instead, all I felt was a deep longing for Gabe, which I knew, however hard I tried, Luke couldn't fill.

Just like how my brain sometimes broke when My Depression returned, something in my relationship with Luke had broken. Something in the core of us had died. A little light we kept for each other had gone out. I couldn't tell when it had happened, not the day, month or year, and it wasn't only about sex. It was more than that.

Each time I returned home after seeing Gabe, I wanted Luke to ask me what I'd done, who I'd seen, to take an interest. Instead, most of the time, I walked through the door, received a perfunctory kiss and an 'okay?' before he assumed the usual position in front of the TV. I felt like a naughty child, pushing its parents until they responded.

After the initial meeting between Gabe and Luke, I had high hopes for double dates, dinner parties, all manner of other middle class young professional activities. In my head it was all going to be exactly like the drama about a house of lawyers we watched some evenings — *This Life*.

Instead, having met Gabe, Luke's curiosity seemed satisfied, so I heard nothing more from him—no suggestions of dinner together, no trips to the theatre, nothing.

As I got to know Gabe more I realised A's attending anything was about as likely as getting the prime minister to join us in Heaven one night. But inside, I still hoped Luke would ask after Gabe, take an interest, feel jealous, like Matt had.

Instead, every time I pushed it further, weekends away, nights out, hoping he'd object, but Luke didn't respond.

One evening, while Luke served us dinner, mine with a portion of carrots, despite the fact I never ate carrots, I remembered other incidents over the past few months, which in isolation meant not much, but strung together meant a lot more.

The week before, I had looked up from *Attitude* magazine and said I was going to join a gym and get fit the following month, would he like to join me as something to do together?

Without pausing for thought, he continued to stir the food and replied, 'I bet you don't.'

'I will,' I had persevered, hurt by his dismissive comment.

'You always say you will, but in the end, I bet you don't. Better to save your money, buy a nice pair of jeans or something. That's more you.'

That's more you?

Some weeks before, after a string of night shifts, exhausted, I lay on the sofa, flicking through the TV magazine and noticed a film with Goldie Hawn had premiered the previous night. I asked if he'd taped it for me to add to my collection and, without looking up from his phone, he replied, 'I didn't realise, sorry babe.'

'Didn't realise what?' I wanted to check if he remembered how much I was obsessed with Dame Goldie of Hawn.

'You'd be bothered. I flicked over and it just looked like all her other films. Didn't watch much of it in the end.'

'Oh.' I couldn't believe it.

'We can buy it on video if you want. It didn't look that great anyway, so no harm done.'

No harm done?

I remembered how I set a cup of coffee next to him one Sunday, as he read the papers, and he didn't even look up or say thank you. Nothing.

Now, pushing the carrots to one side of my plate, I thought, *Do I really want to be with this person, in this relationship until the day I die?* I imagined handing him a drink in twenty years, me grey and him bald—I had my grandfather's genes, so was sure I'd not go bald—with no response from his bald head. I imagined us on a future, gay friendly version of *Mr and Mrs*, the game show where partners have to answer questions about each other, and him getting no points, despite proudly saying to the host at the start, 'We've been together twenty-five years, not a cross word between us.'

I looked at my plate as each little orange baton mocked me in my so-called perfect life, with my so-called perfect boyfriend. I put my cutlery down and, desperate to rescue the situation, desperate for the little flame not to have died, I jumped on our relationship and gave it mouth to mouth. I proclaimed I was full, then said, 'Fancy a bath?'

He looked up. 'What?'

'A bath, or a shower, together, like we used to.'

'I'm still eating, anyway, why, I had one this morning?'

'Not with me,' I persevered. 'Did I tell you, when I was on nights, after I wrote all my care plans, and all alone, in the staff room during my break. Did I tell you, I couldn't stop thinking of you, and couldn't get to sleep. If you know what I mean…'

'Yes, I know what you mean, you don't need to do a drawing you know.'

'So to get to sleep, I… you know…' I wasn't sure why I couldn't tell him exactly what I meant, since I'd shared much more with Gabe, including favourite positions and fantasies in full Technicolor lurid detail. Anyway, I persevered. 'So wouldn't it be fun, together in the bath?'

'Okay, you run a bath and get in, I'll come in a bit.'

I kissed him on the head and did as he suggested.

I lay in the bath until the water was cold, in the dark, quietly crying to myself. I was the only person who came to the watery funeral of my relationship with Luke.

I walked into our bedroom and mentioned the bath. He gave me a look that was the exact opposite of come to bed eyes: his eyes said *go fuck off.*

Chapter Twenty-One

Completely out of character, but in desperation, I rang Dad and invited myself to his for a weekend. 'I need to… get away… to see you…'

After a sniff and a drag on a cigarette—he must have sensed the tension in my voice—he explained he wasn't working, so anytime was alright with him. 'What's up, son?'

'It's Gabe.'

'I thought it was Luke, your fella?'

'It is, but it's complicated.' I paused as I wiped my eyes. 'Not on the phone, eh?'

'Come when you want, I'm not going anywhere.' He put the phone down.

I arrived at his fourteenth floor flat near Portsmouth city centre, after leaving Luke a note explaining Dad had asked me to help him with something for the next few days.

Dad stood in the doorway, the yellow council door covered in street grime behind my almost as grimy dad. He patted me on the back, and hugged me awkwardly, showing me in.

'Will the car be okay there?' I nodded over the concrete balcony to the tiny car park far below.

'It ain't a Beemer, is it?'

'I don't earn that much.'

'It'll be fine, fancy a cuppa tea, or do you want coffee?'

He showed me the tiny spare room, where he'd pushed all his fishing paraphernalia, old newspapers, unused exercise bike and roller skates into the far corner, giving me just enough space for my bag on the floor.

'What coffee you got?' I asked, already really knowing the answer but hopeful nevertheless.

'Nescafe,' he replied, like there was no other type.

'Tea, thanks.'

From the kitchen he shouted, 'I'm down to me last few bags. We'll nip to the shop in a bit.'

'Okay. What we eating tonight?'

'Hadn't thought, what do you fancy?'

I walked into the kitchen: Formica work surfaces, small folding table against the wall, metal sink full of washing up, and a few tea towels hanging on the side, all in need of a good wash. 'What you got in?'

He opened a few cupboards, revealing some pasta twirls, a tin of corned beef and a mouldy quiche in the fridge.

'When did you last work?'

'Few weeks, maybe more. I didn't sign on straight away. Couldn't cope with the forms. They do me head in.'

'But you've signed on now?'

He nodded. 'Reenie next door helped with the forms. She did another one for me, so they're paying me rent and council tax now. I gave her some ciggies as a thank you. I dunno if I'll bother getting another job as it goes.'

'You gave your neighbour cigarettes because she filled in some benefits forms for you?'

He nodded quickly. 'What's wrong with that?'

'Nothing,' I didn't have the energy to delve into this world much longer, for fear of what else I'd uncover.

I found one of the worst things about going to uni, getting a 'professional job' whatever that meant, was inadvertently I became painfully very middle class. I had all the right signs: angst about the 'right' brands, angst about not being too showy with said brands, worries about the environment.

Dad liked what he liked and thought everything else was shit, or too fancy. Much simpler.

Mother used to be like that too, but not since she inherited her mum's money. Since then, one of her neighbours once said if you had a cat, Mother would have an elephant. It was all 'oh the Mercedes is two years old, I must get a newer one…' or 'on the other side of the village green, a woman had a conservatory put on, so I thought I'd add an orangery,' when a few years before she'd not have known an orangery if it had landed on her lap, and never noticed neighbours, never mind what they did with their houses.

Now, I looked at Dad, tin of corned beef and spaghetti on the work surface next to an overflowing ash tray, and rather than broaching the subject of benefits, the advantages of working, and being a good neighbour, I said, 'Shall we get some bits for the next few days, while I'm here?'

'What with?'

'Don't worry.'

He went to the hall to put on his coat. We got in my car, despite his protestations about the corner shop, 'It's got it all, no need to go anywhere else,' and drove to a proper supermarket.

As we worked our way around the shop, Dad handled most items I threw in the trolley.

Mozzarella. 'What you meant to do with this?' (Later, when I opened the bag and cut it into slices with one of the vine tomatoes, he asked what to do with the water it came with. I told him I just poured it down the sink, which was met with a puzzled look.)

Smoked salmon slices. 'This is raw fish, isn't it?' (Chewing it later, he said he could see the attraction.)

Brown sugar to go with the coffee and cafetière I'd packed. 'What's wrong with white sugar and instant?'

'Brown sugar with coffee. What's right with instant, Dad?'

Steak and mushrooms for stroganoff. 'Bit extravagant isn't it? It ain't your birthday is it? Have I forgot?'

As I put the paprika in the trolley, he picked it up like it was an ancient artefact in a museum. 'What's this for?'

I explained about the need when making stroganoff, and he shrugged, before checking the price and shouting it loudly. 'I'm paying for it, remember Dad.' And he threw it back in the trolley.

I broached the subject of breakfast, and not impressed with his response of 'Black coffee and toast does me,' I grabbed bacon and eggs, which, both mornings I stayed, he completely cleared his plate of.

That evening we sat in his living room eating stroganoff from trays on our laps.

'Not bad, son, not bad.'

'Glad you enjoyed it.'

'You'll make someone a good wife one day.'

I smiled. 'Err, thanks?'

'You know what I mean, I don't mean, cos you're like a woman. Not that it… It's good. Good to cook.'

'I know, Dad. It's okay.'

He quickly filled his mouth with food.

As we finished, he collected our trays and, for a moment, I thought he'd wash them up, but instead he returned with two Snickers ice creams and threw one at me. 'Get into that, son.'

We chewed together. I knew I wanted to talk to him, but didn't know where to start. I couldn't remember how to talk to Dad about serious things, probably because I never had done.

'So this bloke, Gave…' he said between mouthfuls of Snickers.

'Gabe.'

'That's him. I can't get me head around you seeing him behind that Luke's back. Such a nice fella that one. Didn't understand that ceremony you had, and it was a shame I had to see your mum, but it was nice. Didn't understand it, but it was nice. So why you throwing it all away?'

'I'm not.' My whole body was reluctant to talk to him about this, but I couldn't face the thoughts going round my head any more.

'You seen what it did to your mum and me. I wasn't a good husband. I didn't just do it once, I kept doing it. It's like an addiction. Once you get away with it, you think, I'll try it again, do it riskier, see if I get found out. And you don't, so you do it again, and again, and again.'

'He's just a friend, Dad.'

'Aren't they always. That's how it starts.'

'No, really, we are just friends.'

'And?'

'And nothing.'

'What's wrong, what you doing here then? Do you want to be more than friends?'

'Maybe.'

'What about Luke?'

'What about him?'

'What's he think to this new little friend of yours?'

'He doesn't exactly know everything.'

'Does he hit you?'

'Gabe?'

'No, your proper fella, that, Luke.'

'Course not.' I wanted to add, because we're not in an *EastEnders* storyline, but kept it to myself, not wanting to spoil the considerable inroads we'd made to father and son bonding.

'Is *he* playing around with some fella?'

'Not that I know of.'

'What's he done, then?' Dad shuffled in his chair.

'Nothing.'

'Nothing?'

I nodded. 'That's the problem, see. It's not one big thing, he's not hit me, he's not cheating on me, he hardly argues with me most of the time. He just sits there, lets me get on with what I want, go out with Gabe, no questions, nothing.'

Dad put cigarette paper and tobacco in the wooden musical gondola, on the coffee table, closed its lid and removed a perfectly rolled cigarette, the gondola turning slowly to a song from *The Barber of Seville* while the lid was open. 'So what's wrong?'

You have no idea how kitsch that is was on the tip of my tongue, but I bit it back. 'He just doesn't care anymore.'

'He cooks for you, he's at home, looks after that dog, what else do you want?'

'I want someone who cares for me, not the house, not the dog, *me*. He doesn't even ask me when I'm coming home when I tell him I'm out with Gabe. I want him to ask, I want him to take an interest.'

He nodded slowly as he took a drag from the cigarette, closing the lid of the wooden gondola, the musical interlude ended.

'What's Mum's favourite film?'

'What's that got to do with the price of cheese?'

'Humour me, what is it?'

'That one, with the thin one, learns to talk proper, flower girl. Move your bloomin' arse.' He snapped his fingers. '*My Fair Lady*. She loved that film. Course, now I expect she says it's some highbrow one with French subtitles, but definitely when we was together, courting, married, that's what it was.'

I told him about the Goldie Hawn film Luke hadn't taped. He listened, rolling another cigarette with the gondola, which distracted me a bit, but also provided a bit of light relief from the awkwardness of telling my dad about my love life, and the sadness of remembering how I felt when he told me he hadn't taped it.

'When I was a lad…'

'…you lived at the bottom of the garden in a paper bag.'

'No need to take the piss, Dominic. You're not too old to get a slap.' He saw the look in my eyes change in an instant and realised what he'd said. 'You know I don't mean it, son.'

'Anyway, when you were a lad…'

'If I kept a job, gave her a few kids, that was it. I came home from work and that was it. I was too tired to take an *interest* in your mum.'

'But you knew her favourite film.'

'I did, son, I did that.'

The next day we went to a building site to meet 'Mick,' as he'd given Dad a sniff of some work coming up in the next few weeks. After a campaign of persuasion—I pointed out surely he didn't want to sit at home all day, staring at the walls—he admitted he was going a bit 'round the twist' and did enjoy eating nicer food. 'It's hard to get that salmon on the dole,' he said.

'That's why you should get a job, let's go, and put one foot in front of the other, to the building site, to meet this so-called Mick.'

We left the flat, avoided the lift, as it smelt of death soaked in urine.

We arrived at the building site, Dad approached the Portakabin and shook the hand of a large red-haired burly man (not burly in a sexy way, more burly in a 'had a hard life, seen a lot of things, not going to be fucked about with' way, but burly all the same).

Dad introduced me. 'He's a nurse, a male nurse, looks after a whole ward, he does. Tells 'em what to do and everything.'

I shook Burly Man's hand, noticing the rough fingers. He nodded his head and smiled before gesturing to Dad to follow him into the Portakabin. I sat near the door, reading the one magazine available that didn't promise Huge Jugs.

I wasn't just pleased with persuading Dad to come for this chat—you could hardly call it an interview—but touched how he'd introduced me to Mick like that. A couple of years after coming out, Mum told me how much stick he'd taken about having a poofy son, as well as all the awkward questions he'd been asked, like didn't it make him feel sick thinking about his son with another man? Or was he worried about catching something from my mug or toothbrush?

Even years after the event, through my mum, it still hurt. Not just for how angry I was at their ignorance, but how it would have made Dad feel at the time. How he had to carry on working with those men, because he had no choice, taking their comments and saying nothing.

I suppose now he had something to tell them about me, other than just 'He's gay'—now I was a big success: my own flat in London, my own car, and a job where I saved people's lives and told everyone what to do. Put like that, I realised it was something he could be proud of.

Now, he tapped my shoulder as he left the Portakabin and we soon ended up in a pub.

'Any joy?' I asked.

'Depends what you mean. Do I have to work, or can I sit around and do nothing for another few weeks?'

'Did you get the job?'

'No. Something'll turn up. Always does. Fancy a pint, or is it wine bars now, in that London?'

'Eighties, Dad, that was the eighties. Whatever you're having's fine.'

A few pints later, Dad was telling me about the moment he knew it was over for him and Mum. 'I was on me way home one night, and I noticed the lights on. I thought, fuck it, she's up, I've gotta talk to her. And all I wanted was to sit alone and watch me TV.'

'How old was I?'

'About this high.' He gestured to the height of the table.

'You must have loved her though, at one point.'

'Course. I still do.'

'Do you?' I asked, surprised.

'I don't like her, but I do still love her. She's your mum, I'll always have some feelings for her. I don't want anything bad to happen to her. We *were* in love, that doesn't just go away you know. You can't turn it off like water from a tap. I wasn't in love with her anymore. Not like I was at the start. It was like we'd said everything we could to each other. Nothing more to say, I didn't want to spend time with her.'

'You stayed with her for years afterwards.'

'Course, that's what I had to do. And it was a habit I suppose.'

'It's so sad.'

'Son, it is what it is. Some ways, when she left me, took you away, she had the guts to do what I probably would never have done. Put it out of its misery.'

'It?'

'Us, your mum and me. The relationship.'

I stared at my pint.

We cleaned his flat; I bought enough cleaning products to start a business, and showed him why people opened curtains and windows.

He sat in the kitchen, surveying the gleaming work surfaces, flicking ash onto the floor. 'Very nice. Won't take much to get it messy again, though. And I'll have to do it all over again.'

He wrote down my recipe for beef stroganoff, his handwriting of block capitals and no paragraphs covered the pages. He proudly read it to me after he finished, adding, 'I'll make it next week, if Irene helps me out again with the forms.'

Chapter Twenty-Two

I pressed the buzzer next to the eight foot metal gates, one with a large C and the other with a large A across them, to gain entry to the gravel carriage driveway.

Mother greeted me at the door, flanked by timber pillars, which were echoed either side with more fake Tudor touches on the house that Carol Anne built. 'Darling, it's so lovely to see you. Still got that car I see. They can't be paying you enough at that little hospital of yours.' She kissed me on both cheeks and led me to the bottom of the stairs in the middle of the double height hallway. 'Leave your bags there; Rose will put them in your room.'

I followed her to what she later explained was the 'Reading room,' surrounded by fake books, built in oak shelves, and green Chesterfield leather chairs and sofas.

She pushed a button in the arm of her chair, and the TV disappeared behind fake books and oak shelves. 'Now, darling, do tell me what this is all about. I do so look forward to getting you all to myself, without that Luke of yours!'

A small Filipino woman glided in and placed a tray of nibbles on the table between us. Mother said, 'Tea for two, Rose.' The woman disappeared as suddenly as she'd appeared, and Mother continued, 'How is work, are they keeping you busy at your little hospital?'

I briefly told her about my ongoing battles with Di Anne and being the Keeper of the Off Duty. She listened, her hands clasped across her tweed covered knees.

'That sounds marvellous. I'm so glad I don't have to work any longer. I honestly don't know how I'd fit it in, you see. Between the Women's Guild, the Village Action Group and running this place, I barely have time to get my hair done weekly, so I've no idea how I'd work too.'

'Village Action Group?'

'Darling, I'm sure I told you about it, the beastly council want to build some sort of waste disposal centre in the village. They said it will help the environment, something about recycling, but I said to the councillor, when I read my statement at the meeting, I explained to him: the villagers just *do not need* to recycle in that way. Most of us have relatives to whom we can pass on items of clothing, electrical items which no longer fit with the colours of our new kitchen, etcetera. So the last thing any of us need is a waste disposal centre here.'

Whom, indeed. I replied, 'You are very lucky, having this place. Not everyone's that lucky.'

'Luck, it's nothing to do with luck, I built this place myself. I designed every little corner of it: where the TV aerials are, where each plug socket goes, right down to the shade of marble for the bath and the exact blue of the swimming pool tiles. All me. It's got nothing to do with luck, darling.'

Tiptoeing around the issue, I said quietly, sipping tea, 'I meant Nan giving you the money to do it.'

'Oh, Dominic, she was never a Nan, or a Granny, you know as well as I do, she was always Grandma. Besides, that's not luck, that's breeding. Breeding coming back to its rightful place. Never should I have married beneath me in the first place. Your grandma was right to cut me off until I'd severed all ties to him. That horrible man.'

'Come on, that's my dad you're talking about. I told you I saw him not that long ago, didn't I?'

'Perhaps.' She sipped her tea from the bone china cup. 'You know what he put me through. You know what he was like to live with. He might be a chirpy old man now, but he wasn't then.'

'I know. But people change. *He's* changed. We had a lovely time together. And I never thought I'd say that about him.'

'That man deserves everything he's got.' She looked out the window, blinking quickly. 'Anyway, I'm sure you didn't come all this way to talk about him, did you?'

I started to tell her about my how feelings for Gabe had grown, alongside my feelings for Luke withering somewhat.

She listened, not asking any questions while I spoke. 'In my experience money usually helps with any doubts you may have.' She looked at her bright gold and jewelled watch. 'Goodness me, is that the time, I must buy an appropriate dress for tonight's party. You'll be alright here won't you, darling? Or do you need something more formal to wear? I could always hire you a dinner jacket while I'm looking.' She put the cup on the table, then stood.

'Party?' I asked. 'What party? I didn't know you were going out while I was here.'

'No, darling, it's my party. A small affair, fifty or so guests, a cocktail party really. Nibbles, champagne, that sort of thing. I must go…'

I shouted after her, 'I'll come with you, I wanted to see *you*.'

'How sweet, darling, you've just seen me.' She reappeared at the door, obviously anxious to leave. 'I am touched, but I really would prefer to shop alone, you'd be awfully bored. One gets used to doing things alone after a while. I'll pick up a dinner jacket for you, what size are you?'

'Forty inch chest, medium length.'

'Marvellous, make yourself at home: swim, watch a film in the home cinema, there are shelves of films for you to choose from.' And she was gone.

And then that happened.

I came to see you, not your bloody house. Still, keen to make the most of the opportunity, I slowly walked around the six bedrooms. The pool was larger than our garden, all bedrooms were en-suite, the staircase split from the middle of entrance hall, both sides curling elegantly to the first floor. After almost losing my way from the TV living room to the kitchen, I bumped into Rose sweeping the kitchen floor.

I made myself a drink and offered her one. She refused and asked, 'Where is Miss Carol Anne?'

I told her and Rose tutted, continuing to sweep the floor.

'You are her son, yes?'

I nodded, motioning to a stool next to me for her to sit.

She shook her head, put the broom away, and started to empty the dishwasher. 'I have a lot to get ready for tonight.'

'What's she like to work for?' I asked. 'Why did you tut?'

'Miss Carol Anne is nice lady to work for. But if you my son, I would stay here—spend time with you. I would not go to shops for dress. But that's me.'

'Do you have children?'

She showed me a picture of a teenaged boy. 'Here he is thirteen years. I have not seen him since ten years. But I have this; I keep it with me all the time to remind me why I am here.'

'Why can't you see him?'

'It is too expensive. It's many miles to fly. I send most of my money home every week to help him, my husband, and our parents. Without my money they cannot live.'

Taking this in for a moment, I asked what his name was.

She replied with a long Filipino name, which I tried to copy. She smiled at my attempts. 'Here I call him James. A good strong name. James.'

'Is he married?'

'Here, I call her Mary. It's easier here. She's a lovely girl. She makes him very happy.'

I told her about Luke, skipping the part where I spelled out I was gay, as I knew how she'd react.

'Do you have a picture?' she asked after I told her how long we'd been together and about our commitment ceremony.

I showed her a picture I always carried in my wallet.

'He is a strong man. He has a strong heart. A good man. He makes you happy.' She said it as a statement, not a question.

I sipped my drink in silence and blinked as my eyes filled with silent tears. 'He used to. But now, I'm not sure.'

'Come, I have to do ironing, but I can listen. Come.' She led me to the utility room, filled with dry clothes and sheets. She got an ironing board and iron from the cupboard and began to quickly iron my mother's clothes while I told her everything.

She ironed sheets, huge king sized bed sheets, pillowcases and duvet covers.

'She makes you iron them too?'

'Miss Carol Anne likes things done a certain way. It makes her happy. So I do them this way. It is easier like this.' She continued ironing, pausing to spray water on sheets occasionally.

'What should I do?' I asked hopefully.

'In my country we have a saying: throw your heart out in front of you, and run after it.'

I heard the front door shut, gave Rose a hug and returned to the kitchen.

There Mother appeared, surrounded by a few string-handled bags. 'Darling, where were you? I swear I heard you in the utility room.'

'Here,' I said. 'I offered Rose a drink when I made myself one.'

'You don't have to do that. She's perfectly capable of making herself a drink. I've told her hundreds of times, she can help herself to anything, except the champagne.'

'I wanted to. It was nice to talk to her.'

'You must be careful with that,' Mother said. 'One moment it's how's the weather, next they're crying about their family back home. It's important to maintain a respectable distance from staff. Otherwise, it can get awfully messy. Trust me, some neighbours have lived to regret it. I left your dinner jacket at the bottom of the stairs.'

'Did you get what you wanted?'

'Perfection. I went a bit OTT actually, ended up buying three cocktail dresses. Mind you, it's not like they'll go off. An investment overall. Now, I must find Rose to go through the menu and ask her to run me a bath. Where did you say she was?'

'Utility.'

'Marvellous. I don't know how I managed without her, I really don't. She's my little Filipino angel.' She left for the utility room.

Soon the guests had arrived, Rose circulated with trays of tiny fashionable nibbles, while Mother circulated me between groups of guests, each time introducing me as: 'My dear son, Dominic. He works for the public sector. n a little hospital. It's terribly interesting,' before leaving.

Each time, just as I got past 'Oh isn't that interesting,' and 'do you have to see blood?' or similar questions, and was starting to get to know the group of guests, Mother appeared and steered me over to another group of guests, repeating the whole cycle.

After enough repeats that I forgot how many, I hovered near the vol-au-vents and mini prawn cocktails, grabbing handfuls at a time in complete ignorance of her advice before the guests had arrived. She appeared behind me. 'I'm not ignoring you darling, I just want you to circulate amongst my friends. Do be a dear won't you.' She left after depositing me at another group of guests talking about house prices, council tax, how difficult it was to get good staff, or school fees (delete as appropriate).

A few hours later, the guests left, their empty glasses and plates the only reminder they were ever there. I started to take them to the kitchen. Mother appeared. 'Don't do that darling. That's what I've got Rose for.'

'I don't mind.'

'But I do, darling. I've told you, it's a slippery slope, being friends with staff.'

I took the plates and glasses I'd collected into the kitchen and returned to Mother, laying on the chaise longue in the living room, holding her brow. 'I want to talk to you, Mother.'

'Darling, I've talked to people all night. It's so tiring hosting these things. I've hardly stopped all evening. All I want now is to remove my makeup and put my Crème de la Mer on my face and hands and retire with my Penny Vincenzi; it's over eight hundred pages, so I've a lot of work left. '

'It'll wait till morning. Night.' I kissed her cheeks and watched her walk upstairs, leaving the house exactly as her guests had left it.

Despite Rose's protests, I helped her clean up before going to bed.

The next morning, over breakfast (me fried egg sandwiches, Mother half a grapefruit, no sugar), I told her the real reason why I was there.

She listened, slowly chewing each segment of grapefruit fourteen times before swallowing it. 'You know, my marriage to your father did make me happy once. At the beginning, I was so happy. You know what happened. I did try to find someone else, someone to look after me, someone who could keep me in shoes and makeup, who could give us a nice roof over our heads. That's all I wanted then: some shoes to keep the rain out, and a house for us all. What I didn't realise was how hard it would be. How hard it would be to get a man to take a look when I had a young boy. I met men at work, that wasn't too hard. It was keeping them, keeping them interested, making sure they stuck around, which was harder. The ones who didn't mind staying around, turned out to be no better than your father. They were going nowhere. And I knew I didn't want another one of them. I'd had years of it already. No thank you.'

'No one was any good?' I was keen to hear more, but still unclear how it related to our discussion about my love life.

'Most weren't even half good, never mind good. Or they just left after they got what they wanted, if you know what I mean.'

'Yes, I know exactly what you mean, Mother. Thank you very much.'

'So I tried it with younger men, men twenty years younger than me. Must have thought I'd be a Mrs Robinson. It was fun, mostly, but the number of times I had to tell them my varicose veins weren't on purpose, I could have screamed. And every time I thought about them meeting *my* mother, I came out in a cold sweat— imagining her asking where their fathers went to school, like a man of expectations.'

'So Grandma died, and then what?' I tried to hurry her story before one of *us* died.

'Yes, I'm getting to that darling, don't rush me.' She flapped her hands in front of her face. 'And once she died, I didn't need to worry about someone buying me shoes, or a house. But then, I didn't want people to get to know me. I didn't want them knowing what I *had*, in case they were only with me for the money. I worried they'd see my huge house and think of me differently, want to be with me for the wrong reasons. It's terrible isn't it?'

'It's certainly *something*.'

'What's that supposed to mean?'

'Bet you're pleased you don't have to work anymore.' I knew that would set her off again, distracting her from my comment.

'Oh, it's marvellous, I don't know how I had time to work. Between all the good work I do, for the Women's Guild and various other local groups, I could never fit a job in as well.'

'So what should *I* do?' I asked, keen to bring the conversation back to its original point.

'Oh, darling, you're so sweet. I thought we were just sharing stories about our relationships. Don't ask me that, I'm hardly qualified to answer, am I? Just do what you think best, how's that?'

Marvellous.

She continued, 'Do you want me to ask Rose for another tray of tea?'

I smiled and shrugged my shoulders.

Later that day, swimming in the pool, I reflected on the chat with Mother. If that was her idea of good advice, I could do without any more.

I dried myself and sat in the conservatory reading, enjoying the last afternoon before returning to work and my real life. Rose appeared with a duster and polish, and asked me if I was okay.

'I think I will be.'

'Miss Carol Anne does not know what she misses with you,' Rose added, her back to me as she dusted the table. 'My son, he writes to me, tells me everything he is doing. When I read I can hear his voice. She can hear your voice but she does not listen. This is very sad thing.'

I packed and said goodbye to Mother; she kissed me very quickly on both cheeks, exclaiming, 'It's so lovely to see you, on your own especially. And I do love it when we have our little mother and son chats. Did Rose help with your bags?'

'She's done more than enough. Bye Mother.'

Chapter Twenty-Three

A month without seeing Gabe. It felt like a decade. There was still no sign of Matt either.

What had surprised me was how my parents had helped (or not) with the situation. After the initial awkward introduction, Dad was so helpful, in his own way.

Mother, on the other hand, just didn't seem to be able to see it from my point of view, constantly feeling the need to bring it back to her and her problems. The space away from home, in her mansion, had helped; it had given me time to think about what to do next. Rose's words swirled around my mind as I shaved for work early one morning.

My God, I look old. The face of a man ten years older than me stared back from the mirror, bags under his eyes, so large and dark they could have gone with the decor of our lounge curtains. I concentrated on getting ready for work, one step at a time, all other thoughts too much at this time of the morning. Shower. Uniform. Work bag—full of the off duty I'd tried to break the back of last night, and instead ended up staring at, while Luke talked about his day at work.

Luke.

Ah yes, the matter of Luke. I dressed in the bathroom to avoid disturbing him before he had to get up for work. I also didn't want any awkward 'I love you, kiss me' conversations to deal with either. But I told myself the main reason was the light.

I crept out the house, closing the front door quietly, arriving at work an hour early, grateful for the quiet time before the day shift arrived, sitting in my office tackling the off duty, but actually staring at the paper, lost in my thoughts.

At eight fifty am, Di Anne arrived, flustered, carrying her mobile phone. I sat back: this should be good, I wondered what would be wrong this time?

'Morning, Dominic, cup of tea?' She put her bag next to the computer.

'You're meant to start at eight today, aren't you?' I started gently, ready to ramp it up if needed.

'Well, what happened was, you see, my next door neighbour had a fridge delivered, early, but they weren't there. So I was just about to leave, and I got this knock on the door, right. I opened it, and there's this man stood with a big fridge. I thought, funny, I didn't order a fridge, I wonder what he wants…'

'Is there a point of this, any time soon? Cos I've got to finish this, and have a pile of work for you to do…'

'A pile of work, I've only just got here, how can there be a pile of work?' Her eyes widened.

'Things which could do with being done, and you're just the woman to do them. Ongoing things, new things, you're going to love it.'

'Right. Tea did you say?'

'Yes, but first I want to hear why you're almost an hour late.'

She sat, then took a deep breath. 'So this bloke with the fridge, right. He's stood there, and I said, what's this, and he said to me, it's for next door, can I sign for it. So I thought, it's good to be neighbourly isn't it, they even say something about it in the Bible don't they? So I signed for it, and he wheeled it into my kitchen see. Then cos it was in the way, it took longer to make breakfast, and there were other things with the fridge, so it wasn't just the fridge, there were drawers and shelves and stuff. So by the time it's all done, I was late, and so I got here late.'

'I see.'

'Nothing I could do about it, Dominic. Nothing.'

'Well, admirable as it is to be such a good neighbour, you will have to do your good neighbour act on your own time. You can either make it up today, shorter lunch or stay longer, or tomorrow. Your choice.'

'Make it up?'

'The time, Di Anne, the time.'

'Can't today, see I've got to go, dead on four, I've got to pick something up for the house.'

'Okay, lunch time?'

'So, I've got to have half an hour, not an hour cos of this fridge?'

I nodded slowly.

''Spect I could today. But I've not brought anything in today, didn't have time to make a cake like before. And I kept putting weight on too. So I'll have to get something from the canteen.'

'That's fine. You can make up the rest tomorrow. White one sugar, thanks.'

'What? Oh yes, I'll be back soon...' And she was gone.

I stared at the off duty and reflected how someone who always seemed to have endless amounts of time off in lieu could have four weeks' holiday at a time and still leave enough for another four weeks scattered around the year, yet still never seem to work even five minutes longer than expected. *Time off in lieu of doing what?* was on the tip of my tongue during the previous conversation, but I didn't want to overload her and cause her to go off sick with stress, as had previously happened.

Di Anne returned with our drinks and my phone rang. It was Luke, wanting to know what colour ideas I'd had for the New Year's Eve party, and could I buy some party poppers, hats and napkins on my way home. I listened as he enthusiastically described what he'd done so far, including invites, buffet plans and music choices. I told him I'd do my best on my way home, but didn't know when I'd finish.

I put the phone down and rolled my eyes.

'Was that him? Luke, your husband is it, called?' Di Anne asked, sipping her tea.

'Yes.'

'Having a New Year's Eve party, are you? I'd love it if my Andy planned a party. I'm lucky if he remembers my birthday. Must be so good being gay.'

I looked up from my papers, my interest piqued by her comment. 'How come?'

'Well the gays love a party don't you? I love the gays—my cousin's gay, you know.'

Please don't ask me if I know him, I don't think I could bear it.

'And he's so funny. So camp.' She flicked her wrist in an exaggerated way, smiling. 'I must bring him to work, you'd love him, I just know it.'

I mumbled.

'So, how do you know who's going to do what?'

'For the party?'

'No, everything. Is there an effeminate one and a manly one? Is that how it works? Does one do the cooking and cleaning, and the other one all the DIY? I'd love it if my Andy put something in the oven sometimes. But he doesn't. Mind you, he's useless with a tool box and all.'

'It doesn't work like that, Di Anne. You just do whatever you're best at, and the other person helps where they're better. Teamwork.'

'But how do you know who's going to be the woman? I've always wondered.'

'There is no woman, that's the point, Di Anne.' I turned back to my papers.

'When I found out you were going to be the new ward manager, and you were gay, I couldn't wait to meet you. I knew we'd have so much fun. So much to laugh about.'

I laughed quietly, looking at the papers, signalling the conversation was over.

She didn't take the hint. 'So if he's planning the party, does that mean he's the effeminate one, and you're the manly one? I can't see it myself, I think you're pretty effeminate as it goes, but I don't know what your Luke's like, so I've nothing to compare I suppose. Mind you, my cousin, he's so effeminate! He's hilarious. I'd love to have a New Year's Eve party. I've never been to one. It would be so much fun. We normally go to the local until midnight, and back home to bed. It must be so much fun, a party full of gays, you're all so much fun. It's gonna be such a fun party.'

I turned from my papers. 'We're not *all* fun, you know. Some of us are *horrible*, some of us can be *vile*, some of us are nice. We're not all the same. I've known plenty of gay people you wouldn't like at all. Some of them wouldn't have very kind things to say about you.'

'Me? What about me?'

'People can be very unkind about size, you know. Can you log onto your computer, I've sent you an email with a list of things.'

'Me, what about my size?'

'The computer, Di Anne, the computer please.'

She tapped her username and password in and waited for it to load up. She saw four emails and jumped back from the screen. 'What's all this, all these emails, when am I meant to do that then? I'm only here till four, I told you that, didn't I?'

'One at a time, read them and ask if you have any questions.' I rolled my eyes to myself and properly started tackling the off duty. It was going to be a long day.

'But I suppose it would only be a joke anyway, cos that's what you're like, isn't it?'

'What?'

'The gays, if you're nasty, it's always a joke, isn't it?'

'The *emails* please, Di Anne. The *emails*.'

I worked through lunch, talking to concerned relatives about their elderly mother's recovery after her hip operation, finally finished the off duty — ready for it to be criticised and to receive a plethora of requests for changes from the staff — and dressed an elderly man's wound on his leg, while talking about how he missed his dead wife every day.

Would I miss Luke *every day* if he died?

I knew the answer to that, but wasn't quite ready to say it out loud.

I wasn't wishing him dead, no, far from it, but missing him every day...

By the end of the shift, I realised I'd survived solely on tea and cigarettes. I told Luke I ate at work, as it was too early when I left, and easier than taking something from home. In actual fact I did neither, but I knew he wouldn't notice either way.

Among all the uncertainty, feelings of my life swirling out of control, missing Gabe but knowing I should miss Luke instead, the only thing I felt in control of was my weight.

During December, I repeated this routine and gradually lost one and a half stone. Luke, between party plans, commented how my face looked more gaunt and asked if I was eating at work. I simply said yes, and he piled on more potatoes to my evening meals, which I chased around the plate before discarding them.

Among the daily Di Anne and other work challenges, I did my best to look after people, glad of the distraction from my own problems, as I carefully looked after my patients, staff and their paperwork, often well into the night.

Sometimes it became too much, and I retreated to the staff toilet to cry silently alone. All the feelings I was dealing with came to the surface: a kind word from a colleague about how lucky I was to have a man at home waiting for me; a patient's husband reading a book aloud by the bedside, holding hands. These displays of love reminded me how alone I felt in my relationship with Luke.

After being appointed as ward manager, I often felt someone would find me out, realise that I wasn't qualified or able to do the job. I often looked down at my name badge and wondered, *Is this really me, am I really good enough for this?* before continuing with the business of the day.

But never before had I felt a similar imposter in my private life. I usually spoke of nothing but Luke this, or Luke that. But since knowing Gabe it all felt so pale in comparison. Gabe had showed me what it could be like, and what I had, in reality, been missing for so long from my and Luke's relationship. That, combined with a visual reminder from another couple, was often too much to take and sent me to the staff toilet to compose myself.

A couple of times one of the senior sisters knocked on the door, asking me if I was alright. I pulled myself together, wiped my eyes and returned, blinking to the bright light of the ward, while the senior sister rubbed my arm, offered to make me tea and asked what was up.

I think I've fallen out of love with my boyfriend, and I haven't told him yet, which means the whole life I've created is wrong. Oh, and the man I am probably supposed to be with, has agreed that we shouldn't see each other again, for both our sakes.

Hardly trips off the tongue does it? Hardly something you can deal with in a fifteen-minute comfort break over tea and Hobnobs?

Instead, I smiled, wiped my face, and said, 'Director of nursing told me I've got to save money, so I've got to let some staff go.'

This, combined with a healthy dose of self-interest, was always sufficient to quench their inquisitiveness. So I continued in silence.

I continued in silence during December.

Chapter Twenty-Four

1989

We'd met in a nightclub in the eighties, at first trying to outdo each other's costumes every Saturday night. We didn't know it, but we'd unwittingly become Hampshire's Club Kids, like Michael Alig and James St James—swanning into clubs for free, spending all our Saturday job money on latex, fake blood and inflatable costumes. Well, I say Hampshire's; what I really mean is Portsmouth and Southampton's Club Kids. Nowhere else had clubs where we could have been kids of any kind. I'd gone drinking one night in Winchester and, stumbling on the pavement, asked someone where the nearest nightclub was, eager as I was to stretch my clubbing wings. 'Southampton, mate,' came the reply.

The costumes gave me some confidence, a mask to cover how intimidated by the scene, sex with a man, drugs, alcohol, everything, I really was. After months of camp costume duelling, we established there wasn't anything *sexual* between us. Both drunk, for wont of anything better to do, one night we leant in and tentatively started to kiss each other. A second later we both pulled away and burst out laughing. 'What were we thinking?' he laughed.

'I know.' I wiped my mouth and smiled.

One night, both well beyond nodding terms, but not at the stage of having each other's numbers, I had found Matt crying on the floor in the corner of the club. 'I don't know where it's gone, I've lost it. Can you help me find it?' he whimpered at me, like a little boy.

Sat on the floor with him, after lots of patience, bottled water and time, I found out he meant his mind. He'd done so many drugs over the preceding months he literally didn't know what or who he was. He'd walked to the toilet and heard a loud crack inside his head— apparently a chemical reaction, from consuming so many narcotics over a prolonged period your brain sort of snaps. And he looked to me to help fix him.

Having established what I was dealing with, I led us to the chill out area. We lay on squashy leather sofas; I stroked his hair and hugged his head to my chest as he shook. I smiled sweetly at a passing member of staff who brought two juices over with a brief roll of her eyes that said 'rather you than me'. After a while, he stopped shaking and looked up from my now wet metallic T-shirt, wiped his eyes and asked if I'd come home with him. 'In case I lose myself again,' he explained. We lay there until his legs were stable enough to walk, then jumped into a taxi where he pulled himself together sufficiently to remember both his parents' address and his name. He held my hand during the whole taxi journey. After that were well beyond nodding terms and called each other at least every few days.

So I fixed him, and in return he made me seem much more exotic than I really was: just a suburban boy from Hampshire, spending his money from a Saturday job on costumes and drinks. With Matt, we were the yin and yang of club kids. He wanted to turn up with an axe wound in his neck, wearing hospital nightclothes and pushing a drip stand. I preferred less horror movie looks and arrived in a bright red puffball skirt, blue stockings and platform boots, topped with a T-shirt covered in white feathers from a pillow. I taught him to eat fruit and vegetables and how to iron a shirt when he was normal Matt, and he showed me how to really let go in the clubs.

Together we were both fabulous, and unstoppable.

Chapter Twenty-Five

Christmas 1999

As a compromise for hosting the New Year's Eve party, we agreed to have a very quiet Christmas: Luke and me in the house together. I couldn't think of anything worse than pretending to play happy house with our parents, so instead it was just us two.

I came down with some sort of fluey cold so stayed well away from any food preparation. Christmas Day morning, I lay on the sofa, surrounded by tissues and wrapped in a duvet, watching Disney film repeats and the Top of The Pops Christmas Special between sniffles, as Luke prepared a feast large enough to feed us and three houses either side.

Initially I thought just us two for Christmas would make the awkwardness easier — no need to put on a show for anyone. However as it happened, it actually highlighted the dysfunctionality between us: there was no one to make small talk with, no one's problems to hide behind and discuss in detail. The only two living things capable of a conversation in the room were Luke and me, and after Christmas shopping, talking was the last thing we wanted to do.

A few days before Christmas, Luke had suggested driving to Lakeside, a huge out of town shopping complex on the outskirts of London. When I pointed out it would be like a zoo, and why had he left it this late, he explained he'd been so busy with prep for the party he'd completely forgotten to buy any of his family (or me, he subtly added) any presents. 'We can get it all in one place, throw it in the car, and it's done,' he'd optimistically offered.

In my drugged up, fluey state, that was the last thing I wanted to do, but instead of an argument, I agreed. We, along with the whole of Essex and north London, descended on the shopping centre, fighting for space among the crowds. We fought right from the queue for a car park space to the queue to pay for the presents he picked for our parents, and every queue in between. I stood back as he picked something for Mother, then Dad, carefully asking me if I thought they'd like his choice. I nodded and continued behind him as he strode off to pick something for his parents.

I stood behind him in the queue, watching hundreds of pounds worth of presents rolling along the conveyor belt as he handed over our joint credit card.

'Now, you can amuse yourself while I slip off to get some other things... alone!' he added with no mystery whatsoever. 'Feel free to make use of the time if you need to get any surprises for me.' And he was gone, disappearing amid the crowds of Lakeside.

I stood, surrounded by our communal purchases, then made my way slowly to the car, where I loaded them into the boot, tears slowly dripping from my face. I felt as if I were viewing this scene from my life from afar—like Ebenezer Scrooge in A Christmas Carol, when the three Ghosts of Christmas show him the options for different Christmases. I sat in the car and wondered what alternate

Christmases I could have had, apart from this one; this miserable pantomime of a Christmas I was stuck in now.

I stared through the windscreen as tears continued to drip down my face.

After a while—I couldn't say exactly how long—Luke returned to the car, arms loaded with bags and a smile across his face, pleased with his haul.

'Where did you go for mine? No, don't tell me, I want it to be a surprise. Let's face it, if you tell me you went to Top Man I'll know it's clothes, and Boots is pretty much a giveaway too.' He opened the boot and placed his bags among the communal ones. He raised his voice slightly, poking around the bags in the boot. 'Can't see any new bags here, Dominic, you did get some, didn't you?'

'No,' I replied, holding my breath for an onslaught.

'Oh. Are you too ill?'

'No.'

'What's wrong, then? Come on, you can tell me.'

'I'm not really in a very Christmassy mood.' I let it hang there, halfway between us in the air of the car.

'Why not? This is nice, us shopping together, for family.'

'Is it?' I avoided eye contact.

'Yes it is, isn't it?'

'It just feels a bit fake.'

'Why?' He touched my shoulder.

'I don't want to have this conversation in a car park. Let's go home.'

'With that just hanging?'

'Maybe I'm being overdramatic, I am sick. I don't feel a hundred percent, I'm tired. Maybe I'll feel better when we get home.'

'And start wrapping them?' he responded hopefully.

'That's it.' I started the engine and reflected on my silent retreat from my point, quickly accepted by Luke.

Surrounded by gifts, wrapping paper and Sellotape, we started to wrap our purchases. Luke handed me his dad's presents, and he started on Mother and Dad's.

I stared at the gifts in front of me: my sort of father in law's laying on the floor, about to be surrounded in shiny paper and a ribbon. I looked up and Luke was already finished with one of my parent's gifts and had moved on at great pace to the second, searching for a ribbon to complete the look.

He looked up at me. 'Do you want some ribbon?'

'I can't do it,' I replied, wiping my eyes.

'I can cut the paper for you so it's the right size, come on.' He shuffled on the floor and sat next to me.

'Not this.' I gestured to the wrapping. 'This, all this, everything, you, me, us.' I waved my hands around at the living room. 'I can't do any of it anymore.'

He hugged me as I cried silently, tears no longer coming, but my throat choked. 'It can't be that bad, we've been through worse, tell me what's wrong.'

I waited for the choking feeling to pass. 'Us. That's what's wrong. How can you pretend everything's alright?

Getting ready for Christmas, when you know it's not. How can you just think about us buying presents for each other, when you know it's not right between us, and hasn't been for a long time?'

'I thought if I made it the perfect Christmas, it would sort it out.'

'Really? You really thought that?'

He nodded slowly.

'So you knew something wasn't right?'

He nodded again. 'I didn't want to say anything because I didn't want to hear the answer to the question. So I didn't ask it.'

'And what was the question?' I looked at him, sniffing slightly.

'Are you having an affair with Gabe?'

I pushed myself away from him, wiped my eyes and looked straight into his eyes. 'No.'

'Are you sure?'

'I think I'd know if I was. And I think I know what you'd define as me having an affair: sleeping with him, being with him like he was my boyfriend. So no, I'm not having an affair with Gabe.'

'Okay, I believe you.'

'Good, because it's true. Why didn't you ask me before?'

'I thought if it was true that it would just fizzle out. New best friends come and go, friends at work leave. People lose touch.'

'He's gone now. I haven't seen him in months.'

'Three, isn't it?' Luke asked.

'How did you know?'

'That's when you changed, that's when I really noticed you weren't happy here, with me. So what's wrong? Why are we both so unhappy?'

'You're not happy?' I asked. This was news to me, I'd thought he was the usual Luke.

'Not at all, not for a long time.'

'So why didn't you tell me?'

'I thought you were having an affair. I wanted to be the positive, supportive boyfriend you return to after it's all over.' Luke stared at me.

'When we started going out, it was so much fun. It was so many happy moments of pleasure all in a line next to one another. Now it feels like a chore. We're always so busy with work, the house, family, I can't remember where we are in all that. I can't remember the last time we did something just us two, just *for* us two.'

'Shopping was kind of fun?'

'It was for others. I mean laughing together, sharing a joke. Telling each other about our days at work and really listening. And how are we meant to feel connected to each other if we never have sex?' I blinked away a tear.

'I thought you didn't want to, so I didn't try.'

'It's all I wanted to do. It's what I thought would save us. I thought, if you kiss me, it'll come from there and we'll be back in the saddle, so to speak. You never came to share the bath with me.'

'All you talked about was Gabe and how much fun you'd had together. All I could think about was you kissing him, so I didn't join you in the bath.' He stared at the half-wrapped presents on the other side of the room.

I put down the scissors and folded my arms, taking a deep breath. 'I used to be so in love with you. It was all I could do to contain my excitement each day before seeing you in the evening. But lately I've been avoiding you, working late, leaving early without disturbing you, because it felt so wrong when we were together. I'm so sorry.'

'Me too,' Luke said. 'I've stayed in hotels more than I needed to, travelled away whenever there was the option to stay or travel. Always stupidly hoping when I came back, it would be like it used to be. Magically!'

'But it never was,' I replied quietly.

'No.'

'All you wanted to talk about was the party, or big grand plans for next year, when the basics of us were so wrong, or just making small talk, pretending to be happy, not really talking about what was wrong. It felt like a pantomime of a relationship.'

'I thought if we pretended for long enough, played the role, eventually we would be…'

'Happy?'

'Like we used to be,' Luke paused as we both absorbed what had so far been said. 'I do love you, you know. I do still care for you. It's just…'

'…you're not in love with me?'

He nodded. 'Sorry.'

'Don't be sorry. Same here. We have tried, we've been through such a lot, such hard times, which would have split up other couples, and we stayed together. But now, now it's like we used it all up, and all we have left with no more moments of pleasure, is us both trying to hold on to each other, to stay together. For no reason other than just staying together.'

'A relationship shouldn't be this hard, should it?' He shook his head.

I looked at the presents in front of me on the floor. 'What are we going to do about this lot?'

'We can't take it back until after Boxing Day.' He paused. 'Give it to them anyway?'

'Alright.'

He wrapped a ribbon around his finger, then asked, 'If you weren't having an affair with him, which I do believe, why did you stop seeing him and why did it hit you so hard? I could practically see the sadness oozing out of you afterwards, like some black snake.'

'You really want to know? You want to hear this and have this conversation?'

'I asked you, didn't I?' He unwrapped the ribbon from one finger and started to wrap it around another one. 'I have to know.'

'Okay.' I took a deep breath and told him about how meeting Gabe made me realise how I'd lived such a cautious life, always staying away from risks, sticking with the known option (including Luke himself) and it then felt like a life half lived. I admitted the nearest I'd come to *risky* was the club kids scene where I'd met Matt, but that too was just a facade of debauchery—no drugs, no sex, just the costumes, dancing and quietly looking after

Matt. I explained how with Gabe, our time together was one moment of pleasure, laughter, joy, after another. How even when he'd told me about The Hydra, it gave our friendship a fresh honesty and clarity, sweeping away all the niceties and dancing around politeness you have with new friends, cutting straight to the core of our relationship. Without a sexual element, being there for each other, showing each other things in a new way, regaining the freshness and joy of moments of pleasure in our lives that we had both, up to that point, lost for different reasons. I told Luke if he didn't want to return to that, or something approximating that, with me, then our relationship, as it was, would be over.

Luke said, 'I knew there was something else going on with him: the phone calls, the emergencies. Now it makes sense. The Hydra, eh. Are you still seeing him?'

'I was never *seeing* him, *seeing* him. We've stopped being friends. We almost made a big mistake, because we both needed to sort out our own relationships before we could take that step. We thought it was best to have space apart to sort our own relationships out, rather than… making it messier than it already was.'

'Have you slept with him?' He couldn't look me in the eyes.

I pulled his face up so I could look him in the eyes. 'No. I would tell you if we had. I promise.'

We sat in silence for a few moments. I expected him to fly at me in a rage. Instead, he sat quietly, not looking at me. I briefly told him about the kiss with Gabe, wanting to show him that was as far as it had gone, no further.

He listened, without interrupting, and finally asked, 'Do you think we can still be friends?'

My gut reaction was to ask *what for*, as we'd done it all, said it all, what more was there left for us to be friends *with*. Over the years, we'd used it all up, and towards the end of our relationship, that was all we really were: two friends sharing a flat and a bed, but nothing more. Knowing this would hurt him immeasurably, instead I replied, 'In time,' before slowly standing up, walking to the spare bedroom. I paused to see if he'd put up a fight for us, for our relationship. Nothing. I closed the door and fell into a deep, yet fitful, broken sleep.

Over the next few days, we agreed not to go public about the split until the New Year. Even I could see that announcing it at our New Year's Eve party would somewhat dampen everyone's enthusiasm.

We also didn't discuss any of the still being friends issues after that conversation. Instead, we muddled along next to each other in the house, politely offering tea, cooking around each other, and putting on a big smile when others asked how things were. During January as friends asked after us, we gradually told them what was really happening. There was no big Luke and Dominic announcement, no 'That's all folks': we just drip fed the news to our friends as and when we spoke to them.

On the second of February 2000, I packed a weekend bag with clothes and toiletries. I walked around every room, remembering the day we had moved in, all those years ago.

My little corner of suburbia. It had all seemed so perfect. The house was in Isleworth, outer west London. I remembered looking for places to buy, relocating from a tiny studio flat in West Kensington, Luke suddenly came over all estate agent: 'It's cheaper than Richmond, and surrounded by parks, but only forty minutes to central London, it'll be perfect!' So we had bought it in 1994 — a year squeezed in the West Kensington studio flat was more than enough. On the day we moved in, the neighbours — a middle aged couple who'd lived there for twenty odd years — referred to the road as 'The Avenue,' before giving us a detailed explanation of why we should insist on including Middlesex on our postal address. 'Despite it technically being London Borough of Richmond, we think Middlesex has a much better *tone*, don't you?' the woman had asked. I'd just smiled and made a mental note that tone was all important now we were in suburbia. As we unloaded furniture from the removal van — I say unloaded, it was more in a management supervisory capacity if I'm honest, as the burly removal men lifted it from the van — the neighbours had sized us up. At first they looked for any evidence of a woman moving in with us. Mrs Middlesex had sidled up to me and asked if it was just us two moving in. Very subtle. Gone was the lovely anonymity central London had given us, we were now officially in suburbia. 'Yes, just us two,' I had replied, striding off to carry a pot plant from the removal van, enjoying her contorted face as she tried to work out *the setup*.

We had gradually decorated and filled it with the spoils from trips to Ikea together, doing the smug couple conga with others who were filling their nests. Over the fence, it was clear to Mrs Middlesex we were a couple, but she never actually asked the question, although every fibre in her body was itching to do so.

Now, I waved to Mrs Middlesex — I still didn't know her real name — closed the door, and left our marital home. *And then that happened.*

Chapter Twenty-Six

February 2000

Sat on the floor in my room in the nurses' accommodation block at the hospital, I reflected on the ten years with Luke and the three months with Gabe.

I had swapped safe, dependable and constant for always seeking the new and exciting. Only, I hadn't swapped, as I now had neither of them in my life. Despite Luke's pleas to stay in touch, I remained resolute that we needed at least six months apart before we could rebuild our relationship as friends. I also knew if I kept him too close, it would be all too easy to move back into the house, into the bed, and into the life once again. And I knew that was the wrong thing, and having the conversation with him hadn't changed how I felt for him, or how he felt for me. We would just have been hanging onto each other as constants amid a sea of massive change and sadness, when ultimately we were both the cause of the sadness in each other.

Still high on the feeling of being completely and utterly honest with another human being, I told Mother how she'd leant on me as a child, far too much. How her drunken behaviour as a recovering alcoholic was not acceptable and I would not look after her any longer, and I would no longer pander to her every whim for fear of offending her.

She listened silently before replying: 'He told me you've moved out you know.'

'Luke?'

'Of course, Luke, who else would it be?'

'So?'

'So, I understand darling. I know what you're going through. I know where this is all coming from — this, this anger, vitriol, venting. Lord knows I did enough of it when I was with your father. So just let it all out. Mother is here to listen.' She paused for a moment. 'Then I want to know what you're doing for Easter. Rose is going away, and I simply can't bear to be in the house if it's dirty, so I want to stay at yours. That is okay isn't it, darling?'

'Mother, there is no ours anymore. He lives there, I live here. We're selling the house. There are no Easter plans as a family; I don't know where I'll be living then. I might be in Australia, or Africa.'

'Why would you want to go there, darling? Australia is full of convicts, with no culture, and Africa, there's not one bit you could pay me to visit. Flies, starvation, dictators who spend all the money on gold thrones while the commoners don't have food or clean water. I simply can't imagine why you'd want to go there.'

'I might. I might go anywhere. I was making a point. I might go there, because I *can*, Mother, whether you like it or not.'

'You won't though,' she said quietly down the phone.

'What did you say?'

'I simply said, I doubted if you'd go. Now, can we stop this silly conversation please, darling?'

'I've had enough of this: biting my tongue so I don't upset you. No more. Just because I haven't so far, doesn't mean I won't go to Australia in future. I'll do what I like, I don't need your approval. It's not all about what you want, by the way. My life is not there for your exclusive pleasure and use.'

'Darling, come on, no need to be like that…'

'Oh, and while we're at it, you are a pretty terrible listener. Mothers are meant to be there to support and guide their children. Not you; it's always just back to you after I've said a few words. I don't need you, or your crappy selfish advice. I'll send a post card from Australia.' I put the phone down.

I didn't go to Australia, America, Africa, or anywhere starting with an A. But I could have done. But I didn't call Mother back either. I screened her calls; whenever she rang my mobile I let voicemail pick it up. A holiday from Mother was exactly what I needed.

I concentrated on not losing my job. I was good at my job, I now realised, and I needed to keep the one constant in my life amid all the other change and loss.

As I now lived two minutes' walk from work, I stayed later and arrived earlier than ever before, throwing myself into work and its regular challenges and problems as a perfect antidote to the chaos outside. I shouted at myself to get out of bed and into the communal shower down the hall every morning. 'Come on, Dominic, get up, get dressed, today can't be as bad as yesterday.'

When every fibre of my body willed me to stay in my bed, under the duvet, away from the world, for as long as I could get away with. After shouting and dressing myself, I strode purposefully across the car park, listening to a particularly motivational song on my CD mix of dance songs: 'What is Love', by Haddaway seemed particularly appropriate one morning; as did 'Believe', by Cher, because I really did believe in life after love; I skipped 'I Feel Love', by Donna Summer, because at that point, I didn't. And so the mornings continued.

I smiled at myself as I completed a particularly challenging off duty late one evening, bending over my desk in the office, while the night staff put patients to bed.

I celebrated with myself when I finally got Di Anne to understand she could only take time off *in lieu* if she had actually worked extra hours in the first place.

I treated myself to a microwave meal the evening after I got her to finally tell me what really made her habitually late every morning (her sister's baby since her sister had been admitted to hospital with severe post natal depression). It felt like I'd climbed a mountain when Di Anne told me that, and we agreed to change her hours so she could start later and finish later — which she subsequently stuck to and was much more productive.

All these challenges were far preferable to returning to my room to another letter from Luke's solicitor about the division of assets in the house. I thought getting out of the joint mortgage was hard enough — harder it seemed than some others getting divorced — but unfortunately that was just the tip of the splitting up iceberg. We appointed separate lawyers who then produced endless letters about furniture, debts, market rate of the house, and even who got custody of Princess, each of them landing on my doorstep, much to my dread most mornings.

I tried to keep it separate from work, but one morning I sat staring at a letter from Luke's solicitor asking me what I wished to do regarding shared ownership of the three piece suite and 'electrical kitchen equipment, namely: washing machine, dishwasher, food mixer…'

I closed my eyes and noticed a mug of tea appeared next to me. I looked up and one of the senior sisters, Alice, smiled gently. 'Do you want to go outside for some fresh air?'

'Can I go outside of my life for a new one? Can I take it back to the shop I bought it from and ask for a refund?' I asked, staring at the letter in disbelief.

'No, you can't. Can I?' She pointed to the letter so I handed it to her, sipping my tea.

After reading it, she put it back on the desk, put her hand on my shoulder and said, 'It's just stuff, things. It's not worth fighting over them. You loved him at one point, didn't you?'

I nodded — because I had, I'd really loved him, *at one point*. I had been very much in love with him. Just not now. Not amid all this separating of property palaver.

'Let him have what he wants,' Alice said. 'Split the house, and the rest is just stuff. It's not worth falling out over a washing machine. If you ever want a chance to be friends after all this is over — and it will be over, trust me — don't let yourself fall out over stuff like this.'

I put the letter to the bottom of my work bag, took a deep breath, and continued with the business of the day, business I could do easily and well: nursing other people and managing the staff on my ward. I had four appraisals booked for the senior sisters that day, so between them, and seeing patients, and the usual challenges from Di Anne, I hardly had time to stop, never mind think about the letter.

That night I sat in my room writing a reply to the letter. I felt a degree of satisfaction as I put it in an envelope ready to be posted the following morning. My reply should stave off further similar letters, based on Alice's advice. I felt lighter, simpler, clearer, knowing what I'd written.

I turned to my box of memories, the only non-essential thing I'd collected from our house: tickets from concerts we'd been to, brochures from holidays we'd been on, the estate agent's details of the house we eventually bought... all piled together were ten years of memories of Luke and me.

Amid the separation of the goods, and me moving out, it all felt so senseless, so pointless — ten years together for nothing. Some evenings alone, I could barely breathe, the sadness was so heavy pressing down on me. Returning to the house for some of my personal things, I had found my box of memories under our bed and unconsciously put it with the pile of things to return to my room in nurses' accommodation.

Now, I found myself flicking between recent and ancient memories of our relationship by touching artefacts in the box. Because I had so many feelings about the now dead relationship, and no one to talk to, instead I wrote about the feelings on a paper pad I'd started at work late one night. Now more than half-full, it contained my thoughts and feelings about each memory-inducing artefact I found in the box.

At first it was nothing but pain, aching, dull pain running through my chest and heart, but as I continued, slowly, each night, home from work, I noticed some of the memories weren't all perfect, weren't like a scene from a rom com with Jennifer Aniston and Brad Pitt. Some memories were sad precisely *because* they weren't perfect, they showed how even early memories of us weren't perfect.

In my recent memories, I had conveniently categorised my relationship with Luke as follows: early perfect; recent wrong.

Now, I wasn't denying that the overall direction it had gone was that, but somehow it helped that amid the early memories were indications of things not being perfect. I remembered how I'd not so much moved in with him, but just never really left after our first night together. I hadn't thought it was too soon to make a proper informed decision, I'd not thought anything, I'd simply allowed Luke to take over, to think for me as well, and so I had moved in.

And amid the recent memories, I still found moments of tenderness and pleasure. After Gabe told me about The Hydra, I had descended into a very black depression, and Luke had tried everything he knew to lift me from it—showing me my favourite bright films, buying me books he knew I'd like, and although it hadn't worked, the effort itself was touching. I saw that now, that he had been trying the best he could.

One morning, I arrived at Dad's flat, with the box of memoires and the paper pad on the passenger's seat.

After a few loud buzzes, he eventually established I was his son, and not some teenager or drug addict wanting to mess up the stairwell, and he let me in. He met me at his door, unshaved, old dressing gown gaping at the front, revealing a vest that had seen better days, striped pyjamas and socks, which his big toes emerged from triumphant into the light on both feet.

'Alright, son?' was all he managed to greet me, accompanied by a one armed hug, his other hand busy with a cigarette.

I nodded as he hugged me, feeling him blow smoke over my head and my eyes prickling with tears.

He led me to the kitchen where he made a pot of tea, then washed two mugs. I stood in the doorway, watching him prepare the tea, cut two slices of cake, place them onto small plates, and carry everything on a tray to the living room.

He put out his cigarette, handed my tea and cake and reclined in his favourite chair. 'What's up, son?' he asked, sipping tea.

I showed him the box of memories, pulling a bus ticket stub from the first few weeks I knew Luke.

He took it and examined it slowly. 'What's this then, eh?'

I explained and he listened, before putting it back in the box. 'Why you doing this to yourself, son? Nothing good's gonna come of this.'

'I've written things down too. Stops it going around and around in my head.' I showed him the paper pad.

He flicked through it, resting on a few pages long enough to read a few words, before putting it down on the table next to the memories box. 'Eat the cake, it looks like you've not eaten for weeks.'

I told him how I was living in nurses' accommodation, and missed Luke so much, but knew it was the right thing to do. He asked why we split up and I tried to explain about the moments of joy and pleasure, which Gabe had showed me, making me realise how few there were with Luke. Dad listened, chewing on his cake and sipping his tea. When I finished he went through the rigmarole of making a rolled up cigarette with the rotating wooden musical boat on the table, which made me smile slightly as the familiar song filled the room. He lit the cigarette, took a deep drag and slowly exhaled.

'Did he hit you? Cos you read about these blokes in the paper, two fellas, and one of 'em used to beat the living shite out of the other one. Battered wife, I mean husband. It's just as bad, you know what I mean.'

'No.'

'Did he cheat on you?'

'No.'

'Did you cheat on him? Now, no lying son, it's me here, no point in lying.'

'No, really I didn't.'

'So you stayed together, while all your mates were dying of *the AIDS* around you, and you watched them. You got through that, and now it's over cos he doesn't take you ice skating? Is that it, son?'

'It's not just the ice skating, it's everything.'

'You've just told me he doesn't do stuff with you, like this new fella, young Gabe does. And mind you, I'm not sure what he's doing if he's got a fella of his own, poor old soul, at home while he's out gallivanting with you. I'd be right pissed off.'

'You can talk,' I muttered.

'What'd you say?'

'Nothing.'

'You're not too old to get a thick ear, whether you're sad or not.' He paused, blowing smoke over his head. It formed a cloud in the middle of the room. 'Dominic, I just don't understand you kids. I mean, it was all I could do to get my head around you liking fellas, and then you found a nice one and had this "wedding" thing.' He added the quotation marks, as he always did.

Dad had come round for the idea of the wedding for my sake. 'Course I was gonna come, you're me son,' he'd told me. 'I was always gonna be on me best behaviour for you, even if your mum was there.'

Mum and Dad hadn't physically seen each other for more than twenty years. Not until mine and Luke's commitment ceremony in 1997. We sat them on separate tables, at opposite ends of the room, and the whole time my heart was in my mouth whenever I thought they might come into contact with each other. Luke had planned the day for so long, I wanted everything to be perfect, and perfect didn't include fireworks between my parents.

He later told me, he'd found the whole day bizarre. During the speeches, fiddling with his piece of paper, he said the only words he'd ever said which made me cry: 'When Dominic was born I didn't think I'd have to make a speech at his wedding. Cos it's the bride's dad who does that.' We'd laughed at that. 'Mind you, I never thought I'd not be with his mum, but there you are... And here I am, divorced from Carol — she'll always be plain old Carol to me, before her airs and graces and the extra Anne. And here I am, making a speech at Dominic's wedding to another man! Pigs could fly. And I couldn't be more prouder of him. My son and Luke.' We had all toasted and cheered to that.

Now, Dad looked at me. 'So you married your Luke, I got used to that. And now you're just ending it with him — seemed a nice enough lad to me — all because of... of...'

'We've fallen out of love with each other. I still care for him, but not in that way.'

'Not in *that* way?' he mimicked me. 'Look, I'm your old dad, and I know I've not been perfect, right. And I understand why your mum up and left. I do, I really do. And I don't blame her, even now. But I can tell you this much: you can't expect to feel the same about someone after ten years as three months. I stayed with her, even though I knew I didn't feel the same way about her — because we had a little boy together.'

'But there is no little boy. It's just us two, and the dog. So even though people say it's love, whether it's two men, a man and a woman or two women...'

'Two women, now you're talking,' he laughed.

'Anyway, returning to the point Dad, it's not the same if there's no children. There's not the same pull together, sometimes it's just easier to walk away.' I thought about the sadness of that for a moment, realised it was too much to cope with, and asked Dad for a roll up from his wooden musical boat instead.

He handed me the cigarette, the boat still spinning to the comforting song from *The Barber of Seville*. 'Marriage is something you work at, it doesn't just happen, Dominic.'

'Mum gave up on yours, and you had a kid together. We did work at it, we worked at it for ten years; we might not have been legally married, but we might as well have been: mortgage, bank accounts, all that, all shared.'

'So why stop now? Why after all this time?'

'You said Mum put your relationship out of its misery. And even *now* you remember her favourite film.

For me and Luke, something just wasn't there anymore. And it was only because I saw how it could be, I realised how it wasn't with Luke. Yes, it's work, but a relationship shouldn't be that hard, not all the time.'

'I wouldn't know, son. Apart from your mum, I've never had what you could call a relationship. So what do I know?'

'It's better to leave him, rather than live a lie and stay together, pretending, just through habit. I couldn't carry on like that with him, because I do care for him.'

'You got a funny way of showing it.' He smiled, trying to lighten the mood.

I shrugged. 'Dad, people do so much in their lives they have to do. Loving someone, pretending to love someone, shouldn't be one of those things you have to do, should it?'

We sat in silence for a few minutes, smoking and sipping tea.

I resumed the conversation. 'Now you mention Mother, you'll never guess what I did.'

'Look, I'm not one of your new men you know. I don't think I can handle any more of this touchy feely stuff, I think it's bringing me out in a rash.'

'You'll laugh, honestly, you will, Dad.' And so I recounted my conversation with Mother, how she was a bad listener, and he listened in complete silence until I reached the end.

'Brave stuff. I'm proud of you, son. Priceless. You heard from her since?'

'She's called a few times, left messages, but I don't call her back. It's still all the same stuff: can I suggest a theme for her spring garden party, can she stay at ours at Easter, that sort of thing. I don't need it, Dad.'

'Fair enough, son. More tea?'

Chapter Twenty-Seven

Weeks became months, and as I got used to the fact that the room in the nurses accommodation block was my home, I made it more comfortable — buying some curtains, a new duvet cover, towels, some candles — and I gradually got used to spending time on my own, and actually enjoying it.

I discovered baking; there was something very therapeutic about mixing flour, sugar, eggs and butter, pouring it into a tin, and watching it rise in the oven, ready to be decorated, iced, creamed, jammed and served to colleagues the next day. Staring at the finished cake or muffins gave a clear sense of achievement from the morning spent in the kitchen, rather than stewing in my own juices, scribbling more in the paper pad or handling artefacts of our past relationship from the memories box.

The whole time I baked, I thought of nothing else except baking: I just couldn't.

Once I put some chocolate muffins in the oven and returned to my room to watch some TV, but instead a photo of us at my twenty-fourth birthday in 1995 caught my eye. We were surrounded by friends, some of whom were no longer alive, in a red-roped-off section of the VIP area in Heaven, London. I looked from smiling face to smiling face, mentally ticking off those who were no longer with us, then quickly moved onto a happier memory of the night itself. I hadn't known anything about it, as Luke had organised a surprise party, inviting friends from my address book. I thought we were just going for dinner together, until he led us through the queue for Heaven, into the VIP room, to a corner of our friends. Topless buff waiters had circulated all night with a mêlée of camp canapés: tiny vol-au-vents, mini toad in the hole, mini fish and chips, and enough champagne to keep Eddie and Patsy afloat for a series or two. We danced until the end, and scrabbled up the stairs into bed, grabbing at each other's bodies when we arrived home.

I sat on the floor in my room and blushed at the memory of the end of that night, until I smelt burning and ran to the kitchen, where my chocolate muffins had smoked the kitchen and set off the fire alarm. I opened the windows and left the kitchen, waiting for the fire brigade to arrive. I'd set alight the oven and filled the kitchen with smoke. The fire brigade arrived, two large engines, sirens blaring and lights flashing. *And then that happened*, I thought to myself.

When a particularly hunky fireman asked what caused the fire, I felt so embarrassed I wanted the earth to open up and swallow me whole as I said, 'Muffins and memories.' It just came out without even thinking.

'Make sure it doesn't happen again.' He walked back to his fire engine, rolling his head slightly as he explained to his colleagues what I'd just said.

So, after that incident, I remained focused on baking, while I *was* baking. Complete and total immersion in the moment, which was exactly what I needed. I loved the reaction one of my creations brought to my colleagues;

each time it was like I'd discovered a cure for cancer, or had personally spilt the atom in my bedroom, when all I'd really done was follow a recipe and make a cake. Di Anne didn't believe I'd made it myself, and when I had told her how much sugar and fat went into it, she realised why eating chocolate cakes for lunch wasn't such a good idea.

After weeks of baking in my spare time, I decided to leave the nurses block to explore what the world had to offer to me now I wasn't part of a couple. For the first time in ten years I didn't have to visit a parent or parent in law, didn't need to traipse around a DIY or home wares shop, had no friends demanding my attention—it was a long time since I'd heard from Matt.

Without this list of activities to structure my time off, I didn't know what to do. What did I want to do with this time? If I could do anything with this day, what would I choose to do? It had been so long since I had just done something for me, on my own, I'd forgotten what I liked to do on my own.

I walked to my car—Luke had let me keep that since my solicitor's letter about the house contents—and drove out of suburban London to countryside proper. Spaced out Tube stations and parks gave way to forest as I crossed the M25 into Hertfordshire, the car seemed to remember driving nearby all those months ago with Gabe. I continued through country lanes and soon arrived in a small town called Ware. I remembered Gabe saying something about it, and that's *where* the car ended up.

Once parked, I stood in the car park, again at a loss for what to do with myself. I wasn't used to having no one telling me where we had to go, what we had to see. I looked around to see if anyone had noticed the strange man in his late twenties, dithering in the car park, but no one had. I strode purposefully towards the town centre and gradually, slowly got used to seeing where the day took me, following my nose and feet, exploring things as I came across them, moving on when I'd had enough.

I walked into a small pet shop, looking at dog leads before hastily retreating; the sad loss of Princess was too much to bear. We'd tried to agree sharing Princess, but in the end I agreed for her sake, bearing in mind where I was moving to, she would be better staying with Luke. Since I had been the one to start the conversation about us splitting up, since I had been the one who'd met someone else even if I hadn't gone all the way with him, the least I could do was to leave Luke in the house to lick his wounds, and to move out myself. I followed optimistic brown tourist signs towards the town's museum and was pleasantly surprised to while away a happy hour or so reading about the little town's history, seeing artefacts from Roman times, to the Second World War. I slowly got used to the sensation of not having to hurry myself up as someone else was waiting for me. What I found harder to acclimatise to, was not having anyone next to me to share views about what I saw. I found myself talking quietly to myself, as I used to when at home alone with Princess.

I discovered an independent book shop and happily browsed there for a while, eventually settling on a celebrity autobiography from an actress in *EastEnders*.

I took the book to a park next to the river that ran through the town. I managed thirty minutes of just sitting. Not bad for me. Then I walked along the riverside path, nosing into the yuppie flats and sheltered accommodation, which alternately backed onto the river. After a while, I took a fork in the path, away from the river, into a clearing surrounded by trees and a bench. In the distance, I saw the motorway whisking cars away and started thinking about all the other people's lives, worries, loves.

I saw a man and woman walking arm in arm along the riverside path; my mind snapped back to Luke and I meandering around Soho early in our relationship.

I opened the book and quickly became lost in the world of the *EastEnders* actress. *I'll just read a chapter.*

I looked up and noticed how cold I felt, used the receipt as a bookmark and closed the book. I had sat on the bench reading alone for over an hour. I was now well into the book and, if it hadn't been so cold, would have stayed longer.

I walked back to the car, thinking about dinner. Since losing so much weight, baking had given me an easy route to putting it back on again. I reached into my pocket to call Luke, ask him what was for dinner, if he wanted me to get anything on my way home, then took my hand out again slowly.

Had I really done the right thing? Or should I have just stayed with Luke, muddling along? My hand still resting on my mobile, I considered calling Gabe, remembering the fun we'd had in the countryside at his parents'. I remembered keeping the secret of The Hydra to myself, and how that had affected me, how My Depression had returned, with an extra vengeance. I concentrated on how that had passed, just like this feeling I now had would pass. The feeling of a heavy stomach, filled with dread — dread about what I was never sure, but just dread.

I closed my eyes and concentrated on the whoosh of the motorway, the breeze on my face. I felt the pages of the book in my hand, squeezing my eyes shut.

Over the next few weeks, I continued to throw much of my energy into work, but also gradually got used to spending my free time alone. Eventually I actually enjoyed it. It wasn't better or worse than being with someone, just different. A different I hadn't experienced for many years.

My life settled into a new rhythm. I found myself crying less frequently; I could now think about the past, flashbacks of me and Luke together, without crying.

I managed to separate the sadness about the loss of my relationship with Luke from the guilt for letting it happen. I realised it wasn't only my fault, it was also his: we had both stopped putting the time in, stopped humouring each other, allowed life and its every daily grind to get in our way, rather than taking time to care, love and share moments of pleasure with each other.

I realised it wasn't ten years wasted, it was still mostly ten years of love and laughter, but it had run its course. We had both needed each other in the eighties, amid all the overwhelming sadness around us; we had both needed something, someone to hang onto amid that. And now things were more settled, we'd weathered that storm, we didn't have that to hold us together, we had been left wondering what there was to keep us together except a dog and a house full of possessions.

We both knew now, that wasn't enough to keep a relationship together, but it didn't mean we couldn't still have each other in our lives, in a different way, as friends. Even now, that concept was too foreign from how I currently felt, and I knew it would be at least a year until I could think about that.

I'd bumped into him a few times, returning to the house to collect my things. Each time, I felt the tension, the pull we had to each other, as I packed my things into a bag while he watched me from the doorway, making polite conversation. One time I went back, and all I could think of was ripping each other's clothes off and fucking like animals on the hallway floor. I had been completely disinterested in sex for so long—even with myself it seemed—but by that point something had reawakened inside me, something was ready for sex again, and I knew how it could be with him. It would have only taken me to lean in and kiss, and we'd have soon been on the floor, sucking and fucking, sweating hard until it was over. But I knew it wouldn't bring *us* back together; it would just mean we'd had sex for the first time in months, but this time after we'd both told each other we weren't in love any longer.

The worst kind of sex for exes.

And I knew my heart and head couldn't handle it.

I made a big fuss of Princess, who every time was so pleased to see me. I poured all my love and urge to touch Luke into her. So I resisted, kept it on a friends only basis, not touching him, waiting as we both reformulated ourselves post 'us' in time in readiness for a new 'us' as friends.

One night, as I collected my things from the staff room, I brushed past someone as we crossed in the doorway. The smell instantly took me back all those months ago. To our first meeting.

I looked up and he stared back at me, his large brown eyes, his long dark eyelashes, and his smile which illuminated the room. My stomach jumped.

'Alright,' Gabe said, extending his hand for me to shake.

I shook it stiffly and repeated his greeting back to him.

'You going home?'

I nodded. 'You on nights tonight?'

'Yeah.' He paused, leaning against the door. 'Shame.'

My head told me to continue walking, but my body, every fibre in my body from my heart to stomach, told me to stand still. 'We could, I mean, if you're not...'

'Coffee or something?' He raised an eyebrow. 'I mean, not now, but tomorrow morning... unless you're...'

'No, I'm not... I'll...' And I mimed a phone with my hand.

'I've still got the same number.' He leant to kiss my cheek and I leant towards him; his lips brushed my cheek and electricity went immediately south.

'I know.' I smiled and watched him disappear into the staff room, the door closing behind him. I walked into the corridor, not quite believing it.

And then that happened.

Chapter Twenty-Eight

I arrived back to my room in the accommodation block, repeating what had just happened in my head. During the evening I was tempted to return to the ward to resume our conversation, but I knew it would be rushed, knew it would be in snatched moments between him working and would be accompanied by disapproving and confused looks from the night staff: 'What are you doing back, Dominic? Don't you spend enough time here already?'

So instead I sat down to watch some TV on the tiny portable set I had removed from our spare bedroom. I couldn't concentrate on the TV, so after picking up a book and reading one paragraph four times, I went to the kitchen and baked, and baked, until I ran out of flour. I baked a dozen chocolate muffins — not burned this time — a dozen orange muffins; a Victoria sponge — decorated with fresh cream and strawberries — and finally a lemon cheesecake before collapsing on my bed and falling into a deep sleep.

Grateful for the distraction, my mind couldn't rehearse what I would say to Gabe the following morning.

My alarm woke me at eight, just enough time to change out of the clothes I'd slept in, splash my face — have a cat lick at the sink, as Mother used to say when she was just plain old Mum — and walk quickly back to the ward for quarter past eight when the night shift finished.

I leant on the wall in the corridor outside the ward's entrance, staring at the ground, not wanting to make eye contact with any day staff, having to face questions about why I was there on my day off.

I felt an arm rest on my shoulder, looked up and his face greeted me. 'You look worse than me, and I've worked all night,' Gabe said gently, smiling.

'Shall we?' I replied, leading him away off the hospital grounds to a small café out of earshot and away from prying eyes of staff.

He followed me without question or small talk, seemingly grateful for the decisive action.

We sat opposite each other in the old fashioned café and ordered, and I took a deep breath, partly from the walk, but partly from the realisation that he was once again in front of me. I took in his face and chest in the nurses tunic, imagining undoing the poppers to reveal his perfectly hairy chest—the image still on my mind since we'd swum together.

'I still can't believe you're here,' I said, sipping my tea.

'It's not like I emigrated or anything.'

'I know, but I thought we couldn't see each other again.'

'We still might not.'

'Oh,' I replied, surprised at this so early.

'Nothing's changed for me, and if we feel the same about each other, "us" isn't possible still.'

'You're still with A?'

He nodded. 'What about you and Luke?'

'No, I'm living in the nurses' block next to the hospital, have been for a few months.'

'When did you split up?'

'I moved out in February.' I told him everything, including my awful Christmas, how meeting him had showed my relationship with Luke had died, and getting used to being single again.

He listened, and then asked if I had any spare cakes cos he was starving.

I smiled and replied, 'Just a few I whipped up last night. So that's enough about me, what about you?'

He explained how A was becoming more and more ill, as he didn't, or couldn't, take his medication for The Hydra. He'd booked A into the special clinic, and for GP appointments to discuss alternatives treatments, but A had simply not gone to any of the appointments.

'But what about his night class?' I asked.

'He went once, but then said it was too much, so now he doesn't go any more. He just stays around the house, calling me at work to tell me we've run out of milk and bread, so I can pick it up on my way home from work.'

'But he's at home, can't *he* get it during the day?'

He smiled sarcastically. 'You'd think, wouldn't you?'

'Why doesn't he take the medication, surely it's bad for him?'

'Of course it is. He says it makes him feel sick, so he doesn't take it. I even picked it up from the chemist for him—and the looks you get when you pick up one of *those* prescriptions, I can tell you. I told him what the doctor told me: you have to take the meds at the same time every day, for the rest of your life. That's what makes it manageable. A manageable chronic condition is what the nurse at the clinic told me.'

'What happened then, what did A do?'

'He took them for a week, then just stopped. I found most of them stuffed under the bed a month after I'd collected them, hardly touched. I told him, if you stop taking them, the...'

'...Hydra?'

'Yeah, it gets resistant to those meds, and you have to try another mixture of meds. So it's worse than not taking them in the first place.'

'What did he say?'

'He lay back on the sofa, lit a spliff and asked what was for tea.'

'I see. Makes me wonder if I did the right thing, leaving Luke.'

'Why?'

'It just seems like a load of little gripes next to that. Maybe I rushed into it. Maybe I should have tried with him.' I stared into the distance.

'You *were* trying; you had been trying for years. Years before I came along. It's all you did, you told me.'

'I suppose.'

'I know. Sometimes things just run their course, things end. Everything ends.'

'I know that. It's just... I didn't think me and Luke would end like that. Somehow, I had this romantic vision in my head, where one of us would sit beside the bedside of the other, mopping his brow, two old men together. Not like this, not now.'

We sat in silence for a few moments, both taking in the recent conversation and the fact we were sat here together, once again.

'You tired?' I asked.

'That light drunk feeling after a night shift. You know?'

I nodded. I knew exactly how that felt. 'You working tonight or what?'

'Or what.' He smiled.

'Funny, no seriously, are you?'

'Not working tonight, not working today. All I've got to do is get back to the flat, see what state he's left it in, and prepare myself for the next battle he's lined up for me.'

'Why don't you leave him?'

'It's not that simple.'

'I did. If he's making you miserable, and you're not getting anything from him, then go. How's the gentlemen friends for the night count?'

'A few, here and there.'

'On your own, or with A?'

'Just me. He indicated he had someone interested, but I didn't pry. Wanted to stick by the rules.'

'What about the guy you wanted to see again? What did we call him?'

'Hercules. What about him?' Gabe's eyes closed, then he jerked himself awake.

'Well, did you… see him again, even though it sort of breaks your rules?'

'I can't sit here anymore.' Gabe stood. 'I'm falling asleep. Either we go for a walk, or I go home to bed. Which do you want?'

'I'll pay.' I walked to the counter. 'Gunnersbury Park?' I asked when back at our seats.

'You what?'

'For a walk. It's not far.'

'I know where it is, I only live a few miles away. Okay, Gunnersbury Park it is.' He looped his arm around mine as we left the café then asked, 'Got any chocolate, could do with a bit of caffeine.'

'Have I got any chocolate? Why don't you come back to my room, have a shower and you can stock up on cakes for our walk?'

As he took a shower, I laid out clean clothes for him on my bed, just as Luke used to do for me. I shook the memory away quickly. This was completely different. He hadn't taken much persuasion; he had immediately accepted my suggestion of borrowing some of my clothes for we weren't too dissimilar in size.

I picked my only rugby shirt—a too large and inappropriate gift from Mother in an attempt to make me part of the sporting middle classes—to accommodate his slightly broader frame, a pair of jeans, and dithered for a full five minutes over socks and pants. Was it disgusting to lend your friend pants, or was it just normal—whatever *that* was—and friendly? Would he be okay wearing his, inside out? *Oh good lord, what's a guy to do?*

In the end, I settled on a new pair of pants I'd not yet worn, still box fresh from buying them a few empty 'what'll I do when I'm all alone' weekends ago. *The Birds of a Feather* theme tune had become my own personal theme tune during gaps in my schedule, which would have previously been filled with *boyfriend duties*: Luke's dad, my parents, house chores etc. Increasingly I found myself humming the song under my breath as I walked around shops and towns I arrived in through randomness, having jumped into the car to see where it took me.

One last check of the clothes, and new pants, and I went to the communal kitchen to make tea to go with my cakes. I arranged them on a three-tier cake plate next to a tea pot and mugs I'd rescued from our house. The concept of 'our' house still stung.

Gabe walked into the kitchen, a towel wrapped round his waist, his hair dripping onto his chest where the hair arranged itself into lines running north to south, as the normally furry look was now wet.

I immediately avoided eye-chest contact for fear of doing something I'd regret, and gestured to the spread in front of me.

'Very good.' He looked at the table of food.

'I've laid clothes out for you, it's just this is, err… a shared kitchen, and…'

'Okay, understood, I'll be back in a minute. Must be my Spanish blood, no one gives a shit if you walk around all day naked, no one bats an eyelid.' And he disappeared to my room.

Is it bad that I'm now thinking of him naked and putting on my pants and clothes and that's actually really turning me on?

Is it normal that I'm sat here in my kitchen surrounded by cakes and tea, and have the biggest boner I've ever had? For my friend?

I started to stand, hunched forward to disguise my lust, and suddenly Gabe appeared at the door, fully dressed in my clothes. 'What's wrong with your back?' he asked, eyeing up the cakes and looking much fresher than before.

'Nothing, I must have pulled it at work.' I sat down and poured tea for us both, handed him a plate for cakes.

We chatted about my new-found passion for baking, and how I wished I'd done it years ago. Both full of cake and tea, we left for the park.

Arms looped together, we walked around the park, at first commenting on the bright weather, then on how beautiful the daffodils and crocuses were, as a sign of spring's arrival.

I took a deep breath and asked the question I wanted to ask ever since seeing him again: 'Why didn't you call?'

'Why didn't *you* call?' He looked at me, frowning.

'What we agreed. Not to see each other. I didn't want to properly fall for you when I was with Luke.'

'Fall, as in fall in love with?'

'Err, yes.'

'I see.'

'You knew that. Luke and I didn't have this whole open relationship framework rules shebang going on, so I just thought it was better to step away. I thought I at least owed him that. And you?'

'I didn't call you cos we agreed to not see each other. Remember? I thought calling and not seeing you would be too painful.'

'I see.'

'What about after you left Luke?'

I knew this was coming, and this was something I'd found particularly hard to deal with in the weeks after I moved out of our house. 'After ten years with Luke, I was suddenly on my own. I didn't really know who I was. It had been so long since I'd done anything really, on my own, I just didn't know where to start.'

'But you knew you liked me.'

'I didn't want to run to you just because you weren't *him*. I wanted to run to you because you are you. Make sense?'

'I think so.' He indicated a bench and we sat down.

I lit a cigarette.

'Still smoking, then?'

'Some days it was the only consistent thing I had to hang onto. My whole world, everything I knew had disappeared around me, so yes, I am still smoking. That alright with you?'

'Just asking.' He smiled, taking a drag on his cigarette.

'I could have been with anyone else cos they weren't Luke, not just you. But instead, I wanted to be with me for a while.'

'Have you worked that out yet?'

'I'm getting there. What I do know is, I definitely want you in my life.'

'And me, you.'

We both smiled, until he raised the issue that had popped into both our minds. 'I can't leave him.'

'You can't stay with him either.'

'But I can't just leave him.'

'Why not?'

'You know why not: who would look after him, where would he live, he doesn't work, he can't work.'

'You know all that's fixable, you know that's not the real reason.'

'It is.' He stood up. 'Look, if you're going to have a go at me, I'm going home.'

I stood and held his shoulders so his face was a few inches from mine. 'I'm not having a go at you. I want you to admit the real reason you won't leave him. Say it out loud. Go on.'

His face scrunched up and his eyes filled with tears. 'What have I done?'

'You don't know that, not for sure.'

'I got sick sooner. He was fine, when I was sick, but we both tested because, well, it's what they ask you to do, so we tested together.'

'When you did it, you didn't think anything was wrong, did you?'

'No, it was years until *I* got sick. We just thought it was a cold or something: a cold I couldn't shake. We were both fine before that.'

'Did you force him?'

'Fuck off, course not, what do you think I am?'

'I know that, but I want you to say it, to hear you say the words yourself. You both wanted it?'

He nodded. 'It just happened. We didn't plan it.'

'I know, who does?'

He wiped tears from his eyes, and snot from his nose. 'Most of the time we did bother, I always insisted. That's what we'd been told, especially if you add in the gentlemen friends for the night. We only didn't bother once or twice. By accident. He said not to worry, it would be fine. That's how much he cared.'

'You've taken him to the clinic, got him meds, bought him food, let him live with you?'

'Whatever I do, it's not enough, he'll always be sick, cos of me. I'm dangerous, me, I don't know why you even want to be friends with me, never mind anything else. If I were you, I'd run away, leave me here. Damaged goods, that's what one guy said to me.'

'I hope you told him to fuck off.'

'Didn't have to, he was gone, soon as I told him.'

'A is not your responsibility. He's not a child, he has his own life. You have done all you can to help him. You can't just stay with him cos you feel guilty.'

'Easy for you to say, mister perfect. Mister having sex with one man for ten years.'

'You know I'm right though. This, this thing, isn't a reason to cling to him. He still needs to be a good boyfriend to you; he still needs to love you, to love each other. The Hydra isn't love.'

'How can I tell him?' Gabe looked at me, tears in his eyes. 'It'll break his heart.'

'Don't you think he knows it's really over already? You don't do anything together now, do you? You're really only going through the motions.'

He nodded.

'And all the stuff about where he lives, all that, it's fixable. You do have a choice, you don't have to stay with him. You can leave him and live your life again; we can sort out the practicalities together, make sure he's not on the street. Okay?'

'Okay.' He nodded, his face wet with tears. 'You sure?' He wiped his face with his sleeve.

'It's the only thing you can do, or you're going to end up like Jo Orton and his boyfriend in their little flat.'

'What happened to them?' Gabe asked, his inquisitiveness pricked.

'Tell you later, come on, fancy lunch?'

He nodded and I led him out of the park to a café where we ate toasted sandwiches and drank gallons of tea. We talked for hours: about where we'd like to go on holiday together—just as friends, he clearly pointed out— the Maldives we finally agreed on; whether my Mother was actually a robot planted to test my patience; and whether Di Anne was more of a lazy nightmare than his ward clerk Tracey.

Chapter Twenty-Nine

1989-1993

I met Luke in 1989. We were both eighteen and I'd only just come out, and had maybe snogged a few other guys, but nothing more. Matt and I had just fallen out with each other *again*, something suitably dramatic about me not understanding him; he was seeing three guys at the same time and hadn't told any of them, and I—Mary Whitehouse—disapproved and had told him to make a decision. Matt said, 'You've not got a clue, you. Why am I listening to you, you've not even gone past kissy wissy.' And he walked out our local gay pub. So I was left alone, in the pub, without my left arm, with whom I'd gradually explored what the gay scenes of Portsmouth and Southampton had to offer.

I counted on my fingers the stages of sex we'd both agreed when making our first forays into the arena of gayness—Matt was a bit less hesitant in his forays than I—kissy wissy; touchy feely; icky sticky; rumpy pumpy. I repeated them a few times, pleased with how they rolled around my head. Ticking them off my fingers made me look so decisive, forthright and occupied as I sat alone in the pub. I knew I was none of these, but I didn't want them to know that. Rumpy pumpy, the holy grail of sex to which I'd not even reached the outer suburbs.

For wont of anything better to do, I walked to the toilets past a man playing pool who asked if I wanted to play. Even now, I still don't know my cue from my pocket, but he looked kind and had nice arms, so I smiled and said, 'Why not?'

When he realised how clueless I was at pool he offered to teach me. And slowly, round by round — if that's what they're called, I still couldn't tell you either way — he explained about angles of cues, black balls, pockets, chalk and all manner of things, most of which I've long since forgotten. And the whole time, I thought to myself, *he's got nice arms, if I play this right, I might just get up to icky sticky.*

A few more drinks later, we were laughing and joking about music taste, and what he studied at college — business, as it turned out. We went back to his student house together and fell onto the sofa, where he kissed me so hard and vigorously, with a stubbly face, I had beard rash for weeks afterwards and spent the whole time making excuses to my parents every time I saw them. That first night, on the sofa he pulled my jeans and pants off and busied himself with something between icky sticky and rumpy pumpy I wasn't at all prepared for. Coming up for air, he took his T-shirt off, revealing the sort of chest I'd only dreamed of to that point. Conscious of someone walking in, I reluctantly pushed him off and suggested we move to his bedroom. He rearranged himself in his trousers, I grabbed my jeans to cover myself up, and he led me by the hand to his bedroom. A wooden desk stood by the window, covered in piles of paper and folders, a clothes rail bent slightly under the weight of his clothes, and a large double bed stood in the middle of the room, perfectly made. He pushed me onto the bed and closed the door with his foot. Both being eighteen had its advantages: we slipped and slid around his bed until the early hours of the morning, coming up for air and water from the kitchen a few times, and spooning under his warm duvet. Each time exploring more and more of each other's bodies. In the early hours of the morning, he'd laid on the bed and, after a bit of awkward condom action I left to him, followed by a nod from Luke, I gently lowered myself onto him, enjoying the new fullness I felt and leaning forward to kiss him as we moved together. We soon finished in a sweaty heap, him kissing my chest. It was my first time—well, our fourth that night—and we'd gone all the way to *rumpy pumpy*, much to my surprise and joy.

The following morning I nursed a cup of tea, covering myself up with the duvet.

'Not much point to that,' he said, smiling lasciviously. 'My lips have been all over every bit of your body now, and have practically memorised it!'

He asked me if I had anywhere to be later that day, and as I hadn't I shrugged and soon the morning after became the evening after, and we settled down with a takeaway together.

I was surprised he wanted me to stay around, and since falling out with Matt, I wasn't in any hurry to return to my real life any time soon. Every time there was a lull in conversation, which wasn't too often, my mind drifted back to my argument with Matt, and it filled me with sadness.

Luke asked what was wrong, and I shook my head, not wanting to over share at this stage. 'I've just had my tongue all over your body, so I think we're past niceties, Dominic.' He smiled.

So I told him about Matt and explained how I felt like I was missing an important part of me, even though we had been friends for only months, we'd been on nodding terms for longer and his absence felt so wrong. 'I don't know who I am anymore,' I explained, while worrying that I'd scare Luke off.

'You're here, in this room with me. And that's just right for me.'

'But what about Matt?'

'He'll come back if he wants to, just leave him.'

And so I put it away in a little box and allowed myself to be swept up with the first moments of a new relationship, when everything the other person says is so interesting, where you're finding out about their life, their hopes, their fears, whether they take sugar in their tea, all at once. All the time, I couldn't really believe he'd not thrown me out straight away, the morning after. I couldn't believe that this, my first time, had been so amazing. Not some awkward fumble in a toilet of some club, or a furtive grope in an alley round the back of a bar—as my friends had told me about, and filled me with dread about my first time. It was in his very own bed, gently, carefully, and safely. Okay, so it wasn't like in the films, the sheets could do with being changed, 'A symbol of our love,'

Luke had laughed at the sheets. There was that awkward moment with a condom, which I instinctively knew was *a good thing*. Who could forget the tombstone advert *AIDS don't die of ignorance*? But I wasn't *quite* sure why *we* needed one, as there was no one getting pregnant. So I was pleased I didn't need to broach the subject, as he'd just taken care of it, and I knew with him, it would all be alright.

Luke listened and offered advice; the following evening stretched into a week; without even thinking about it, as it all seemed to make perfect sense, I moved in with him for the summer. 'It'll be easier, you're always here anyway, so, let's make it official,' he offered. He dropped me off at Mum's house to collect some clothes and toiletries — I was staying with her at the time.

She hardly registered the significance of a man collecting my things and me moving in with him; she was just glad to have my room back. 'I can use it to store my shoes, they're so crowded in the little wardrobe at the moment. It'll give them room to breathe,' she breezed, watching me and Luke carry my things to his car.

'He's called Luke, Mum, he's my...' I looked at him nervously. 'Boyfriend?'

Luke nodded and smiled, putting a box into the boot of his car. We drove into the sunset, Mum leaning against the front door, waving half-heartedly.

We spent every day that summer together. I quickly forgot about Matt: who needed an ex best friend, when I had a proper full-time boyfriend? I wasn't missing anything from my life anymore, I had a whole new person to fill my life with. I moved to London for university, and Luke stayed in Portsmouth, where he finished his business course and started working in retail. While at university, we religiously alternated weekends between London and 'home' when I stayed in Luke's student house and I visited my parents separately, as they were not able to be in the same room as each other then.

While at university, I lost quite a few friends to AIDS; it was still relatively new, and we didn't fully understand it. A friend from my nursing course met me for a drink one evening after uni; he told me he'd gone for 'one of those tests, and it was positive,' and he asked me what it meant. I'd paid less attention to the adverts and leaflets, as by then I'd been with Luke for over a year, and it seemed to only affect guys who slept around. 'It's probably just like flu, you'll be fine,' I reassured my friend hopefully. He was dead before I finished the course two years later.

The papers used to call it a gay plague, or gay cancer. Some columnists said it was us getting what we deserved. What they didn't mention was every one of the AIDS victims was someone's son, someone's brother, someone's partner. Not just nameless victims of something they'd brought on themselves, as they often portrayed it. I read about Princess Diana leaving the Royal summer gathering at Balmoral without the Queen's permission to go to the deathbed of her friend Adrian Ward-Jackson, who was an art dealer. The *Sun* said that her support for AIDS victims was 'both wrong and highly damaging to her' although looking after 'blameless' victims was okay, but it was dangerous for her to show the same concern for men who were infected 'by indulging in sleazy, unnatural sex with other so-called gays.'

All the gays who died left partners, parents, brothers and sisters, devastated, trying to understand why *their* family, why *their* son. The papers never mentioned that; somehow that wasn't such an interesting story because it didn't only affect 'the gays' but it spread into the rest of society, showing that gayness affects the lives of so many other people.

As our relationship progressed, Luke and I went clubbing less often. Friday nights we rented a video, got a takeaway, both exhausted from a busy week studying and working. There was a spate of attacks outside London gay clubs, gay men getting spat at and punched while they made their way home; people were attacked in their local gay pubs, bricks thrown through windows, bombs. That helped our decision of whether to go out or stay in, until if we didn't make a decision, we knew we'd stay in.

I hoped I'd be placed at the Middlesex Hospital in central London, which had the first ever dedicated AIDS unit. I saw the picture in the papers showing Diana opening the Broderic Ward, shaking hands with the one who'd bravely agreed to being photographed holding The Princess of Wales' hand. The papers all commented that she'd been brave enough to touch an 'AIDS victim' without gloves. The papers gleefully told about how the trade union representing the cleaners, porters and kitchen staff on that ward threatened to boycott Broderic Ward as they hadn't had the basics of HIV transmission explained to them. The families of the hospital workers explained they were happy for the staff to play their role, but didn't want them bringing AIDS into their homes. The ignorance was breath taking. The photograph showed that touching an 'AIDS victim' was safe, and compassionate, but it took the public years to catch up with that knowledge.

Unfortunately, not at the Middlesex Hospital, I did placements on medical wards, nursing men with *the concentration camp look*, by now familiar to us all: hollow cheeks, sunken eyes, dark marks on the skin. Well known drag queens from the London scene used to arrive on the wards, fully in drag, and serve red and white wine from the unused cardboard urine bottles, singing to patients their favourite songs, holding their hands. They would stop by the beds of the sick guys, stroking their hands, making them smile with a comment about the male nurses, or other bitchy camp fripperies.

The sick men all told me the one thing they missed was a laugh: as soon as they'd got sick, all they had was a long procession of sympathetic, sad friends with an undercurrent of 'It's your own fault really, that's sad.' So to crack a smile, or heaven forbid *laugh* even, be treated to a drag queen's acid put downs, was a welcome return to normality for them.

For many of us, the gay scene was our only family, so the drag queens became to the younger lads, like a wise old auntie.

As part of my course, I researched HIV, wrote essay after essay about it, and consequently often knew more than colleagues on the wards. Some matrons insisted on putting the men in side-rooms and barrier nursing them — latex gloves, masks, plastic aprons. A friend told me his partner was in the hospital where I worked as a student nurse, and asked me to keep an eye on him. On my day off, I went to his ward, completely ignoring the sign about barrier nursing; the matron stormed up to me and said it would be on my head if anything went wrong.

I stared straight into her eyes, said, 'Leave me alone, I'm seeing a friend. You can't catch it by touch, and it's not airborne. Call yourself a matron,' and pushed past her to the room. She watched in horror as I kissed his cheek and took a sharp intake of breath when I held his hand and sat to read him bits of the book he was reading but was too weak to hold.

During the early nineties, I attended so many funerals I lost count. Soon Luke and I were experts at flat clearances, drafted in after being handed the keys from a hospital bed, to collect all the things any gay guy doesn't want his parents to see. We had such a collection of second hand porn videos, Luke suggested we sell them to pay for a holiday. The charity shop assistant had practically screamed the one time I tried to offload it on them, so having checked with our friends each time as they handed us the keys, we agreed to make good use of it. They normally just said, 'Do what you want with it, just get rid of it, will you?' During that period, it paid for a few *porn stash* holidays for Luke and me, away from all the death and greyness.

After a few years, I sat in the coffee shop at Heathrow, waiting for our flight, tears streaming down my face, and told Luke I'd never felt so sad before a holiday. That week we'd been to the funerals of two of my closest friends from the nursing course, Steve and Chris. Their open relationship and 'it won't happen to me' attitude had come crashing down around their ears one evening when Chris found a lesion on his leg. We cleared their flat; I collapsed in bed that night and then boarded a flight the next day.

'Fuck it, I don't want to wake up tomorrow,' I said, noticing the whooshing of the planes and pushing my tea away.

Luke held my hand, stroking it, and told me it would all be fine once we landed on the beach.

Once I opened my thick paperback, I allowed myself to become completely absorbed in the characters' glitzy lives, listening to the sea lapping against the sand. My mind couldn't take any more thinking about reality for a while.

Luke and I visited Mother after one funeral, and she asked how many we'd been to that year. We tried to count, but stopped at fifteen. Her face looked at us in horror. 'I've not been to fifteen in my whole life, and I'm much nearer death than you two are.' She stared at us. 'I mean, you two *are* alright, aren't you? You look after each other, don't you?'

We nodded and took a sip of the tea she'd made us. We did look after each other; we clung to each other, like a shipwrecked passenger clings to a life vest in a storm. We clung to each other for the familiarity, we both knew we were okay, and we knew we weren't seeing anyone else behind each other's backs. We'd had that conversation very early on. And why would we need to see anyone else? Every weekend escaping from uni, I couldn't wait to see him; as soon as he arrived at my place, we went straight to my room and hungrily grabbed at each other's clothes, pulling them off, dropping them into a pile on the floor. We'd spend the first few hours together in bed, emerging late Friday night to see our friends or clear another one's flat.

The only way we got through that was to just keep on going. I couldn't break down in front of my ill friends. I wasn't the one lying in a hospital bed, coved with lesions, losing my sight. I could go back to bed with Luke, carry on with my nursing course. I didn't have to ask someone to clear out my flat of porn before my parents found it all. So we just carried on, taking each thing as it came and dealing with it. We escaped on holiday, and with each other, locking ourselves away in our bedrooms, sometimes not appearing for the whole weekend unless we needed to.

Luke's mum died of a brain tumour suddenly. No warning, no illness, no hospital trips. One day she complained of headaches. A week later she died in hospital.

And then that happened.

Luke hardly had time to feel his grief. His dad was so beside himself he literally didn't know what to do with himself. We went to his house every weekend, bought him

Delia's One Is Fun cooking book—which Luke said was a bit rich since he'd just been widowed, how much fun could he really have? But I had insisted it was practical.

Luke took two days off work: the day of the funeral and the day after. No more. I told him he could take more if he needed it, just to see his GP and he'd sign him off.

He said he wanted to keep busy. But he was lost without her. Every day he rang me and told me something he would have told her, something she would have laughed at, something she'd have given advice about. 'And she's missing it. I'm never going to see her again,' he said quietly.

'Death, it's pretty final,' I replied, not wanting to be glib, but unsure of what else to say.

He came in from work every night, collapsed in a pile on the sofa, turned on *EastEnders* and started to cry.

I held him tight in my arms. I used to think he was my rock, that he was the one who did the supporting in the relationship. Someone once told me in every relationship there should be a flower and a gardener: someone to tend and look after, and someone *to be* tended and looked after. I always thought I was the flower, nothing about being butch or camp, just that he'd always been there for me, dealing with split up parents, problems with Matt, propping me up as our friends died around us. It never occurred to me that all these things were about me, and that Luke had, up to that point, had a quiet, simple life, not requiring much support from me.

And then his mum died. *And then that happened.* And now *I* was beside *him*, propping him up. *I* was telling *him*, it would all be okay, that it would all pass, and it would get better.

I used to think I didn't have it in me, to be the tender, the supporter, but at the time I just got on with it.

Every time we visited, his dad just sat in his chair, watching *EastEnders*—a soap opera he'd hated when his wife was alive, but now it was a link to her, he wanted to hang onto it. He stared at the screen, commenting that Maeve used to love it, and he found it a bit confusing. Luke lost his temper and shouted that it was no good taking an interest in her now, now she was six feet under, and stormed out.

I made him and Luke eat chicken soup—Jewish penicillin, as one of my matrons had once told me. I played peacemaker between them both, rushing between the kitchen and living room, trying not to take sides, feeling the pain in the air all around me.

Each weekend his dad promised to improve and look after himself. The next weekend we returned we found a sea of takeaway containers and the TV stuck to *EastEnders*. We arrived one Friday night and he was in the same position we'd left him the previous Sunday evening.

After a month, we noticed his dad had started to smell, a mix of musty and boozy. Luke remarked how he was wearing the same clothes as last weekend.

We chose to ignore the booze smell at first, much to our regret.

'I've run out of clothes,' his dad said, scratching himself unflatteringly in the groin, lounging on the sofa amid pizza boxes.

I showed him how to use the washing machine. Next week I added an extra tutorial about whites and darks, having assumed it was obvious, but when he appeared at the door in a pink vest, I knew something was wrong.

Luke explained how the vacuum cleaner worked and pointed out that dust and dirt didn't just clean themselves up. He gestured to the room corners, which had accumulated quite a pile of dirt and hair.

'What am I supposed to do with this shit?' he asked, surrounded by bleaches and cleaners his wife had stored under the sink.

I looked at Luke, slowly looking through an old family photo album. He wiped his eyes.

'I'll take this,' I replied, rolling up my sleeves and explaining the difference between washing up liquid and toilet bleach.

To make sure he left the house, every time we visited, we went to the local pub. After getting over the initial shock, he enjoyed leaving the house. He knocked back round after round very enthusiastically, recounting stories of how much he loved his old Maeve. His eyes filled up when he told us about how they never had a cross word to say to each other, and used to stand next to each other washing and drying the crockery and cutlery after every meal.

Luke looked at me, shrugged, and I said nothing.

'Not sure where he got that from,' Luke said over his dad's head as we supported him under each arm, walking back from the pub. '*She* told me they were about to get divorced, he just didn't talk to her for days.'

We poured him into bed. I left Luke to undress him while I got pint glasses of water.

We woke the following morning to find him crying in his underpants on the floor, trying to put the duvet into the washing machine. 'I can't stand it anymore. It hurts so much. I just want it to go away.'

'Let's sort out these first.' I removed the duvet cover and put it in the machine.

Luke left the room, went outside to smoke, 'To take away the smell,' he explained when I later found him.

He refused to admit his dad had a drink problem, despite the evidence. After weeks of wet sheets and finding bottles in the bread bin, toilet cistern and behind the vacuum cleaner, after his dad faithfully promised us there wasn't a drop in the house, I put them both in the car and drove them to an AA meeting on a bright Saturday afternoon. I told them we were going to the supermarket 'To stock up' to persuade them out of the house.

Luke's dad stuck with the AA meetings, explaining it gave him a reason to get dressed and leave the house, rather than sitting around watching soap operas all day. 'It was full of others, just like me. Worse than me, some of them. They were people who understood what I was going through, and why I drink,' he explained after a few visits to the group.

He found the group helped him resist having a drink between meetings. His sponsor was a man who'd lost his wife in a car crash, then taken to the bottle in a big way — vodka with cornflakes, serious. Luke's dad rang his sponsor when he felt he was about to fall, rather than us, knowing his sponsor could be round much quicker than we ever could, and that the sponsor would talk to him in a way his son and I never would. Gradually, 'One day at a time' he always told us, he stopped drinking and started living again, in a post-Maeve world, which he eventually found he could be in, without alcoholic sedation.

Chapter Thirty

March 2000

Gabe and I gradually rebuilt our friendship, while I worked out what I wanted from my life. We spent much of our time together discussing a tactful and practical way of ending his relationship with A.

One evening, he told A he didn't want to be in the relationship any longer. As expected, A's response was dramatic, and centred on him being made homeless and Gabe throwing him out on the street.

Gabe and I had expected this, so Gabe calmly offered to give A the deposit for a flat, to help him sort out housing benefit, and to pay for a removal van for his possessions, hence dealing with all A's immediate objections. Gabe gave him six weeks to leave the flat and left the room to call from the bathroom, taps running loudly, as we'd previously agreed.

I pointed out to Gabe that A's objections all centred on the flat, and there was no mention of love, the relationship or another man. Gabe said that made him feel he was definitely doing the right thing.

Stage one Gabe telling A he had to leave the flat successfully completed, we quietly congratulated ourselves on the plan so far.

Meanwhile, solicitors' letters continued to arrive and I signed papers when required to do so, until eventually 'our' house was no longer. I returned once more to collect photos and one more box of memories from the attic, before walking around the now empty house, recalling how I'd felt when we first bought it. I breathed deeply and pushed the feeling of sadness down, posted the keys through the letter box and shut the front door for the last ever time.

Gabe called me a while after he'd asked A to leave the flat, frantically babbling down the phone: A had burst into tears that night at dinner, asked who the other man was, and said his life wasn't worth living and he couldn't possibly even think about moving out, before locking himself in the bathroom with a bottle of vodka and pills.

'What did you do?' I mentally prepared myself to jump in the car and drive round his.

'Called an ambulance. They're here now.' Gabe explained that he'd stood by the bathroom door, keeping A talking until the experts arrived. They'd persuaded A to open the door, where they found him on the floor, very drunk from the vodka. 'They checked the pills and he'd only taken a few, so they're taking him to hospital just in case. I'm going with him, I'll call you when I know more.'

'Do you need me?' I offered, unsure what I could do, but wanting to offer anyway.

'Speak to you when I know what's happening.'

'Be strong, you can do this.'

'I know.' He put the phone down.

The next day, Gabe called and explained. A had returned from the hospital pale and quiet. Once Gabe had convinced him there wasn't anyone else — and that in itself had taken a huge amount of convincing on Gabe's part, including swearing on his dad's life that, no, he wasn't having an affair with someone called Dominic, and he never had been — A seemed to calm slightly. Gabe explained they weren't making each other happy any longer, to which A's silence said everything.

Gabe helped him search for flats and completed applications for housing benefit. As the six-week deadline gradually crept closer, and it was quite obvious A would not find a flat and sort out housing benefit within the deadline, Gabe suggested A move in with his mum.

This didn't go down well with A. I found this out as Gabe rang me a while later, sheltering in the bedroom while A threw plates around the kitchen. Apparently, A's mum made mine look like a hippy earth mother, head to toe in kaftan and patchouli oil.

After placating A and clearing up the broken crockery, Gabe convinced him it was the quickest option for him leaving the flat, lest they actually killed each other as part of the warped drama of cruelty they currently found themselves in.

Gabe called his now ex sort-of mother-in-law asking if A could maybe stay with her for a few weeks, just while he, you know, sorted himself out.

'What's he got to sort himself out from this time?' she spat back.

'I think it's best if he tells you.' He handed the phone to a distraught A.

Throughout this, and other numerous, similar altercations, Gabe's constant retort to me, amid the daily updates was 'It's too hard, I'll just leave it.'

To which, every time, without fail, I replied: 'It's not meant to be easy, it's called *breaking up*, it's not called *stroking each other*. Short-term pain for your life back.'

After A's mother got involved, Gabe explained to me, it really started to get difficult: A recounted her regular questions in preparation of her 'so so sick son' returning to her nest. 'She wants to know if it's okay for our toothbrushes to be in the mug next to each other.' And shortly after, 'She's asked me if I have my own knife and fork now.' Then, 'She asked if it's safe for us to share soap.' Followed by, 'She asked me exactly how it happened. My mother's wanting to know that.'

'Tell her it's none of her business,' Gabe had replied.

'She said it *is* her business, if I'm living in her house,' A had replied.

'Tell her we don't know for definite,' Gabe said, desperate to do anything to move this situation on, but also exhausted by her endless idiotic questions.

'She said she doesn't want to talk to you, but she's written a letter, it's in the post.'

Relieved at being spared further interactions with A's mother, after tolerating it during their four years together, Gabe brought me her letter.

I kept it, unopened, promising him we'd open it together, a while after A had moved out.

Gabe never asked me about the letter again.

One week before the original deadline, Gabe confronted A, asking when he was going to start packing—the living room, filled with flat cardboard boxes Gabe had ordered for A, being the only sign of his impending departure.

I later learned A had spent the whole day smoking very strong spliffs, and had a fair dose of paranoia, combined with cabin fever. There followed an argument, the crescendo of which was a very stoned A screaming how much he hated Gabe from the living room window. Gabe would have capitulated were it not for my texts throughout. Gabe started to pack A's things into the boxes while he disappeared into the kitchen.

I had almost real-time updates from Gabe's constant stream of texts during the evening, and as soon as A disappeared into the kitchen, I jumped into my car and drove to their flat.

Gabe opened the front door and A appeared from the kitchen, holding a knife. 'So this is him is it? This is Dominic? Mister Perfect who's ruined my life for the second time. First it was you, Gabe, and now him. Well you're not going to get away with it. I won't let you.'

Gabe tried to calm him, saying gently, 'Now come on, you don't mean that.'

'Don't I? What have I got to lose?' he spat back.

'Imagine your mother, imagine her having to visit you in prison.'

A's hand shook as it held the knife tightly. 'Fuck's sake, I can't even get this right.' He threw the knife to the floor.

I looked at Gabe as he hugged A. 'Did you call the police?'

'Like it's not messy enough already.'

He cried into Gabe's hair as they hugged each other tightly, repeating, 'Sorry, sorry, sorry,' again and again.

I looked around the room, taking in the boxes and knife on the floor.

We all slept there that night, each in separate rooms.

Next morning, Gabe made us breakfast, and over tea and bacon sandwiches A finally agreed to leave the flat for his mother's place in three weeks.

He also agreed, maybe it wasn't healthy for him and Gabe to spend time together, 'As it's all so breathtakingly complicated, and if we want any chance of ever being friends in future, we need to stay as adult as possible now.'

I couldn't have put it better myself, and couldn't quite believe he'd come out with it himself. Gabe later explained A's normally very reasoned and logical mind went totally out the window after smoking pot.

I helped Gabe pack some clothes and toiletries into a bag, before leaving them to say goodbye to each other alone.

We drove to my room in complete silence.
And then that happened.

Chapter Thirty-One

Gabe moved into my room for three weeks. It was both the longest and shortest three weeks I'd ever spent. During this time, it showed me how much I still felt for Gabe. There's nothing like sharing a double bed and bathroom to push that to the front of a mind. After a few days I managed to hide my eyes from staring at his chest when he left the bathroom down the corridor, wrapped in a towel. I also managed to stop willing the towel to drop every time too. Instead I focused my worries on whether the hotel services manager at the hospital might find out I had a room mate, contrary to my tenancy agreement, sneaking Gabe in and out without anyone seeing him.

A few days in, he stood in my room, dripping quietly as I lay on my bed, looked at me and asked, 'Are you going to stare like that every time I have a shower? It can't be that different from Luke.'

'What?'

'His body.'

'Oh… no,' I replied, looking at the floor.

He sat on the bed, then skilfully slipped on pants under his towel, before drying his hair. 'I don't mind, just maybe you need to be a bit more subtle. Or maybe we need to have a sort of understanding.'

'Like what?'

'From experience, sex is on men's minds most of the time, but we're both a bit broken at the moment, so it's best if we don't. Okay?'

'Oh, I didn't mean that, it never crossed my mind,' I replied, staring at the floor again.

'I think we both know that's a big lie. And I don't mind. Like I said, sex, it's always there, just under the surface of most men's minds. So you seeing me like this, you think of one thing. I'm not gonna lie to you, Dominic, it's the same here.'

'With me?'

He nodded. 'Thing is, you're a bit less, how can I say… physically liberated than I am. Must be the Spanish in me somewhere. I grew up in what I suppose English people would describe as a naked house. You obviously didn't.'

'What do you mean?'

'When I was growing up, my parents used to walk in when I was in the bath. I did to them. No big deal, but you, I suspect did not.'

'Bloody right too. There's a word for that.'

'Don't be so ridiculous. It's not sexual, it's just skin. No touching.'

I shrugged, conceding his point, but still being a bit disgusted by the whole thing.

'So you just need to get a complete eye-full of me, get it out of your system, know nothing's going to happen, and get it over with. Then we can carry on as we are. I'm not sleeping on the floor, so you're going to have to do something about your nightly erections.'

I opened my mouth to speak, but couldn't think of anything to say, so closed it.

'Don't deny it. So, what we doing today?'

So that was that: we gradually became used to each other, just being there, with nothing behind it. This was a key factor in me finding it both the longest and shortest few weeks at the same time.

We shared the small double bed, top to tail at first, then, because it was easier to talk, the normal way round. We spent evenings tucked up together, sharing, talking, catching up on all the parts about each other we'd never had chance, but always wanted to discover.

Even after Gabe's 'naked house' discussion, it took four days before I stopped replaying that scene from the film *Beautiful Thing*, when he leans across and kisses his best friend in the bed. I toyed with trying that, but realised we were still both too damaged post A and Luke to give ourselves a decent go at a relationship together. So I held myself back, both physically and mentally. Every night when he clambered in, I remembered his comment about my nightly erections, and mysteriously, suddenly, they disappeared. It wasn't an issue any longer. It just seemed like a dinner guest making a rude joke among polite company — unwanted, inappropriate, not needed. Why on earth would *that* be here in this situation, between these two men, who are only, and can only ever be, friends?

Alongside this tension, it also showed me how easily we could live together, even in such a small space. We quickly fell into a new routine: whoever got home from work first made the dinner. Gabe introduced a rota for us to write which shifts we were working, so we knew when to expect each other every evening.

Over dinner, we finished each other's sentences, listening, really listening, to how our days were. Both paying proper attention and savouring every meal together. It was like the day we'd spent together ice skating and swimming, all those months ago, no talk of A or Luke, only this time it was because they were genuinely not there, not just hidden in the background. It was like we had created our own bubble again, to protect ourselves and learn more about each other together.

'I don't think it's helpful to bring all *that* home with you,' Gabe commented one evening, early into his stay, pointing at my pile of paperwork I'd brought from my office.

'I've told you, I can't do it at work, there are too many distractions, so I just bring it home.'

'And spend your evening, when you should be talking to me. Hello, I'm not getting enough attention here.' He batted his eyelashes in a mock camp way and pursed his lips.

'I have to do it.'

'Tonight?'

'By the end of the week, but we're already halfway through.'

'I do this, I have to do all this too, now I'm a senior charge nurse. Do you see me bringing armfuls of the stuff back here with me? No. And do you know why?'

'No, but I've got a feeling you're going to tell me,' I replied, chewing my cheek camply.

'I put a sign on the office, for an hour each day, saying do not disturb. They know that's when I do my paperwork every day. Five hours a week, uninterrupted — except in an emergency, a proper emergency like someone having a cardiac arrest or something. Not "I need to book next week off and talk to you now" emergency.'

'Does it work?'

'Where's my paperwork?' He looked around the room, lingering on the corner where his bag lay, empty after he'd unpacked it into my draws and wardrobe.

Next day at work, I tried it. At first it was like I'd told them I was walking off the ward, but soon they got used to it. They knew I could both show student nurses how to dress a pressure sore, and sign off annual leave and appraisals on time, but not at the same time.

One night, over dinner, I quietly picked at my food. Gabe asked what was wrong and said nothing wasn't an option. Eventually, after gradual coaxing, I told him I missed Matt and wasn't sure what to do. He listened, without interruptions, told me I was the only person who really knew whether Matt was worth keeping as a friend, and finished by saying, 'The difference between the pain of missing him and the pain of having him in your life will tell you what to do.' He let it hang in the air between us, a fork full of food.

I chewed slowly, hoping he'd add to that last little pearl of wisdom, for useful as it was, I hoped for something a bit more practical.

Thankfully, he looked at me and said, 'I had a friend, I'd known him for years, since before going to uni. He mixed with my uni friends, but only because he had to. I invited him out for my birthdays and he came along, always picking a seat next to me in the bar or restaurant. Everyone else talked and joked, while he whispered in my ear about the latest drama or anguish in his life, or the latest issue he had with me. Endless hours of his friends he'd fallen out with—I'd never met any of them, because he only ever saw me alone, or with my friends. Familiar patterns about falling out over what was said. One time at my birthday meal, after I hadn't seen him for six months, he leant towards me and whispered in my ear, "I've got bones to pick with you." Then he proceeded to tell me how he was pissed off with me for not being as close over the last six months because I couldn't see him for dinner during my final placement. My final placement, which decided whether I got into my final year at uni. I thought it was a good reason for not seeing him, and hadn't really noticed him not being in touch afterwards, but evidently he'd stored up that resentment, and built on it over the following months, and now presented me with a list of issues.

'All around me, my other friends laughed and joked, eating happily, while I got my ear chewed off by someone I'd pissed off, without even knowing it, months before. Friends aren't measured by how long it is between your phone calls, real friends are people you might not see for a year—life happens, people leave jobs, people leave partners—and when you see them, it's just like you saw them the day before. He finished bollocking me for my unknown friendship failures, and I leant back, taking a breath, absorbing what he'd accused me of. I took a swig of beer and asked him why he'd picked my birthday meal to tell me this. It hadn't even occurred to him it might not be the best timing. He said he needed to get it off his chest, and didn't want to dwell on it.'

'And did you?' I asked, riveted by the story, but not *quite* understanding how it related to Matt and me.

'What?'

'Dwell on it.'

'You could say that: instead of returning to my meal, after giving him all the air time to tell me off, and keep a nice quiet birthday—which was what he expected me to do—I told him.'

'What?'

'All of it! I told him how important my final placement was, how I didn't know any of these friends he endlessly talked about, so how was I supposed to really care or comment about them. I told him how he lurched from one group of new friends to another, each time repeating the same mistakes as before and falling out with them all. I told him it didn't matter if I didn't come to dinner that one time, proper friends don't hold things like that against each other. Proper friends don't sit on their hands, not calling one another, seething about a slight done to them months ago, and choose the worst opportunity to air those issues, when the other person can't respond. I told him how I'd tried to keep him at arm's length because every time he met my friends he usually caused an issue with a tactless comment, or argument, just like with his own friends. Of course, by now everyone else wasn't making small talk, they all had ring side seats for this argument between us both.'

'What did he say to that?' I asked, gripped by the soap operaesque story, not completely convinced he hadn't embellished slightly, but enjoying it all the same.

'He stood up, tried to punch me, but was held off by some of the people round the table, told me to fuck off, half tipped the table over, grabbed his bag and coat and left.'

'Was that it?'

'Never saw him again, never heard from him again. Suppose I joined the legions of other friends he'd fallen out with. He's probably telling some new friend all about me and how I disrespected him, or something. Good luck to them, I say.'

'Is there a point to this? It was a very entertaining story, but…'

'Some people don't bring anything but hassle to the party, all they do is take from you. Your advice, your time, but gives nothing back.'

I chewed, reflecting that Gabe had given more helpful Matt advice during that last few mouthfuls of food than Luke had done during our entire relationship.

As I let that thought seep into my subconscious, thinking how it would hit me later and knowing it would hit me like a train, I knew at that moment, as surely as I'd known anything, what I had to do about Matt.

A combination of Gabe's hour-long management idea, realising I'd been staying on for something to do, and the promise of his company every evening, meant I reduced my hours at work back to only a few more than I was actually being paid for, for the first time in months. Even though I returned each evening to a small room with a shared bathroom and kitchen rather than my own house and garden, I couldn't wait to come home in a way I hadn't experienced in years.

Since Gabe's 'naked house' talk, there wasn't any overhanging sexual tension at home. Each night, I didn't return thinking *I should have sex tonight with my husband, because it's been so long I've almost forgotten how to do it* hanging over everything I did, like part of a gigantic cosmic to do list. Instead, an easy familiarity replaced it, making our time together easy, natural, comfortable, fun.

Which was why it was so hard to give all this up when Gabe moved out. The blissful three weeks together had flown by, it felt like three days. I knew it was only ever temporary, while A moved his things out the flat, to give them both space and time from each other. I had told Gabe this was essential if they were to stand any sort of chance of being friends afterwards.

I knew all that, I understood that, I'd been the one to suggest Gabe moving in, but it didn't make it any easier when Gabe packed his things and left me living alone once again.

Chapter Thirty-Two

We sat in the same room, me staring at the same annoying spider plant, next to the same low table with a box of Kleenex tissues. Everything was still the same. Except now I felt less begrudging towards my time with her.

My time with Barbara.

I marched in, post-Luke and mid–Gabe living with me, and proclaimed I was all fine and didn't need to see her any longer. 'Nothing to talk about really. It's all fine. Fine and dandy, in fact, I'm walking on sunshine, as the song goes.'

She wasn't convinced by that at all. She leant forward, asked me gently to sit down, and took her clipboard from the table, pen poised to make notes.

Barbara tried to get me to talk about my parents. 'Tell me about your mother,' she tried hopefully, pen hovering above the clipboard.

'Nothing to tell really. I told her she couldn't carry on like that, and I've not heard from her since.'

She nodded slowly, made a point with her thumbs and fingers—I braced myself for I knew what was coming. 'And how does that make you feel?' she asked, right on cue.

I told her it didn't make me feel anything. She wasn't impressed with that, and tried another tack: 'Your father, what happened there?' Again, the steepled fingers and thumbs.

'I don't really want to talk about my parents actually,' I replied, shocked at how forthright and assertive I was being.

'Interesting. Why is that, I wonder?'

I could see where this was going, and didn't want to give her the satisfaction, so just sat in silence for a full minute. I know it was a minute because I watched the second hand on my watch do a whole circuit. Have you ever sat in a room with someone for an entire minute in silence? It's a long time.

I looked up from my watch. 'Look, I don't see why I have to carry on coming here, if everything's alright. I'm alright. No tears, no sadness, no return of My Depression.' I folded my hands in my lap, waiting for her reply.

It came slowly, after a long deep breath: 'Just because you're well, it doesn't mean you should stop coming here. You wouldn't stop taking the tablets if you felt better, would you?'

I hated the tablets, but couldn't deny they worked. 'No.' *How did she know I was still taking tablets?*

'You keep taking them don't you? Because it makes you feel better.'

I nodded. 'Suppose.'

'This is exactly the same. It's all part of an overall package of care we have created for you to holistically support you with your mental health.'

'My depression.'

'We prefer to say your mental health.'

'You can say what you like, but it's still me crying in a room, tears streaming down my face for no reason other than what's inside my head. My Depression. That's what I call it.'

She explained how it all fitted together, and among the buzz words, I caught the odd word and found I understood what she meant. I finally, for the first time since My Depression had first arrived, realised it wasn't down to me and me alone to keep it at bay. I had a team of professionals on my side—my GP knew about it too, as well as Barbara's colleagues. For the first time, I felt like I had a whole team, Team Dominic, helping me with this. And that in itself took a huge weight off me.

Before, it had always seemed like it was all down to me and only me to keep it at bay. So I plastered a smile on my face and tried with all my body and soul to *be happy*, all day, every day, of every week. And that, in case you've not tried it, is pretty exhausting.

Now, finally, I understood there wasn't really anything to be ashamed of about My Depression; it was a part of me, like The Hydra for Gabe, which I managed, alongside my everyday life.

I smiled, and she asked what that was about. 'Just pleased, it's all fitting into place I suppose.'

She looked at the clock on the wall above my head and pointed out we still had thirty minutes of our time left, was there anything else I'd like to discuss?

Although I felt I'd more than got Mother's money's worth from this session, it seemed like a waste to just sit there silently for another thirty minutes, especially given how long that one minute had seemed earlier. I took a deep breath and replied, 'Now I'm here, I might as well stay. And if I stay, what I'd really like to talk about is... Gabe I suppose.'

'Right... what about him do you want to talk about?' she replied. She turned to a fresh page on her clipboard.

I told her we'd both split up from our boyfriends and said I didn't know how to navigate my way through this next part of our relationship while not jeopardising anything we already had.

She jumped on my use of 'relationship,' which irritated me: who doesn't say that, talking about their friends. You can have a relationship with your teacher, with your pet, with your friends. Nothing more than that. However, Barbara wasn't convinced of this, not convinced at all.

For the rest of the session, I talked about Gabe, living with him, getting used to that, feeling like we were a couple, but knowing we weren't. Helping him leave A, our day trips together in the final months of Luke and I, everything, even me telling Gabe I was falling for him.

I had kept all this from Barbara, I wasn't sure why, apart from that it felt self-indulgent talking about that when it was really meant to be about My Depression, so it should be things about me, shouldn't it?

Barbara replied near the end of the session once I told her I'd confessed to Gabe I was falling for him, weeks before: 'Guard your heart, Dominic. Be careful who you give it to, as it'll break and hurt you very much.'

'I have, haven't I?'

'That's time now, Dominic.' She looked at the clock above my head. 'We can talk about that next week.'

And despite what I'd first thought, there was plenty to talk to her about in the coming weeks, *including* Hercules.

Chapter Thirty-Three

I helped him move back to his flat, once A had got himself together and moved out. We walked around and Gabe commented on how empty it all seemed without A's furniture. Gabe explained it had always felt like A's flat more than his: 'His stuff was everywhere, I now realise.'

We walked around each room noticing the gaps: a space where the bookshelves had stood; no coffee table or sofa in the living room, the carpet marked where they once were.

'It just all feels so sad and empty now.' Gabe disappeared to the kitchen to make a drink; I heard him crying quietly from the living room, and walked in to comfort him.

Through breathless sobs, he said, 'I know I wanted him gone, for so long I did, but now he really is gone, I can't believe it's over. All those years together and now there's a mark where the sofa was. And I don't have any fucking bookshelves.' He wiped his eyes.

'You don't have any books really, so no need for shelves.' I rubbed his back as we hugged.

'Suppose.' He continued, remembering good times together, the early days of their relationship, when everything and anything had seemed possible. 'It was like we'd finally found the other half, you know how people say, he's my other half, well that's what we really felt like at the start.'

I let the silence hang between us as he gathered his thoughts and breath; I saw on his face how the memories were flooding through him like a physical sensation.

'Tell me to shut up, you can tell me to fuck off, but I do feel duty bound to remind you that you were officially having an affair behind his back. For quite some time if I remember rightly.'

'I knew you'd bring that up, Dominic.'

'It's my job. I'm here so you don't descend too far in to the maudlin pit of saccharine memories from the relationship past and call him, tell him it's all been a mistake and soon he moves back.'

'How did you know?'

'It's textbook. Don't you think I've been thinking the same about *Luke* too? It's normal to want to hang on to things which are familiar amid all this change, even if what's familiar is unhappiness. At the moment, you're not remembering how you felt at the end, you're just remembering what it was like at the beginning. You can't remember the end, because you'd felt it so long, it was just the way you felt, a bit like breathing in and out, it's the way it is. You don't think about it.'

'I've done an awful thing, I know I have.'

'Why?'

'Throwing him out, no job, no flat, nothing. Especially after what I did. What sort of person does that make me?'

I knew this was coming, the delayed guilt for reclaiming his life back. 'Relationships are about what you bring to it; it's a partnership, two people. It's not about money, it's about contributing. Each part has to bring something to the party, to support each other and the relationship together. He didn't do that, and you know it.'

'He did at the start.' He stared at the floor where the sofa had been.

'Did he? Did he really?'

'You know what, I'm not sure I can remember it, really.'

'You'd remember it if he did, I'm sure. It would stick, like the other good memories.'

'Fair enough.'

More silence, and I noticed a tear slowly trickling down his right cheek. His bottom lip started to shake before he completely broke down.

I hugged him hard, stood in the kitchen. 'You can't go on blaming yourself forever you know.' I felt his head nodding against my chest, spreading his tears on my top.

He pulled away from my hug, his face red with tears. 'But maybe if we hadn't both got sick, we'd still be together. If I'd not… he'd still be okay. What have I done? What *have* I done?'

'If if if. If I hadn't stayed with Luke, I might not be here now; I might be living on an island with my dream boyfriend. But I didn't, I stayed with him, and now we've split up. All you can do at the time is make a decision, and live your life. You can't spend your whole life looking back thinking, what if, what if, what if. Because you didn't, you did what you did because… well, because you did. You didn't know you were sick. He didn't know. You *were* fine, weren't you?'

He nodded. 'Until it was too late.'

'Exactly. You had no reason to think anything was wrong. Plenty of people do it; fuck's sake, Matt's done it at least twice I know of. He's just been lucky, he dodged a bullet. You didn't. It could happen to any of us.'

'Random luck.'

'Random luck,' I echoed. 'I had a friend, back in the eighties, first time he slept with a man, which was a big thing for him, it'd taken him years to get his head around it, then suddenly he burst out the closet. Met this bloke down at Heaven, I remember him bringing the bloke over to show me, so proud, I can see his chest all puffed up even now. He said, "Isn't he lovely? He's taking me home to show me the ropes." We both giggled at that.'

'What happened?'

'He got it.'

'What, first time?'

I nodded. 'He saw me a while afterwards, couldn't get rid of a cold he'd had for months. Went to get tested and they said he was positive.'

'How is he now?'

I shook my head.

'Oh.'

'Everyone makes mistakes, it's down to random luck.'

'I want to lie down, it feels like my head's going to explode.' He walked to the living room and lay down where the sofa used to be.

More than a bit confused, I asked what I should do.

'Hold me.'

We lay on the floor like spoons.

A while later, we put some loud disco music on and moved the furniture around to minimise the gaps left from A's departure, spreading out Gabe's feeble pile of books onto the one remaining bookshelf dispersed with ornaments from around the flat. We put on the new duvet cover and pillow cases then added the old ones to the charity shop pile as they all reminded him of various sexual exploits with A from over the years.

I looked around the newly spread out furniture.

He walked into the living room, holding a large wooden owl. 'He left it, I can't believe he left it.'

'That?'

'It was a birthday present from one of his friends, he always hated it, and so did I. He couldn't throw it away in case the friend came round and didn't see it, so he just kept it, hidden in our room. But he left it in our bedroom on the one bookshelf he left here. Why?'

'He thought you might want to keep it?'

'It's his, it's not mine. We both hated it.'

'That's why.'

'What?'

'You both hated it, it's a part of your relationship together: he knew whenever you looked at that horrible hideous wooden owl, you'd remember how much you both hated it.'

'Yeah, like the flat hasn't got enough memories of us anyway.' He shook the wooden owl and stared at it.

'The rest is more gaps, spaces where he used to be, this is a reminder that you both shared things.'

'I don't need a reminder of that,' Gabe replied quietly.

Gradually we both became used to being single once again. Between us, we had fourteen years of being in our last relationship, and that's not something you can just shrug off like a bad hair day.

We both fell into a new rhythm, a different rhythm from when we had been with our boyfriends, and different again from when we lived together, but this time it had its own special closeness of two friends, finding their way in the world together.

Gabe started to see people, guys he met in bars or clubs, sometimes with and sometimes without me. I didn't get into the details of exactly what *seeing them* entailed, but he rarely mentioned them other than to comment on how good the sex was. Part of me wanted to ask if he'd been completely honest with them, but another part just didn't want to open up that particular conversation. He was starting to heal himself post A: 'It's like coming out to someone, all over again, and if I think I'm not going to see this person again, it's just for the night, mostly I don't,' he'd explained one evening.

I started to ask about safety, and he nodded his head slowly and replied, 'Of course, I'm not stupid.'

For me, any description of dating, seeing, courting, whatever you wanted to call it, was too much to take. Whenever I saw someone, I immediately started comparing him with Luke, positively or negatively, but my natural inclination was to compare and contrast. Even the thought of sleeping with someone else, after all this time, struck fear into my heart. 'It's like riding a bike, once you start, it'll all come back to you,' Gabe had advised.

Riding a bike or otherwise, I knew I wasn't ready for just a quick ride, as part of me thought it would automatically lead to more. And the thought of anything more than a quick ride, anything more serious, also scared me. I needed more time to get used to myself once again, to rebuild who or what I was, my work, my friends, my family, before I could think about inviting someone else in to share it with me.

It was all starting to become comfortable, starting to feel normal once again.

Then Gabe started to tell me about meeting up with Hercules again. His voice was bubbly and enthusiastic as he described a date they'd been on — already more serious than just seeing him, as with others he'd mentioned. So I listened, while my stomach lurched and jumped in somersaults for some reason.

Gabe's continuation of our code for the guy's name pleased me. It signalled a common language, like The Hydra, a shared understanding, something we could talk about in public without causing looks. These, I knew, were the things of friendship. And that was important to me.

My stomach still lurched, and I continued to feel sick as he carried on with his story.

Gabe explained they met for a drink, after Hercules had got back in touch, moved onto a restaurant for dinner where 'he offered to pay,' but they'd eventually agreed to split it. Gabe added, as if I hadn't realised, 'A never offered to pay, in fact I can't remember going to a restaurant with him,' before finally ending the night back at Gabe's flat.

During the story, my stomach had anticipated that ending, anticipated, but hoped for a different ending all the same. I imagined them kissing and more in the living room I'd rearranged for Gabe not long before. I saw them laying on the sofa I'd helped Gabe buy one Saturday at Ikea. Where had Hercules — and all his strength — been for all that? How come this Hercules had only just swept in now?

'Isn't it amazing?' Gabe ended with. 'I never thought I'd see him again.'

Me neither. 'How did you leave it?'

'Casual, he's going to call me. But I can't wait, I want to call him.'

'And that's casual, is it?'

'I know, I'm a twat, I know, but *he* came back for *me.*'

So, I watched from the side lines as their relationship developed: Gabe gave me regular updates on the phone, for he found it harder to meet face to face between work and his ever increasingly frequent dates with Hercules. They split up, they got back together, then split up again; each time Gabe called me in tears, saying he'd never find anyone else, as no one would want him as 'damaged goods.'

Each time I explained he was no more damaged than any of the rest of us, and he would find someone who'd get him, who'd want him for himself, the whole package. Gabe explained, Hercules at first was absolutely fine about The Hydra, then reconsidered his position, having spoken to his *parents*, who'd warned him off. Gabe was left feeling like a used tissue, thrown on the floor. His private and intimate secrets about his health were now common knowledge among Hercules' friends and family, as if it were about his wisdom teeth.

'I've told no one, Gabe,' I said. 'It's nothing to do with them, so why would I?'

'If you were sleeping with me, with someone who's HIV positive, are you telling me you wouldn't at least tell your best friend?'

'You are my best friend,' I said quietly.

'Okay, putting that aside. Are you saying you'd keep that to yourself, not tell anyone?'

'I don't know. I'm not sleeping with you, am I?'

'No, you're not, Dominic.'

I met Hercules, Gabe's suggestion; the three of us went for a drink in Soho. I begrudgingly admitted to myself he gave good conversation. He asked about me, my job, my home, my boyfriend, listened intently and asked more questions from my responses. He sat next to Gabe, arms entwined, scrabbling to share cigarettes between drinks. I asked him about himself and Gabe, and he replied, carefully covering my questions, and adding that it felt like a job interview.

'I've got to make sure your intentions are honourable, I'm looking out for Gabe.' I smiled, but it didn't quite reach my eyes.

After a couple of hours of intense conversation, including a rather heated political debate about care in the community—Hercules was a mental health advocate—I left them, limbs entwined and staring into each other's eyes.

I realised he wasn't going anywhere fast, and he definitely made Gabe happy, after the initially bumpy ride. And after seeing Gabe so unhappy when he was with A, and after they broke up, I knew Hercules was good for Gabe for all sorts of reasons. He was so distinctively not anything like A, anything he did could only be received by Gabe as a breath of fresh air and relief.

Gabe explained, 'He tells me he'll cook dinner round his, and he does. I arrived and he'd done it, full dinner—with a bit of help from M&S—candles, the lot.' And then, 'He wants to be a chief executive of a mental health hospital, long-term. And he knows how he's going to do it.'

I knew he was good for Gabe in many ways, so I was happy for them both. Because I wanted him in my life, I had both of them: for the sake of our friendship, I put aside my feelings and watched their happiness together.

Chapter Thirty-Four

1989 — 1993

Matt reappeared, six months into my relationship with Luke, both indignant that he'd missed out on this development and desperate for my help.

'I've had a bit of a slip-up, can you come to the clinic with me?'

'Tell me you're joking,' I replied, having already done quite a bit of reading in my first year at uni.

'Sorry, it won't happen again. It just sort of happened… Will you come with me, I can't do it alone?'

'What about the guy?'

'Who?'

'The guy you slept with, doesn't he want to know too?'

'Dunno, didn't ask.'

'Call him, I can kill two stupid birds with one, too kind for my own good, stone.'

'Haven't got his number. It wasn't really like that.'

We went to my hospital where I'd just started as a student nurse. Matt didn't want to risk anyone seeing him back home if he had the test there. I sat with Matt, in the waiting room, looking at the sexual health posters, wondering how he could be so stupid. I felt angry, but still cared about him enough to help, so there I was, once again, in his very own drama.

As we left the clinic, I looked around at the other men, waiting for their name to be called, waiting to hear if they'd dodged a bullet or were to receive a death sentence.

Matt called me a few weeks later, pleased as punch it had come back negative. I could hear the smile in his voice. 'They rang me. Nothing to worry about in the end,' he breezed.

'No thanks to you.'

'Thanks for coming, gotta go, babes.' And he was gone.

Despite everyone's predictions at uni, Luke and I stayed together. I watched numerous other relationships from pre-uni days crash and burn by reading week of the first term. But I knew Luke and I were different. Matt said it was a shame, as I'd missed out on all the action of Freshers' Week, but I was just glad for some stability in my life.

The first year became the second year, and soon we were mid–third year. I was almost a qualified nurse, allowed to look after patients on my own, dispense drugs, write care plans, everything. And Luke was still there by my side, every weekend we saw each other. Despite my best predictions, he'd not just disappeared, and I knew I wouldn't dump him, so we stayed together.

Going through the hard times with Luke, visiting sick mates, clearing out their flats, watching our circle of friends disappear around us, made it even harder when

Matt told me he'd had *another* slip-up, and asked me to come with him to the clinic again.

'You are kidding?'

'Sorry.'

'It's not me you should be sorry to, what about your parents, imagine their faces when you have to tell them. They've only just got used to you being gay, and now this.'

'Will you come with me?'

'Did you read the leaflets, after last time? Or did you just throw them away and think it'll all happen to someone else?'

'It was all so depressing. Pictures of people with marks on their faces. Stuff about drugs and needles. I don't do that, so I didn't need to worry.'

'Or so you thought.'

We went to the clinic together, of course we did. I wasn't going to leave him to go on his own. I wanted him to be taught a lesson, not too much of a lesson, not permanently, just something to scare him.

He left the clinic, walking quickly to the ward entrance, waiting by the lifts for me. I followed. 'What happened?' I asked.

'I've gotta wait a few weeks.'

'They'll call you?'

'If there's anything bad, they ask me to come in, otherwise they call me.'

We arrived at the bus stop outside the hospital and I said I had to go to meet Luke.

Matt hugged me. 'It's alright for you. You've only been with him. All this time, one man. It's like that song — who was it? 'Stand By Your Man.' And you have, haven't you?'

'Tammy Wynette. I'm glad I have, if this is the alternative. I'd have that any day, compared to what happened to some of the others.'

'You love him, don't you?'

'Luke?'

'No, matron. Of course Luke.'

I smiled.

'But do you still get that feeling? When he comes home, and you think, I'm going to see him now, I might get a shag in a minute. And you think about his body and him kissing you, and straight away you go hard. Cos that's what I was like with thingummy.'

'Who?'

'You know, the one before this last one. You met him a few times. Long brown hair, combat trousers round his waist, big trainers. Worked in the shoe shop.'

I trawled my mind, back through numerous ex-boyfriends and casuals Matt had introduced me to, and drew a blank. 'Of course it's like that *in the first month.*'

'So it's not like that now, for you and Luke?'

'When you've been with the same man for, how long is it now?' I counted on my fingers. 'Nearly four years. Blimey, is it that long we've been together. Suppose it is, almost three years training to be a nurse, it's flown by. When you've been with someone that long, come back to me, alright?'

'But you still love him?'

'Course I do.'

It was like morning following night, how the seasons rolled on, it just *was*. Dominic and Luke, they went together. That's what love is isn't it? I hadn't been with anyone else, and I didn't know what it felt like to love anyone else, except Luke. Friends and family, that's different, it's a different sort of love. Love was how I felt about Luke, even if that wasn't how others described it, it couldn't be anything else. Security, safety, caring, they're all parts of love, which I felt for Luke.

Three years after I'd started, I qualified as a RGN, or registered general nurse to you. I had a profession, something to be proud of, something which would make a difference.

Luke was still by my side.

Luke came to the graduation ceremony, of course he did, sitting next to Mum. Dad made an excuse about work and money, but I knew it was more about not wanting to be in the same room as Mum. Luke made small talk with her, united in their pleasure at seeing me do well after all the hard work.

Luke finished his course, worked as an assistant manager for a Dior concession in a department store, working his way up through branch manager at a larger shop in London. Once he had that job, we were both working in London, so it made sense to move into the tiny studio flat in West Kensington soon after, towards the end of 1993.

The difference between an eighteen-year-old and someone who's twenty-three is usually quite obvious. It's often the time between leaving home, training, or studying to be what they want to be, and then being that thing, in the real world. This is exactly what happened to Luke and me, but the things we'd seen along the way meant we both came out the other end, at twenty-three, feeling middle-aged, life worn, smoothed around the edges by what life had thrown at us both.

Chapter Thirty-Five

April 2000

Mother didn't speak to me for two months after our little chat. At first I felt so guilty I could feel it like a bowling ball, swirling around my stomach every day. After a while, I began to enjoy it: no last minute visits, no criticism thinly veiled as passing the time of day, no watching her fall off the wagon and onto the floor.

But, despite all her faults, I realised she *was* my mother, and the only one I was ever going to have. I debated whether to call round to her house, and had visions of me talking to her housekeeper Rose, in preference to my own mother, or turning up to find she wouldn't answer the door to let me in. That sort of highhanded drama would be exactly Mother's style. So I didn't give her the satisfaction. I had more than enough to get on with in my life, settling into the nurses accommodation, Gabe's relationship, both with me, and Hercules, and of course my job. So I played a waiting game.

One day, as I pottered about in the shared kitchen, baking fairy cakes between loading clothes into the washing machine, listening to the radio and thinking life wasn't so bad after all, the entry phone system beeped. I asked who it was, and an unmistakeable voice replied, 'It's the person who gave you life. The person who carried you for nine months. The person who sacrificed her body for you to come into the world.' She pressed the buzzer again. 'Darling, can you please hurry up as I am getting looks from people?'

She smiled as I opened the door, passed me while brushing against my arm—that, I realised, was as much affection as I'd get today. Her face looked slightly more startled than usual, more plastic surgery no doubt; if only I was allowed to hug her, I could check behind her ears for stitches.

She kept her elbow length white gloves and pink pillbox hat on, which matched her little suit from Hobbs that paid homage to Jackie O mid-reign. She carefully ran her finger along the work surface as we reached the kitchen, surveying the whole room in its student mid-seventies shabby, not very chic splendour. 'So, darling, this is where you're living I see? Kitchen's not as small as I'd thought. Somehow, I imagined it to be more like a caravan, but not on wheels. Lots of cupboards I see, and you're baking. Hmm, I won't, thanks, watching the calories.' She patted her stomach, then looked at the chair, laid a handkerchief from her handbag on the seat and sat delicately, resting her hands across her lap.

'It's shared.'

'Sorry, darling?'

'The kitchen, it's shared. It's not just mine.'

'I see.'

'And the bathroom.'

'You're sharing a bathroom. I'm sure that's unhygienic, lots of young people, getting up to lord only knows what, sharing baths. Oh, darling, surely this is enough of this silly nonsense. Can't you just move back to your lovely house? You've made your point; this is just dragging on now, surely.'

'There is no house — well, there is, it's just I don't own it anymore.'

'Is he still there, your friend…?' She waved her gloved hands in the air, trying to summon the name of her now ex son in law.

'Luke?'

'Yes, that's him. Surely he's still there isn't he, darling? You could just pop all this into my car and you'd be home in no time. I can't imagine you have much here to pack really, it's not worth risking it spoiling anything as far as I can see.'

'I don't know where Luke is, actually. I've not heard from him since we sold the house. That's it, it's gone, no more. I am living here now, until further notice.'

'But darling, you simply cannot live here. What will I tell the ladies back home? I've got a Women's Guild meeting coming up, they'll all want to know about my son who lives in London, the successful nurse. I can't say you're living in a tower block next to the hospital, with a shared kitchen and bathroom. I'll never live it down. They'll take me off the committee for the Village Action Group.'

I snorted.

'You may well laugh, but darling, they've done it before. I've seen it.'

One of my flatmates, a student nurse called Cheryl, arrived in the kitchen. Seeing we were in the middle of a delicate conversation, she grabbed some milk from the fridge and left for her room, smiling awkwardly at us both.

'And they just walk in like that do they? These *flatmates* of yours?' Mother asked, trying to grasp the concept of a shared kitchen.

'That's generally what happens when you share a kitchen, yes. Shall we go to my room, no one will disturb us there?' I ushered her to my room while she used her white gloves to test for dust en route.

I sat on my bed and Mother sat on the office chair I used to lay out my clothes. 'So this is your room?' She looked around.

'It's not much, but it's mine. It'll do for now.'

'If the house is gone, you must have some money, you must be able to afford *something* more than this. What am I supposed to tell them back home?'

'Tell them what you want; how are they going to find out?'

'But if they did find out, if they knew I'd lied, oh the shame. You have no idea, Dominic, no idea at all.'

'There's a bit of money left, but after legal costs and some loans to pay off, not much. I don't want to rush into anything, and I'm certainly not rushing into anything so you can save face with your cronies.'

'I can soon go. They are not cronies, they're my friends.'

We sat in silence for a few moments.

She looked up from her hands resting in her lap, back to my eyes. 'What are you doing now? You must be on the lookout for someone else, a rich man this time, or what will become of you? You're nearly in your thirties, these sort of places aren't for people in their thirties, oh no.'

'I'm not looking yet. And even if I was, I'm not interested in what he earns. It doesn't bother me.'

'But darling, there are standards to be maintained. You're university educated, you have a degree—even though it's in nursing, and not history or politics, it's still a degree. You can't just shack up with someone who hasn't even got A levels, where would it all end?'

'I'll be fine.' I paused, wondering if she'd tackle the great break in communication which had preceded this visit.

'I was very hurt and upset at what you said to me you know,' she started. 'I spoke to Rosemary, one of my friends from the Women's Guild: she talked me round, she persuaded me to visit you here. I thought it was all lost, I thought, all these years raising my lovely son, and that's the thanks he gives me.'

'Mother—' I replied before she interrupted me, putting her right palm up.

'No, I'd be grateful if you'd listen please. I need to ensure I have what Rosemary called, closure, so: the words were very hurtful, but I understand why you said them. You were going through a difficult break up with... you know...'

'Luke?'

'Yes, and the emotions during that time affected how you spoke to me. I am looking forward to a time when I can stay at your place once again. Because that's obviously not possible while you're living here. I mean, what am I supposed to do?'

I left silence to the last question, not shocked, but disappointed how she'd completely missed the point of our falling out.

'I could lend you money, help you get out of here. Just say the word; I've got my chequebook in my handbag. Come on, how much?' She reached into her bag and brought out a gold leather chequebook holder and gold pen.

I knew any money she lent me would surely come with enough strings attached to start a puppet show, so I politely declined her offer and promised I'd have my own place as soon as possible.

She stayed to sniff some of my fairy cakes. 'I can't afford the calories, darling,' and agreed a date for me to visit her, 'So I can hear all about your new flat plans, darling.' She hugged me for the briefest of brief hugs, still not long enough to check behind her ears for stitches.

I watched her through the kitchen window, walking to her brand new Mercedes coupe. And she was gone.

I felt relieved she'd returned to my life, but also frustrated nothing had really changed. Still the same judgemental, money-obsessed Mother, completely devoid of emotional support. But she was at least *my* emotionally stunted, money-obsessed mother, and the only one I would have, so I resigned myself to making the best of it.

She rejoiced and included an announcement in the village newsletter when I bought a flat in Fulham six months later. The first time she invited herself round, I braced myself for her familiar return to form, allowing myself a quiet reminder to her about best behaviour, and did she remember what I'd said before. She ignored my comments and soon arrived in Fulham, amid the Chelsea tractors, yummy mummies and wide kerb hogging prams, full of children destined for private schools further into the suburbs. Mercifully, we went to Chelsea's King's Road, 'Just to have a look at the little shops for some little, gorgeous things, darling,' and returned with armfuls of Moroccan bowls and incense burning paraphernalia, 'Gifts darling, all gifts, none for poor little Mother,' she explained. We stopped for dinner at a little Greek restaurant one of her Women's Guild friends had told her about, 'Just for a little celebration, to you, darling, being *back to yourself* again.' I explained I'd never really left, and was of course still the same person, just without Luke and the house, but she insisted my move to the flat — 'Call it an apartment, darling, it's so much better' — was my return to form, and something to celebrate.

This is when the wheels fall off, I thought as the waiter handed us menus and asked what we'd like to drink.

'Perrier water. You, darling?' Mother said immediately after the waiter finished talking.

'Really?' I replied, so shocked with what had just happened. I asked if she minded if I ordered wine and she replied she wasn't a child, or course I could, and that Rosemary had told her she couldn't avoid alcohol as 'it's *everywhere*, darling, simply *everywhere*' but to call her if she felt a weakness.

So it seemed Rosemary had other hidden talents too. She didn't call Rosemary, but instead sipped Perrier water throughout the delicious meal, providing very convivial company and explaining how Rosemary had once woken up in a bus stop, with no recollection of getting there, just clutching a bottle of Sauvignon Blanc. That was Rosemary's wake up, just like my little speech had been to Mother.

'How wrong can I be about the WG?' I asked, keen to hear more about this Rosemary.

'Oh, darling, she wasn't from the Women's Guild. I mean, she is *now*, star baker and she can knit and crochet like her life depends on it, now I've persuaded her to join. No, I first met her in a pub, drinking Perrier water, while I sloshed down the wine like it was going out of fashion. We started talking and she scooped me up and led me to an AA meeting. She taught me how to go out and not drink, I learned that drinking isn't the solution to all of life's problems, in fact it's rarely the solution to any of them, especially the amounts I was drinking towards the end. She also taught me how to bake too; I had so much time on my hands with not going out all the time and getting drunk, I had to have a hobby, darling. That's why I was interested in your hobby too. I even sometimes eat what I bake, but mostly I sell it at fetes and jumble sales.'

I sat, open-mouthed.

'Close your mouth, it'll catch flies.' She pushed my mouth shut. 'Do you know the most extraordinary thing since I've not been drinking?'

I shook my head.

'I've lost so much weight, I can actually have cakes sometimes, without worrying about piling on the pounds. So, every cloud etc, darling, every cloud...' She chinked her glass to mine, winked and squeezed my shoulder.

Chapter Thirty-Six

October 2000

After his pointed comments about me spending so much time with Gabe that weekend at his parents' place, I wasn't surprised when I realised I hadn't heard from Matt for almost six months. It had all just passed so quickly: splitting up with Luke, moving out of the house, then the time after Christmas with no contact from Gabe. Some days it had been all I could do to get myself up and to work each morning.

And it was Matt's standard operating procedure, really — back together with Marcus, that would have been his focus. Thinking about Matt's absence now, I felt relieved, as I couldn't have repeated the same conversations with him again and again, especially while I was going through all my changes.

Another deep debate about his boyfriend Marcus' inability to commit to him, and to actually behave like a boyfriend, would have tipped me over the edge during the past few months. For as long as I'd known Matt his boyfriends were always a bit on and off. They would split up, and Matt would announce he'd never see the boyfriend again and disappear on a plane to find himself and get 'a bit of short term cock,' as he'd termed it so beautifully, only to return a few weeks later back to the boyfriend's arms to repeat the same pattern all over again.

For the first time, in that bar all those months ago, trying to grasp onto our past, I had seen the whole picture of Matt and Marcus' relationship and how that had affected my relationship with Matt. I saw how Matt felt torn between his friends and plans, and Marcus' plans, grateful for any scrap of attention he threw at him.

What I realised after that night was what Matt really craved, what he really envied, was my settled suburban life I'd had with Luke. On the surface, he would sneer at it, commenting that we hadn't gone out and done anything for ages, but I soon realised that covered up a gaping great sore in his relationship with Marcus.

If Luke had treated me as an afterthought, fitting me among his other friends, leaving me out of plans so I could never decide what to do in case something better, involving him came up, I would have treated my friends how Matt treated me. 'I'm not sure if I'm free that weekend, Marcus is thinking about doing something, so I'll let you know.' Or 'I'd love to see you New Year's Eve, but Marcus has been invited to a party which we might go to first.'

This, combined with Matt's burning jealousy for my friendship with Gabe, which came out through bitter comments about me spending too much time with Gabe, not having time for him, and wondering what Luke thought of me spending time with Gabe, made my decision very easy.

When I received a letter to my ward, and I recognised Matt's scrawly handwriting, I sat down in my office, ordered Di Anne to look for some papers from the ward next door and opened it with surprise. Amid the vague plea for us to 'catch up soon' he explained he had 'lots of good news about me and Marcus I can't wait to tell you in person.' I put the letter to one side and continued with the business of the day: Di Anne's request to leave early for the fourth day running; transferring an elderly patient to a hospice for her last weeks; and two senior staff nurses' appraisals and training plans. During all this, Matt's words nagged at me.

I reread Matt's letter when I got back to Fulham. I put my dinner on, then called Matt. I fully expected voicemail, as it was the usual greeting whenever I called him, so was surprised, and had a mouthful of beans and toast, when he answered.

He was pleased his letter had reached me; after getting a return to sender for my house, he assumed I'd still be at the hospital. 'It's been years and you're not leaving anytime soon, so I sent it there.' He told me about his plans to marry Marcus, what the wedding would involve, how they were going to buy a house together, once he'd saved enough to move out of his parents' place, but in the meantime he was staying at Marcus' flat 'practically every night.'

As he paused for breath, I asked, 'How's he been?'

'What do you mean?' He jumped at me in response.

'The way he is with you. The boyfriend stuff. What we talked about, before Christmas.'

'I've moved in, so that's a step in the right direction.'

'What about the friend?'

'He doesn't talk about him anymore, so… Oh look, that's him calling now, I'll call you back.' Click as he put the phone down.

I put mine down and resumed my beans on toast.

During the ten-minute call, he hadn't asked me why his first letter was sent back. He hadn't asked where I was living, what I was doing, how was Luke or how was Gabe? He hadn't even asked how my parents were—usually he relished my latest story about Mother and her exploits. Okay, so we'd been out of touch for a few months, quite a few months, but with good friends, it's like a soap opera: you can drop it for a while and pick it up again, and after a quick chat you know where all the characters are and what they're up to. *If* you ask about the characters and what they're up to.

Matt didn't call me back that evening, and after putting the phone down, I realised I'd missed nothing from him falling out of my life since his phone call on New Year's Eve.

This time, true to form, it was all about *his* life, *his* plans, *his* boyfriend, without even a sideways glance at mine. Since we'd last spoken, my life had changed almost beyond recognition and Matt wasn't in the least bit interested. I realised, not only could I not have the same conversation with Matt about Marcus' treatment of him—because I didn't for one moment believe he would change, whether they lived together, were married, or not—but I also didn't want to have *that same conversation* again. I also didn't want to feel the need to drop in bits of my news among the great dollops of his, like raisins in a cake mix, when I had other friends who were interested in my own raisins of news, just as much as theirs.

Months after Gabe's advice I finally knew what to do. That phone call was the last time I ever heard from Matt.

Chapter Thirty-Seven

Gabe and I went to his parents' place in Stevenage. Gabe wanted to lick his wounds after Hercules had finally, after a long period of vacillating between total acceptance and total disgust, decided he couldn't be with Gabe any longer, and had dumped him. Hercules' friends and family hadn't helped matters, each giving their own changeable and ill-informed views and opinions about The Hydra.

I was exhausted from the vacillating, as I'd been through every high and low with Gabe: each time he called me to relay the latest confession of undying love Hercules had professed to him, or comments from Hercules' oh so concerned friends and family about how dangerous Gabe was to Hercules.

After the final dumping, Gabe had asked me what would become of him now, as no one else would want him, since he was 'dangerous' and 'damaged'—two beautifully cruel words Hercules' ex had used when 'expressing concern about safety,' these words had stuck in Gabe's mind, usually to be surfaced during his darkest moments.

'Who isn't a bit damaged?' I had replied, partly grabbing at straws and partly believing my own hype. I was pretty damaged too, and I was sure Luke wasn't exactly going to Disneyland, skipping down the yellow brick road of life on his own. Matt was certainly pretty damaged by years of mistreatment by Marcus. Mother was definitely a few raisins short of a fruitcake. So really, honestly, when you came down to it, who wasn't damaged in their own way? I had reminded Gabe of this.

Barbara was relieved? pleased? Something like that, I wasn't sure. When I'd told her Hercules was out of the picture, for good, she leant forward, pausing to do the fingers steeple, *how does it make you feel* move, then wrote a whole page of notes as I answered. She listened as I recounted what had happened, only when I finished did she say slowly: 'You still need to be careful, and guard your heart.' After that, our sessions became less about how hurt I felt seeing Gabe with Hercules, and more about me, on my own in a world without a boyfriend, with my relationships to others. Barbara gave up asking me about my parents, I was wise to that one, but gradually I realised: rushing into a relationship with Gabe immediately after Luke would have been as messy and too soon as Gabe and Hercules' relationship had been.

Now, Gabe and I had reasons for the weekend away from London, and against my better judgement, Gabe also wanted to come out to his parents about The Hydra. I told him to tackle one thing at a time: recovering from Hercules was one thing, without having to launch himself into another.

Since Hercules' friends and family knew all about The Hydra, but Gabe's own family didn't, he had questioned how right this was, whether he could or should continue with the deceit. He explained to me, 'No more secrets. Keeping them going becomes bigger than what the secret was in the first place.'

Friday night, we exchanged pleasantries with Gabe's parents before falling asleep in our separate rooms his mum had made up for us. As we finished breakfast on Saturday morning, his mum began to clear the plates and Gabe asked her to sit as he had something to tell them, yes I could stay too.

His parents sat at the table.

Gabe said, 'I'm telling you this now, because since splitting up with A, I feel pretty together. Pretty sorted. My life's not exactly like an episode of *Friends*, but it's pretty near sorted as it can be: I've got my own flat, a job as a ward manager, friends who love me. After I split up with Hercules —'

'Who?' his mum interrupted.

'An ex. After A. Anyway, he made me realise his family knew things mine didn't. Okay, some of the things they said weren't very nice, but I wasn't lying to them. What they said was based on knowing about me. Mum, Dad, you know there are lots of different gay people, lots of different ways to be gay?'

They both nodded.

'Well, there are lots of different straight people, people who are blind, people who have diabetes, people who can't move below their necks. And they all live their lives, gay or straight, these people live their lives all the same. There are also people who have cancer, and some of them live and some of them don't, but in the meantime, they get on with their lives. And there are some people who are HIV positive, and they live their lives and they take their medication and they go to their jobs, and they meet their friends, and they take their friends to their parents' house for the weekend. And that's me.'

Gabe's dad asked, 'You've got cancer?'

His mum replied, 'No it's not cancer, it's…' She struggled to say the words.

'Mum, you can say it.' Gabe looked at her.

'HIV. You're HIV?' Her eyes filled with tears and she put her hand to her mouth.

Gabe nodded.

'What, AIDS?' his dad asked.

His mum started to sob.

Gabe put his hands out, one resting on his mum and one on his dad. 'I haven't got AIDS, I'm living with HIV. I take my medicine, I go to my doctor, I do what I'm supposed to do, and I live my life. Like someone who's living with diabetes.'

'You don't die of that, though,' his dad said.

'You can actually. Lots of people die of it every year, because they don't look after themselves. People die of AIDS too, I know that, but that's if they don't look after themselves properly.'

'And are you?' his mum asked, her hand still covering her mouth.

'Everything the doctor told me, everything they said at the clinic, I do. I eat healthily, I take my medication at the same time every day, I have a flu jab so I don't get flu, to protect my immune system. And look at me, would you know if I hadn't told you?' He held his hands out either side of his body.

His mum started to clear the plates and take them to the kitchen.

'Mum, Dad, ask me questions. Anything you want to know, I'll tell you. It's not like it used to be – people are living with it longer and longer. Every year the medication gets better. For some people the viral load is so low it's undetectable, which means in theory there's little risk of passing it on. Come on, ask me.'

'How long have you known?' his mum asked, putting the plates back on the table, wiping tears from her eyes.

'Just over a year.'

'When did you find out?'

He told her about having a cold he couldn't get rid of, and being admitted to hospital with pneumonia. They remembered that, they'd all thought it was flu, or too much partying, and then suddenly it wasn't talked about any more and Gabe was better.

'And now, are you okay?' She sniffed.

'Do I look it?' He paused as they both nodded. 'Every morning at the same time, I take eight different tablets to treat it. Some of them make me feel a bit sick, some of them make me a bit sleepy, some of them used to give me terrible psychedelic nightmares, but the clinic changed them. Even with those side effects, if that means I stick around, and I don't end up in hospital when I get a cold… if those side effects mean that, I'll take that. I'll take that with knobs on.'

I looked at his parents then Gabe. 'Tell them about the clinic, what they do.'

'Oh yes, I go to a clinic at a hospital every three months, where they take blood, to monitor my viral load—that's how much of it is in my blood—and white blood cell count—that's how much of my blood can fight infections. They ask how I'm getting on with the medication, change it if it's not working, if the side effects are worse than what it's fixing.'

I added, 'It's like a service and MOT, every three months.'

Gabe nodded. 'There's a woman to talk to about benefits and help if I can't work. Two thirds of people don't work again after they're told they're HIV positive. I can't imagine not working, I trained three years to be a nurse, it's what I've always wanted to do.'

His mum's crying reached a crescendo, she wiped snot from her nose. '…such a shame, such a waste, all those years training…'

'Mum, I can still nurse. I *am* still nursing. I've got friends I met at the clinic who're in their late forties, they're still working.'

His dad looked at Gabe then shot his eyes to me. 'What about him?'

'What about me?' I asked.

'Did he know?' his dad said.

Gabe replied, 'Everyone who matters in my life, and some who don't actually, they all knew, except you two. Which is why I had to tell you. Keeping it secret was tearing me apart. It meant I couldn't tell you about certain things, certain places I'd been, things I'd talked to Dominic about. One lie breeds others, until you can't remember what you've told who, and so you don't tell those who are closest to you anything. And I didn't want that, not for you two.'

His mum continued to cry, while his dad sat next to her, stroking her shoulder.

'I'm sorry if I've upset you, it's a shock, and I get that. But I'm not sorry for telling you. Look, do you want to ask me any more questions, or shall we leave you to think while we go shopping?'

His mum, among gurgling tears, replied, 'Shopping, how can you go shopping at a time like this?'

'Mum, I've been shopping since I found out, I'll go shopping again. Life goes on. That's what I want you both to understand, *my* life goes on.' He handed her a piece of paper. 'That's some websites and phone numbers for organisations you can speak to if you don't want to talk to me. We'll be back in a while if you want to ask more questions. There are no stupid questions at this stage. Best to get it all out early.' He stood up from the table and carried the pile of plates his mum had stacked earlier into the kitchen, and we both left for my car on the drive.

In the changing rooms at Top Man he broke down. He'd taken some jeans and T-shirts to try, and after a very long pause, as I waited for him to leave, I heard a muffled sobbing. I quickly followed my ears and made a knocking sound next to the curtain, asking if I could come in.

'I'm fine,' came the reply.

'You don't sound it.' I ducked round the curtain and saw Gabe on the floor of the corner of the cubicle, hugging his legs to his chest.

'I'm happy, honestly I'm happy I've finally done it, after all that time, lying to them, now it's out in the open. So why am I fucking crying? I really don't know.'

'Relief?' I tried.

'It's like a huge blockage has been cleared, and so all these tears come flooding out. And now it's the next phase, we go back home and see what they're like.'

'It'll be fine, they'll be fine.'

'Hope you're ready to pack quickly when we get back. They might throw us both out, never want to see me again. You didn't bring any things you'd mind being thrown out of a first floor window, did you?'

'Don't be so ridiculous. They love you.'

We returned to the house; no bags or clothes were on the pavement. His parents were at the dining room table, pads of paper filled with blue biro. His mum held out her arms and said, 'My baby, come here.' She held Gabe tight. 'We spoke to a lovely lady called Jan, she went through things you do and don't need to worry about. Her son Alan lives with them and he told her just over a year ago. He lost his job, poor lad. They fired him because he was off sick for a bit just after he got the test results. When he came back, he told them what was wrong, and they still fired him weeks later. Before that he was their best salesman, beat all his targets. Jan explained there's legal aid for things like that, if you want. But her Alan's not pursuing it. He's concentrating on getting another job, getting his own place again. She goes with him to his clinic, they go up to London together, she nags him about eating more fruit and veg. We talked for hours, about everything...'

Gabe's dad nodded and allowed himself a slight roll of his eyes. 'Hours it was...'

'That's enough. There was one question I was going to ask you, only, when I told this... Jan, she said there's no point. It won't change anything, people make mistakes, we're only human. It only takes once. It just comes down to luck at the time. Her daughter made another mistake and Jan ended up with another grandchild. Oh.' She clasped a hanky over her mouth. 'No grandchildren, then?'

'Not necessarily, Mum. Not necessarily.'

'So, you and Dominic, you're not... you know?'

'No, Mum, we're not together.'

'Cos I was wondering, how does it work if you find yourself a boyfriend? I mean, what about A, how did that work?'

'He was ill too. I just noticed it first. Maybe you can ask your new friend Jan about that before we talk about it.'

His mum nodded her head.

Gabe later told me how his parents were gradually getting used to the concept of having a son living with HIV. Their questions slowly became less frequent, and less intrusive. They soon stopped asking him, 'How *are* you?'

with that tone and the tilted head every time they spoke, as if he were about to crumble into dust at that moment. Sometimes his dad would drop into conversation something he'd read in the news about 'New breakthrough treatment and research,' and would Gabe's clinic give him access to it? Gradually they became used to it; their family adjusted to the knowledge, and it was mostly not discussed, unless Gabe started it.

Chapter Thirty-Eight

We went to Dad's flat together. He buzzed us up and we climbed the stairs. He stood at the door of his flat, smoking a hand rolled cigarette. He shook my, then Gabe's hands, showed us to the living room then shouted from the kitchen if we wanted tea or coffee.

I mouthed to Gabe the coffee would be instant, so replied we'd both have tea. The flat seemed a bit better kept than last time I'd visited: piles of old TV magazines were only five high, rather than as high as the coffee table; ash trays had been emptied quite recently; the kitchen surfaces were visible as I walked past.

We sat with our drinks and Dad asked, 'Who's this fella, then?' looking at Gabe.

'Gabe, I've told you about him, Dad, remember?'

'Ah yes, I remember.' He reached into the wooden boat on the coffee table and let it do its musical making a cigarette routine, the room filled with tinkly music from *The Barber of Seville*. He took a freshly rolled cigarette, lit it and sat back in his shabby chair. 'Gabe, where's that from?'

'It's short for Gabriel, but no one calls me that.' He looked at Dad.

'What brings you two here then? It can't be the beautiful surroundings now, can it?' Dad took a drag on his cigarette and filled the room with smoke.

'We thought we'd come see you, see how you were, nothing special, Dad.'

He sipped his strong dark tea. 'You two, what they call, *special* friends is it? That why you're here, show me your new special friend?'

'No,' I replied, wishing the earth would open up and swallow me whole. 'We had a day off and I asked if he wanted to come to Portsmouth for the day.'

'Just like that?' he asked, not at all convinced. He took a drag on his cigarette, then looked Gabe up and down.

'Yeah, just like that,' I replied. 'What you got planned today, Dad?'

'Well, after a visit to see the Queen, I was going to go over to France for one of those booze cruise things I've been reading about in the paper.' He smiled. 'Tonight, I've got that Madonna coming round for her tea.'

'No need to be sarcastic. You not got work at the moment?'

'I'm fine, don't you worry about me. You've got enough on your plate with your job up at the hospital. And all that business with Luke. I never did see that house of yours did I? No, I'll be fine.'

Gabe said, 'Me and my boyfriend split up, he moved out of my place not that long ago. It's been a bit manic lately, so we thought it would be nice for a change, come here and see you.'

'Both of you eh? What is it, time of year, something in the water? You both got a lot going on, haven't you?'

We both nodded, relieved he appeared to have understood our stories.

'What about your parents, Gabe, do you see them?'

He told Dad about our visit to his parents, but left out the bit about The Hydra. On a 'need to know basis' it wasn't really essential for my dad to know.

Dad replied, 'I like to keep it simple, just me, none of that hassle with women… or fellas for you two.' He paused and stroked his stubbly chin. 'They just make things complicated, and all I want is a simple easy life.'

I asked, 'Don't you get lonely? Here on your own?'

'I've got me telly, me papers, I see people down the sites when I'm working, or down the pub otherwise. So, no, I don't get lonely as it goes. Why, don't you two like living on your own?'

I replied, 'Takes some getting used to. Gabe?'

Gabe said, 'After years of living together, it's strange to come home to a dark empty place, everything where you left it. A was always there, so I never came home to an empty flat, but that's another issue…' he trailed off.

Dad, bemused and intrigued, asked Gabe: 'Who's this A?'

'My ex—he's gone now.'

'You said, didn't he have a name, this A fella?'

'A long, hard to pronounce name, so I always stuck to A. Abejundio. It means bee. Still, now I don't even have to say that, now he's gone.'

There was a silence as Gabe thought about this, and Dad sucked on his cigarette, rolling his eyes at me.

I jumped in and rescued with, 'You missed the hospital accommodation I was in. It's wasn't much to be proud of. Mother wasn't too impressed. She went around with gloves checking for dust.'

Dad said, 'Where you staying now?'

'Fulham, a little flat just off the North End Road. Mother went shopping on the King's Road.' I looked at Dad, who rolled his eyes. 'There's plenty of pubs around when you come up,' I added hopefully.

Dad replied, 'Fulham, very nice.'

'How are you?'

'Never mind about me. Nothing much changes. Not much to complain about. I've got this place, food in me kitchen. It's you who's got more going on, you alright? Sad about you and that Luke fella; you couldn't pretend once you knew it was over, it was over. Are you alright now it's all done with?'

'Better than I was,' I replied. I told him about settling into my role at work, helping Gabe get his job, and his little management tips. He listened without interrupting, nodding and smoking throughout.

'I never knew there was male matrons, or all this *management* stuff. There was me thinking you just looked after people, made 'em better then sent 'em home. But no, it seems it's a bit more to it than that.'

Gabe replied, 'We do still do that, Mr Davies, as well as the management stuff.'

'Anyone want another cuppa?' Dad stood.

'Unless you fancy something stronger, we could go to the pub if you want, Dad?'

'Don't have to ask me twice, I'll get me coat.' He walked to the hallway where he put his shoes and coat on. 'Ready when you are.' He stood by the door, waiting for us to join him.

Having got the awkward personal conversation over and done with, we were all somehow linked, somehow closer than just half an hour before. Although it was obviously a dad and possibly his two sons walking to the pub, obvious from the age difference, we all behaved more like a group of friends, walking in a line, joking about each other's drinking prowess, jibing each other about who'd get the first round.

I realised it was moments like this I knew I'd miss after Dad was gone. That was the main reason for visiting him: to spend easy, friendly, familiar time together, with someone who's only going to get older and less able to share those times.

'We'll go to *my* pubs, alright? I'm sure there's plenty of *your* pubs around here, but I'm not ready for that yet, alright, lads?' Dad put his arms around our necks as we walked in a line towards the fruit machines at Portsmouth's seafront, which optimistically called itself Southsea.

We tried most of the fruit machines, and the simpler arcade games — Dad didn't want anything too complicated, as he preferred the coin pusher machines. Gabe taught him a simple platform game and after reaching the end of level one and collecting hundreds of gold rings he said he'd had enough: 'No more playing with that fucking hedgehog, I want a pint, come on lads.' So we headed to his local.

As we walked in, three burly men, covered in builders' mess wearing overalls, turned around, one shouting, 'Dave! Who the hell are these two reprobates?' He pointed to me and Gabe.

Dad introduced me and when he mentioned I was his son, two of the men nodded in recognition, saying they'd seen me before. Dad introduced Gabe, explaining we were just friends, and they all shook his hand vigorously while offering to buy us a drink.

I replied, 'Just a half for me, I'm driving later.'

This was met with a chorus of 'I'm not buying any bloody half pints on my round, you'll have a pint and that's the end of it,' so I did, and so did Gabe, and so did Dad.

After two pints, it seemed a shame to depart from the spirit of the moment, so I asked Dad if we could sleep at his that night, as I couldn't drive home.

'You don't have to ask to stay at your own dad's.' He smiled.

Four pints in, as we sang with Dad and his mates, 'That's Living Alright', the theme tune to *Auf Wiedersein Pet* — he explained it was about a group of builders who moved to Germany for work — I told Gabe, unless he hadn't realised, we were staying at Dad's that night. He nodded his head vigorously and said, 'No shit Sherlock,' before taking another sip from his pint.

We lurched in a line together singing *That's Living Alright*, and ended up in one of *our* pubs, not far down Commercial Road, the main street in Portsmouth.

Dad walked straight up to the bar, where a tall drag queen rested her hand on the beer tap, looking him up and down. Taking in his checked shirt and work jeans she asked, 'You going to behave? Cos I don't want any trouble alright.'

I replied, 'It's alright, he's with me, well not *with* me with me, he's my dad, so he's fine.'

'What can I get you, darling?' The drag queen looked at Dad then served him.

We sat at the bar chatting, and drinking — including a depth charge of vodka which Dad insisted we drop into our pints. Dad put his arm around me and kissed me on the cheek. 'I love you, you know? You know I'm *proud* of you, don't you? Whatever you do, whatever you are, I love you. You know that, son?'

I didn't feel awkward, I didn't feel embarrassed, I knew the kiss and what he'd said came deep from the bottom of his heart, and that only after this many pints could he say how he truly felt and show me his love. There was nothing awkward or inappropriate about the kiss, it was exactly the same as if — and it was a rare occurrence — Mother kissed my cheek. It was purely father-son love. I closed my eyes and let myself really feel that moment, the music on the juke box, the warm feeling of being happily drunk, the sloppiness of his kiss on my cheek, his arm around my shoulder, Gabe's hand holding mine. I allowed myself to drink in the moment of pleasure, to cherish its memory. I knew then how much I'd missed after Mother and Dad had split up, how much of this father-son time, I would never get again, and how important it was to cherish it as he got older and less able or inclined to do it.

I opened my eyes and two young guys stood next to us at the bar. I asked them what they were looking at.

One of the guys replied, 'Is he your dad?'

I nodded. 'And?'

'We just want what you've got.'

'What's that?'

'A dad that loves us. We don't see ours anymore.'

They explained their families found out they were together one evening over dinner: one of the lad's sisters started reading out text messages from her brother's phone while they sat next to each other mid-forkful of sausages and mash. They both remembered what they'd been eating as it was the last meal they ever ate with their families. The sister thought it would be funny to read the text messages out, just a bit of teasing, but it actually showed the two lads had been seeing each other for months and planned to have a 'dirty weekend in Scarborough soon.' The dad asked what they'd been doing whenever they stayed over together in his son's room. Neither lad replied, so the dad had replied by throwing plates full of food at them, saying he was disgusted by it all, especially under his roof. They ran out the house, not even stopping to collect any belongings, and hadn't dare return afterwards as the dad shouted he'd kill them if he ever saw them again. So they moved south from Manchester and ended up in Portsmouth.

'It nearly split us up,' one of the lads added. 'What's her name, behind the bar, Shirley, and her boyfriend the landlord, they look after us. Gives us a few shifts, makes us a dinner.'

The other lad continued, 'I never realised how hard it would be without family. You take it for granted, think they're a pain, so when they're gone you really notice it.' He paused, looked at Dad and me. 'Sorry to stare, I couldn't stop looking at you two. Reminded me of home.'

Dad looked at the two lads. 'I'll look after you two. Where do you live?'

They pointed to a tower block out the window.

'If you want anything done, any DIY, painting, anything, give me a call.' He wrote his number on a bar flyer and handed it to the closer of the two lads. 'Now, someone mentioned karaoke, so where do I go for that?' And he strode off towards the stage in the corner.

After singing two Elvis songs very well—during which I looked at Gabe, shrugged and mouthed, 'who knew?'—Dad explained he was a club singer between building jobs, and a pretty good one at that.

Now, he gestured to me and Gabe to join him on the stage. Reluctantly we walked up; he continued to gesture to the two lads, who were still sat at the bar. They joined us, Dad asked what we'd like to sing and the two lads instantly replied, 'The Time Warp from Rocky Horror.' Dad shouted that to the karaoke man and the music started. *And then that happened.*

After one run through, all five of us were singing and doing the actions to the whole song, while most of the rest of the pub copied us enthusiastically. At the *'But it's the pelvic thrusts. They really drive you insane…'* part, I looked to my right and saw Dad perfectly copying the moves with a slightly camp flourish, and smiled to myself. We carried on singing, *'…Let's do the Time Warp again. Let's do the Time Warp again…'* Another perfect moment of pleasure. I would later hug the memory close to my chest.

Back at Dad's flat, he served hot buttered toast and mugs of tea. We laughed and continued singing until his neighbour banged the ceiling. He gave us two blankets and an airbed and disappeared into his bedroom after hugging us both tight, telling me how much he loved me and appreciated us coming to see him, 'Some old codger'.

'*My* old codger,' I said to his back as he walked to his bedroom.

The next morning we were all very quiet and he apologised for making us stay, before adding, 'But it was worth it, what a night? Wait till I tell the lads at work. *It's just a jump to the left. And then a jump to the right. With your hands on your hips…*' He continued singing as he walked to the kitchen.

We arrived in London just about in time to wash, change and make our way to our respective hospitals for a judiciously rearranged late shift that afternoon.

Shortly afterwards, Dad visited my flat in Fulham. This was something he'd said he would do when I lived with Luke, but somehow it never happened. I was so proud to show him my own flat, amid the activity of Fulham. He wasn't bothered about its closeness to a nearby rival football club of his; instead he took me to B&Q for shelves he fitted in the living room, and plumbing for a dishwasher he also installed. We sipped tea on my new sofa as he looked around the room, looking at the pictures on the walls I'd told him about carefully choosing. He stood to touch the wallpaper he'd explained over many phone calls how to hang then said quietly, 'You done well, son. You done well here.' He returned to the sofa and hugged me awkwardly, squeezing me tight and kissing my cheek roughly.

Chapter Thirty-Nine

July 2002

Gabe and I were at my flat in Fulham—on a Friday night, both exhausted after a busy week's nursing/managing. We'd decided to have a night in together. Not that we needed much of an excuse for that.

Long gone were the days of clubbing and bars, although we still did the scene for birthdays and other special occasions. But tonight, having flicked through the channels and realised there was nothing worth watching, we reverted to our two favourite comfort viewing films: *Death Becomes Her*—as it reminded us of when we first met: Goldie's line, 'Look at me Ernest, I'm soaking wet,' was still one of our most popular jokes—and *Housesitter*, with the one and only Goldie Hawn perfectly confusing and beguiling her onscreen husband, Steve Martin.

Gabe had come round to mine after changing and showering at his—he had moved to Fulham too, having realised how much he loved the central London buzz of the 'Chelsea borders,' as Mother still referred to it. He brought a takeaway pizza, and having opened the wine as soon as he arrived, we were set for the night.

Between mouthfuls of pizza and large glugs of red wine, we reflected on the years we'd known each other. I laughed at how the randomness of him being assigned a shift at my hospital, and me working that night, had caused us to meet—amid all the other hospitals, shifts and staff that night, we happened to meet at just the perfect (or imperfect depending on your point of view) time in our lives. 'Not seeing anyone at the moment?' I asked.

Gabe shook his head, his mouth full of pizza. 'Can't be arsed with it all.'

'Maybe that's where you're going wrong, Mister. That's exactly what you need to be.'

'Very funny. The luck I've had lately, I'm giving it a rest.'

'What about that guy you went out with, a year ago? What was his name?' I scrunched my eyes and snapped my fingers, trying to wish the name to appear before my eyes.

'How long ago? When?' Gabe smiled.

'Twelve, maybe eighteen months ago, you met him when you went to a club, got chatting in the coat check queue.'

'He always used to cry after sex. Every time—and it wasn't that many times if I remember rightly—he'd lay there crying, sucking his thumb. At first I thought it was just the relief of getting a shag, or maybe I was so amazing he didn't know how to cope. But when he did it next time, I thought, hang on, something's not right here.'

'Where *do* you pick these people up?'

'You can talk; what about when you joined that dating site and met that guy, sounded perfect, and lots of texting and flirting by email, then you looked him up on the internet. Turned out he was in the middle of a really horrible divorce *from a woman*. Something about she was actually gay, but he'd married her so she could stay in the country, she…' he trailed off.

'…If you please, it's my story.' I laughed. 'She used to see women when they were married, so he thought he'd have a go, and started to see men too. But it turned out he actually preferred them to women. And when *she* found out, she wanted a divorce, and that's when the fighting started, over the car, over the CD collection, everything.'

'Brings the worst out in people, that sort of thing.'

I nodded. 'It's amazing how petty people can get. That's why his story got into the papers, they were fighting for custody of who got to keep the dog.'

'What was he like when you met him?'

'All he talked about was her, and how he'd never let her have the dog. By the end I felt like I knew her, and actually I sympathised with her a bit too.'

'You never saw him again, did you?'

'What do you think?' I looked at the finished pizza on the coffee table. 'Pudding?'

'Now now, Dominic, it's dessert, as you well know. You simply cannot refer to it as pudding…' Gabe replied, mocking Mother's accent.

'Still, I can't think of anyone else I'd want to be with me, over the years, through the good boyfriends and crap ones, promotions and knock backs.'

'I wonder what they're up to now?'

'Who?'

'Luke and A. Don't you ever think about him still?'

'I did a bit of internet stalking, just to see if I could find him. If I wanted to.'

'And?'

'I looked at his profile and friends and suddenly this wave of nostalgia hit me like a train. It would have just taken one click and we'd be connected now.'

'Why didn't you?'

'Have you looked for A?' I asked, knowing he wouldn't have done, or he'd have told me.

Gabe shook his head. 'It's sad, but some things are best left in the past.'

I nodded.

'It's hard to remember what it was like before I met you. I mean, I know there was *Life Before Dominic*, but apart from that, it just feels like you've always been here.'

I rolled my eyes. 'Talking of sickeningly sweet things... I've got rocky road ice cream, Vienetta, some cakes I made earlier, or a bread and butter pudding. It was originally a Delia, but I've messed about with it a bit; she's quite conservative when it comes to her recipes, so it's much more *now*, and a bit less seventies austerity.' I enjoyed showing off my culinary expertise, as it had developed over the years. By now I could bake a Victoria sponge with my eyes shut, and my crème patisserie was the envy of the management corridor at the hospital. Such was my cunning and wiles; I was renowned for persuading fellow board members through sugary bribes to ensure my nursing budget didn't take as hard a beating as originally planned.

Gabe made balancing motions with his hands. 'Vienetta, bread and butter pudding? Hard to say?'

'I'll do both, and you can open another bottle.' I disappeared to the kitchen to prepare the desserts, reappearing shortly after with a tray and about four thousand calories divided into two bowls.

'Three years,' Gabe said, as I sat next to him.

'What?'

'Since we met, it's three years last month.'

'Doesn't feel like it. Feels like a few months. Last year one minute we were talking about going to Sitges for summer and next it was Christmas divided between our parents' places.'

'Having to explain that no, we didn't want to share a room, and no neither of us had boyfriends still.'

'*Awkward.*'

He took a large spoonful of dessert and chewed thoughtfully. 'Do you have some friends, who you've known for years, but all they talk about is years back, when you first knew them? It's like your friendship is stuck on pause?'

'Because you don't actually do stuff with them now, it's all things you've done before?'

He nodded, mouth full.

'What makes you say that?'

'Nothing, I was just thinking. Cos it's easy isn't it, to let things slide, to let your relationship or friendships only live in the past. I suppose it's like a pet, you've got to keep feeding it, keep making an effort, or it just…'

'…dies?' I offered.

'I was going to say, withers away, but dies works too.'

I stared into space and felt one small tear form on my cheek, which I blinked away quickly. 'Three years, and I was with Luke for ten.'

'We've still not beaten me and A.' He paused. We sat in silence, both thinking about our exes. 'I meant what I said about it feeling like I've always known you.'

'I know. Me too.' I smiled through a tear. 'Shall we put the film on, or we're never going to watch it?' I wiped my eyes then blinked quickly. 'It always surprises me how upset I get when I think about *him*. Even now.'

'I know. It was the right decision, even if it hurt at the time.'

I nodded. 'Wonder if I'd have done it if I hadn't met you.'

'We'll never know, will we? But seriously, I don't think you could have gone on like that for much longer. I think I just helped you see it.' He paused, smiling at me. 'What you got planned tomorrow?'

'I thought we'd do something really wacky and wild.'

'Not go to the café up the road, walk along the river people-watching, have a sniff around the shops in Hammersmith and the over-priced boutiques in Chiswick, then dinner here?'

'I wouldn't go that far, no,' I laughed. 'We could have a walk around Richmond Park, it feels like we've left London, but it's only a short drive away?'

'So not too wild and wacky, then?' He smiled.

'You can see why they asked us if we want to share a room, can't you?'

'Who?'

'Our parents. Fuck's sake, even Dad made up the sofa cushions into a double bed on the floor in the living room.'

'That's a conversation I *don't* want to have again anytime soon.'

'I know, my dad, who'd have thought it? What did he say?'

'Something about us fellas always being together, so he just thought, you know…'

'That was as near as he'd get to saying it I suppose, that and making us a double bed. You can see why though, can't you?'

'Haven't really thought about it,' he replied, filling our glasses with a generous glug of wine. 'The first rule of Fight Club, no one talks about Fight Club.'

'Err, excuse me, what are you talking about?'

'The film, *Fight Club*. That's what they say.'

'Okay, I get that, but there's nothing else we don't talk about. I mean, *literally* nothing. You know everything about my sexual fantasies, me yours. How much of a loon I can be in a relationship, being too clingy, checking in my brains at the door, suddenly turning into a dumb blond. I know about your worries about The Hydra, people's reactions, how much they hurt you. So why don't we talk about *this*?'

'We've both been in a few relationships, and they've all ended, right?'

'Right.'

'And some of them ended well, and others, not so well.'

I nodded.

'If we talk about *this*.' He gestured around the room at us both. 'Then it *is* something, and as soon as it *is* something, it's something which can go wrong, which can end.'

I took in what he had said, sipping more wine, enjoying the slightly light-headed sensation it had now given me. I felt at the perfect point between stone cold sober and completely plastered: I was in the nirvana of drunkenness.

'And anyway, there is no *us*. We don't share a bed because we don't need to. *That* is not there with us. Never has been, never will be.'

'Except when it was. Except when I told you I was falling for you, and when we kissed. There's always been something, someone getting in the way. That's why it didn't happen.'

'It's not there, not like that anyway,' he replied, folding his arms and crossing his legs.

'You're telling me.' I looked into his eyes. 'You've never laid awake at home, one night if you can't sleep, thinking about me, thinking about my body—cos let's be honest, you've seen it enough, the number of times we've changed with each other. Wondering what it would feel like to lay with me, to touch me, to kiss me? Cos I have.'

'Have you?' he asked, incredulous.

'And so have you.' I sat back on the sofa, my arms behind my head, allowing my T-shirt to ride up and reveal my belly button. I saw Gabe's eyes look there, before quickly returning to the opposite wall. 'I saw that,' I added.

'What?'

'You know. And don't tell me I don't know why you always keep your pants on under your pyjamas when we share a bed. I can see it now; you've crossed your legs.'

'Okay, hands up, you're right, I'm wrong. But what if it fucks everything up? What if we're a worse fit for that, than we are now? Cos once we open that box, there's no closing the lid. Once it's out it's out.'

'Who said anything about boxes, I've not got a box, and from what I've seen, neither have you,' I replied, attempting to lighten the mood.

He stared into my eyes, leant towards me and kissed my lips. I closed my eyes as my mouth opened and his tongue explored my mouth. We continued to explore each other's mouths while a jolt of electricity went straight to my groin. The fact that I hadn't had any action, of any kind, icky sticky, never mind rumpy pumpy, for so long, and that I'd imagined this moment so many times, meant that for a moment I thought I would be all over before we'd even begun.

I gently pushed Gabe back and suggested we take it slow, asking if he was sure. He nodded and said, 'As sure as I've been about anything. I love you.'

'I love you,' I replied, staring into his eyes.

We sat on the sofa, kissing and necking like teenagers, for what seemed like hours. Part of me, and it was obvious which part, wanted to rip his clothes off and fuck like animals there on the living room floor. Another part of me wanted to savour every moment, every familiar glimpse of his body, every gentle stroke of his hairy chest, every tender touch and kiss from him onto my skin. Never before had I felt so comfortable and excited at the same time. Years of knowing each other, sharing jokingly what turned each of us on, no holding back, meant I knew exactly what he liked, and he for me.

I pulled away and asked if he wanted to take a shower together — I knew how much he enjoyed it.

He nodded, smiling, and we walked to the bathroom, holding hands. There we undressed ourselves quickly, and before I could think any more we were both stood stark bollock naked in front of each other, our desire for one another abundantly obvious. We both started laughing at the ridiculousness of the situation.

Gabe spoke first, through laughter. 'So, this is what I look like naked. Like I'm wearing a woolly jumper I suppose.' He smiled.

'Yeah, and this is me.' I put my arms out to my sides, then laughed.

He walked closer to me, so I felt his hairy stomach and chest pressed against mine. He kissed me, holding my bum with both his hands, pressing me towards him. We stood like that, kissing for a while. He pulled back from the kiss and traced his hand slowly down my smooth chest. He smiled at me, one hand on my bum and the other resting on my chest.

'Shower?' I looked into his eyes.

He nodded, so I leant into the shower to turn the water on and adjust the temperature, knowing exactly how hot he liked it. He led me into the shower by the hand. He stood behind me, his arms around my chest, I felt him hard against my back. I wanted him against me, inside me, filling me, moving faster and faster, there and then. I turned my head back and kissed him angrily, grabbing him with my left hand. 'Have you got any…?' I managed, my throat strangled with excitement.

'Let's shower first, there's no rush,' came his reply with a smile.

We took turns under the water, soaping each other's bodies, kissing while the water rinsed off the soap. I ran my hands through his wet and curly chest hair, we gently pulled at each other before leaving the shower. I watched his face twist in pleasure as I continued to pull. And then he stopped. I started to put his hand back, but he led me out of the shower and handed me a towel. We started to dry ourselves in the bathroom before running to the bedroom and collapsing in a damp heap on the bed.

I lay on my back, while he very ably did one of *my* favourite things. He pressed down onto me, gently rubbing his whole body and himself against me, gradually increasing in speed together. I responded by moving myself back and forth in time underneath him, enjoying how our bodies rubbed and slipped together. He leant back and grabbed both of us in his hands, pulling us together, quicker and quicker. I knew how much *he* enjoyed this, as he'd told me on many occasions. I smiled at him and nodded for him to continue. We looked into each other's eyes then down to what his hands were doing, making us even more turned on. He continued pulling on us both, faster and faster, harder and harder, until we both, exhausted and sweaty, lay on the bed in a sticky pile. We held onto each other for a few moments, enjoying each other's body heat and salty smell.

He rolled off me and lay on his back, his arms behind his head, showing more dark hair.

I looked to the side and started playing with his chest hair. 'And then that happened.'

He nodded. 'Shower?'

'In a bit.'

We lay there on our backs, listening to each other's breathing, both admitting we wished we'd done it years ago. I enjoyed the salty smell our bodies made together.

After a little doze, when he lay behind me, his arms holding me tight and his body pressed tight against mine, and some more chatting and laughing about what we'd just done, no regrets, just the fact it had taken us this long, we took a shower together. The shower was another opportunity for us to explore each other's bodies.

Afterwards, we started the film and watched it in the darkness of the living room, stroking each other's hands on the sofa, laughing at the same parts we always laughed at, trying to beat each other to favourite quotes throughout.

He turned the TV off when the second film finished, turned to me, holding my hands, and said, 'I love you Dominic, and I want to be with you always.'

'I love you too, Gabe, my angel.'

We returned to my bed, where he whispered into my ear something *he* really liked to do, and asked could we give it a go. I knew he liked this, as he'd told me before, only now, it was something I'd have to participate in, rather than listen to. I wrinkled my nose at the thought and he said if I didn't like it we could stop, but could I just give it a go, please?

I lay on my back with my arms above my head, and he slowly kissed me, moving from my lips, down over my chest, gently biting my nipples in turn, down to my belly button, until I gasped as he reached his destination. I lay still, my arms above my head, not moving, exactly as instructed, as he continued kissing and teasing. In one deft movement, he rolled a condom onto me and lowered himself. I caught his eye as he sat, his legs either side of my chest; he bobbed in front of my eyes, pointing skyward with excitement. He nodded, smiling, and started moving forward and back on me; sometimes he tensed himself, which squeezed me tight, so I took a sharp breath, thinking I would finish. But as instructed, I lay as still as I could, while he moved slowly on me, bobbing in front of my eyes and hitting my chest with each movement.

I relaxed and leant into the feeling, closing my eyes. It was a feeling I'd never experienced before, of laying back and being completely passive, while someone used me in this way. I'd always thought of myself as the other partner, the one in Gabe's position, but only because I hadn't liked the idea of this role. Luke and I had fitted how we had fitted, and never felt the need to change anything. Now, this felt like the most natural thing in the world, another way I was meant to fit with Gabe. His smile beaming down at me, certainly showed how much he was enjoying it.

He leant back, arching himself towards me, and it was over for him, narrowly missing my forehead. He lifted himself off me, kissing me as he moved, then he lay beside me, pulling at me, kissing my chest and squeezing me with one hand until it was over for me. He kissed me.

And then that happened.

Laying together, me behind him this time, I played with his chest hair. 'That was fun.'

'I knew you'd like it once you started.' He kissed my hand and squeezed it tight.

'We can still… can't we?'

'We can do anything we want. Anything we both enjoy.' He kissed my hand again. 'I knew my extensive sexual experience would come in handy. And next time it's your turn, your favourite position, I remember what you've told me.'

I smiled, feeling myself tense with anticipation. 'And I've got what I always wanted, right from when I first met you.'

'Even then, you wanted to sleep with me?'

I nodded, my chin rubbing on his back.

'That's gotta be the longest courting and foreplay I've ever heard of.'

'I don't like to rush these things, you see.'

He laughed, and turned his head to kiss me, his bristly face rubbing against mine. I kissed him back before falling into a deep contented sleep.

If someone had told me I'd be doing *that* in bed, I wouldn't have believed them. If someone had told me I'd be doing that with a man other than Luke, I wouldn't have believed them. If someone had told me I'd be doing that with someone I had been friends with, again, I wouldn't have believed them. But if someone had told me I'd do all those things with someone who was living with The Hydra, I'd have said they were mad, that's not the sort of thing I do.

It's funny how life turns out, isn't it? Despite all the plans, hopes, wishes you have, sometimes something, someone comes along and throws all that up in the air and makes you see what you wanted isn't right for you at all. Not one bit.

The next time life throws you an *and then that happened*, just remember, this might be the one that answers all the questions you've been asking for so long, in a completely unexpected way.

And then that happened.

The end.

About Liam Livings

Eight things about Liam Livings, one is untrue, can you guess which one? Email him with your answers.

He lives, with his partner, where east London ends and becomes nine-carat-gold- highlights-and-fake-tan-west-Essex.

He was born in Hampshire with two club feet (look it up, it's not nice) and problem ears, needing grommets: this meant he was in plaster from toe to groin until he was two, and had to swim with a cap and olive oil soaked lamb's wool over his ears—olive oil bought from a health food shop, before it was sold by supermarkets.

He started writing when he was fourteen: sat in French lessons during a French exchange trip, for want of anything better to do, he wrote pen portraits about his French exchange's teachers. He wrote for his school's creative writing magazine and still writes a diary every day.

He grew up on the edge of the New Forest—not in the New Forest mind, but on the edge. Now it's a national park, it's so much more glamorous. He went to uni in London and never really left.

One evening, flicking through the channels, he stumbled across the film, Saving Private Ryan, and it took twenty minutes of not seeing Goldie Hawn in an army uniform, before he realised it wasn't actually the film, Private Benjamin.

When not writing, he also enjoys baking.

He avoided any sport at secondary school by having an orthodontist appointment between the age of fourteen and sixteen, and when he was old enough to drive, just drove home instead of playing rugby/hockey/whatever.

He is a car geek, his particular passion is old French classics, and his every day car is what is popularly referred to as a 'hairdressers car' a Mazda MX5 in powder blue — Muriel.

Connect with Liam

liamlivings@gmail.com
http://www.liamlivings.com/blog
https://www.facebook.com/liam.livings
https://twitter.com/LiamLivings
https://www.goodreads.com/author/show/7424798.Liam_Livings

Printed in Great Britain
by Amazon

19597896R00212